THE PLÉBISCITE

OR

A MILLER'S STORY OF THE WAR

BY ONE OF THE 7,500,000 WHO VOTED "YES"

HE ROBBED YOU, THAT'S ALL.

THE PLÉBISCITE

OR

A MILLER'S STORY OF THE WAR

BY ONE OF THE 7,500,000 WHO VOTED "YES"

TRANSLATED FROM THE FRENCH OF

ERCKMANN-CHATRIAN

ILLUSTRATED

NEW YORK

CHARLES SCRIBNER'S SONS

1903

LIST OF ILLUSTRATIONS

INTRODUCTORY NOTE

THE present volume serves to emphasize the important connection, so generally now lost sight of, between the *plébiscite* of 1870 in France and the war with Prussia which so speedily followed. Under the administration of Ollivier, which promised an attractive extension of popular liberties, it will be remembered, the *plebiscitum* of the Roman Constitution was borrowed, to give an air of popular approval to the strongly attacked Imperial *régime* by taking the sense of the people through universal suffrage as to the continuance of the Imperial authority on its then existing basis. Of the web of chicane and corruption by which the election was brought out an overwhelming triumph for Imperialism, MM. Erckmann-Chatrian give a clearer and more impressive notion in this book than could be obtained from entire volumes of parliamentary reports and whole files of newspapers. But they make it especially clear how the people were persuaded to return a majority of " yeses " so enormous as to make it impossible to account for it on the theory of mere corruption and chicane. It is evident from this narrative that the people were made to believe that the Empire meant peace abroad and freedom from foreign complications then threatening, as well as tranquillity at home, and that therefore one of the profoundest instincts of twenty millions of peasantry was utilized in order to be subsequently betrayed.

No authors could have been so happily chosen to write the story of the struggle which followed. Alsace and Lorraine, at once the scene of the earliest campaign of the war and the victims of its result, furnish the most appropriate background of such a picture. In reading these adventures, sufferings, meditations, and discussions of the simple yet shrewd Alsatian miller and his neighbors, the reader will take in almost at a glance the causes, incidents, and consequences of one of the greatest of modern wars. The corruption of the office-holding classes, the ignorance of the army officers whose ranks had been filled by favoritism, the bravery of the private soldier ill-equipped, ill-fed, and disastrously led, the contrasting system and discipline of the Prussians, the awakening by Gambetta of the national enthusiasm, and the determined and dogged fighting under Chanzy, Faidherbe, and Bourbaki, how the peasants fared at the hands of the enemy, and how the enemy conducted themselves during the brief campaign are all unfolded before the reader with a combined fulness and incisiveness difficult to encounter elsewhere in narratives of this momentous conflict.

THE PLÉBISCITE

OR

A MILLER'S STORY OF THE WAR

CHAPTER I

I AM writing this history for sensible people. It is my own story during the calamitous war we have just gone through. I write it to show those who shall come after us how many evil-minded people there are in the world, and how little we ought to trust fair words; for we have been deceived in this village of ours after a most abominable fashion; we have been deceived by all sorts of people—by the sous-préfets, by the préfets, and by the Ministers; by the curés, by the official gazettes; in a word, by each and all.

Could any one have imagined that there are so many deceivers in this world? No, indeed; it requires to be seen with one's own eyes to be believed.

In the end we have had to pay dearly. We have given up our hay, our straw, our corn, our flour, our cattle; and that was not enough. Finally, they gave up *us*, our own selves. They said to us: " You are no longer Frenchmen; you are Prussians! We have taken your young men to fight in the war;

they are dead, they are prisoners: now settle with Bismarck any way you like; your business is none of ours! "

But these things must be told plainly: so I will begin at the beginning, without getting angry.

You must know, in the first place, that I am a miller in the village of Rothalp, in the valley of Metting, at Dosenheim, between Lorraine and Alsace. It is a large and fine village of 130 houses, possessing its curé Daniel, its school-master Adam Fix, and principal inhabitants of every kind— wheelwrights, blacksmiths, shoemakers, tailors, publicans, brewers, dealers in eggs, butter, and poultry; we even have two Jews, Solomon Kaan, a pedler, and David Hertz, cattle-dealer.

This will show you what was our state of prosperity before this war; for the wealthier a village is, the more strangers it draws: every man finds a livelihood there, and works at his trade.

We had not even occasion to fetch our butcher's-meat from town. David killed a cow now and then, and retailed all we wanted for Sundays and holidays.

I, Christian Weber, have never been farther than thirty leagues from this commune. I inherited my mill from my grandfather, Marcel Desjardins, a Frenchman from the neighborhood of Metz, who had built it in the time of the Swedish war, when our village was but a miserable hamlet. Twenty-six years ago I married Catherine Amos, daughter of the old forest-ranger. She brought me a hundred louis for her dowry. We have two children—a daughter, Grédel, and a son, Jacob, who are still with us at home.

I have besides a cousin, George Weber, who went off more than thirty years ago to serve in the Marines in Guadaloupe. He has even been on active service there. It was he who beat the drum on the forecastle of the ship *Boussole*, as he has told me a hundred times, whilst the fleet was bombarding St. John d'Ulloa. Afterward he was promoted to be sergeant; then he sailed to North America, for the cod fisheries; and again into the Baltic, on board a small Danish vessel engaged in the coal-trade. George was always intent upon making a fortune. About 1850 he returned to Paris, and established a manufactory of matches in the Rue Mouffetard in Paris; and as he is really a very handsome tall man, with a dark complexion, bold looking, and with a quick eye, he at last married a rich widow without children, Madame Marie Anne Finck, who was keeping an inn in that neighborhood. They grew rich. They bought land in our part of the country through the agency of Monsieur Fingado, the solicitor, to whom he sent regularly the price of every piece of land. At last, on the death of the old carpenter, Joseph Briou, he became the purchaser of his house, to live there with his wife, and to keep a public-house on the road to Metting.

This took place last year, during the time of the Plébiscite, and Cousin George came to inspect his house before taking his wife, Marie Anne, to it.

I was mayor; I had received orders from M. le Sous-préfet to give public notice of the Plébiscite, and to request all well-disposed persons to vote " Yes," *if they desired to preserve peace;* because all the ruffians in the country were going to vote *No,* to have war.

This is exactly what I did, by making everybody promise to come without fail, and sending the *ban-gard* * Martin Kapp to carry the voting tickets to the very farthest cottages up the mountains.

Cousin George arrived the evening before the Plébiscite. I received him very kindly, as one ought to receive a rich relation who has no children. He seemed quite pleased to see us, and dined with us in the best of tempers. He carried with him in a small leathern trunk clothes, shoes, shirts —everything that he required. He was short of nothing. That day everything went on well; but the next day, hearing the notices cried by the rural policeman, he went off to Reibell's brewery, which was full of people, and began to preach against the Plébiscite.

I was just then at the **mayoralty house** wearing my official scarf receiving the **tickets,** when suddenly my deputy Placiard came to tell me, in high

---

* An old word, probably from *ban garde ;* now *garde cham-pètre,* a kind of rural policeman.

indignation, that certain miserable wretches were attacking the rider; that one of them was at the "Cruchon d'Or," and that half the village were very nearly murdering him.

Immediately I went down and ran to the public-house, where my cousin was calling them all asses, affirming that the Plébiscite was for war; that the Emperor, the Ministers, the prefects, the generals, and the bishops were deceiving the people; that all those men were acting a part to get our money from us, and much besides to the same purpose.

I, from the passage, could hear him shouting these things in a terrible voice, and I said to myself, " The poor fellow has been drinking."

If George had not been my cousin; if he had not been quite capable some day of disinheriting my children, I should certainly have arrested him at once, and had him conveyed under safe keeping to Sarrebourg; but, on giving due weight to these considerations, I resolved to put an end to this awkward business, and I cried to the people who were crowding the passage, " Make room, you fellows, make room! "

Those enraged creatures, seeing the scarf, gave way in all directions; and then discovering my cousin, seated at a table in the right-hand corner, I said: " Cousin! what are you thinking of, to create such a scandal? "

He, too, was abashed at the sight of the scarf, having served in the navy, and knowing that there

is no man who claims more respect than a mayor;
that he has a right to lay hands upon you, and send
you to the lock-up, and, if you resist, to send you as
far as Sarrebourg and Nancy. Reflecting upon
this, he calmed down in a moment, for he had not
been drinking at all, as I supposed at first, and he
was saying these things without bitterness, without
anger, conscientiously, and out of regard for his
fellow-citizens.

Therefore, he replied to me, quietly: " Mr.
Mayor, look after your elections! See that certain rogues up there—as there are rogues everywhere—don't stuff into the ballot-box handfuls of
Yeses instead of *Noes* while your back is turned.
This has often happened! And then pray don't
trouble yourself about me. In the Government
Gazette, it is declared that every man shall be free
to maintain his own opinions, and to vote as he
pleases; if my mouth is stopped, I shall protest in
the newspapers."

Hearing that he would protest, to avoid a worse
scandal I answered him: " Say what you please;
no one shall declare that we have put any constraint upon the elections; but, you men, you know
what you have to do."

" Yes, yes," shouted all the people in the room
and down the passage, lifting their hats. " Yes,
Monsieur le Maire; we will listen to nothing at all.
Whether they talk all day or say nothing, it is all
the same to us."

And they all went off to vote, leaving George alone.

M. le Curé Daniel, seeing them coming out, came from his parsonage to place himself at their head. He had preached in the morning in favor of the Plébiscite, and there was not a single *No* in the box.

If my cousin had not had the large meadow above the mill, and the finest acres in the country, he would have been an object of contempt for the rest of his days; but a rich man, who has just bought a house, an orchard, a garden, and has paid ready money for everything, may say whatever he pleases: especially when he is not listened to, and the people go and do the very opposite of what he has been advising them.

Well, this is the way with the elections for the Plébiscite with us, and just the same thing went on throughout our canton: at Phalsbourg—which had been abundantly placarded against the Plébiscite, and where they carried their audacity even to watching the mayor and the ballot-box—out of fifteen hundred electors, military and civil, there were only thirty-two *Noes*.

It is quite clear that things were making favorable progress, and that M. le Sous-préfet could not be otherwise than perfectly satisfied with our behavior.

I must also mention that we were in want of a parish road to Hangeviller; that we had been promised a pair of church-bells, and the *Glandée,*

or right of feeding our hogs upon the acorns in autumn; and that we were aware that all the villages which voted the wrong way got nothing,
whilst the others—in consideration of the good
councillors they had sent up, either to the arrondissement or the department—might always reck-
on upon a little money from the tax-collector for
the necessities of their parish. Monsieur le Sous-
préfet had pointed out these advantages to me;
and naturally a good mayor will inform his subor-
dinates. I did so. Our deputies, our councillors-
general, our councillors of the arrondissement, were
all on the right side! By these means we have already gained the right to the dead leaves and our
great wash-houses. We only sought our own good,
and we much preferred seeing other villages pay
the ministers, the senators, the marshals, the bishops, and the princes, to paying them ourselves.
So that all that Cousin George could say to us about
the interest of all, and the welfare of the nation,
made not the least impression upon us.

I remember that that very day of the Plébiscite,
when it was already known that we had all voted
right, and that we should get our two bells with
the parish road—I remember that my cousin and
I had, after supper, a great quarrel, and that I
should certainly have put him out, if it had not
been he.

We were taking our *petit verre* of *kirsch*, smoking our pipes, with our elbows on the table; my

wife and Grédel had already gone to bed, when all at once he said to me: " Listen to me, Christian. Save the respect I owe you as mayor, you are all a set of geese in this village, and it is a very fortunate thing that I am come here, that you may have, at least, one sensible man among you."

I was going to get angry, but he said:

" Just let me finish; if you had but spent a couple of years at Paris, you would see things a little plainer; but at this moment, you are like a nest of hungry jays, blind and unfeathered; they open their bills, and they cry ' Jaques,' to call down food from heaven. Those who hear them climb ᵤp the tree, twist their necks, put them into the pot and laugh. That is your position. You have confidence in your enemies, and you give them power to pluck you just as they please. If you appointed upright men in your districts as deputies, councillors-general, instead of taking whoever the préfecture recommends, would not the Emperor and the other honorable men above be obliged then to leave you the money which the tax-collector makes you pay in excess? Could all those people then enrich themselves at your expense, and amass immense fortunes in a few years? Would you then see old baskets with their bottoms out, fellows whom you would not have trusted with a halfpenny before the *coup-d'état*—would you see them become millionnaires, rolling in gold, gliding along in carriages with their wives, their chil-

dren, their servants, and their ballet-dancers? The
préfets, the sous-préfets say to you: ' Go on voting
right, and you shall have this, you shall have that '
—things which you have a right to demand in
virtue of the taxes you pay, but which are granted
to you as favors—roads, wash-houses, schools, etc.
Would you not be having them in your own right,
if the money which is taken from you were left in
the commune? What does the Emperor do for
you? He plunders you—that is all. Your money,
he shows it to you before each election, as they show
a child a stick of sugar-candy to make it laugh; and
when the election is over he puts it back into his
pocket. The trick is played."

"How can he put that money into his pocket?"
I asked, full of indignation. "Are not the accounts
presented every year in the Chambers?"

Upon this he shrugged his shoulders and answered: "You are not sharp, Christian; it is not
so difficult to present accounts to the Chambers.
So many chassepots—which have no existence! So
much munition of war, of which no one knows anything. So much for retiring pensions; so much for
the substitutes' fund; so much for changes of uniform. The uniforms are changed every year; that
is good for business. Do the deputies inquire into
these matters? Who checks the Ministers' budgets?
And the deputies whom the Minister of the Interior
has recommended to you, whom you have appointed
like fools, and whom the Emperor would throw up

at the very first election, if those gentlemen breathed a syllable about visiting the arsenals and examining into the accounts—what a farce it is! Why, yesterday, passing through Phalsbourg, I got upon the ramparts, and I saw there guns of the time of Herod, upon gun-carriages eaten up by worms and painted over to conceal the rottenness. These very guns, I do believe, are recast every third or fourth year—upon paper—with your money. Ah, my poor Christian, you are not very sharp, nor the other people in our village either. But the men you send as deputies to Paris—they *are* sharp, too sharp."

He broke out into a laugh, and I could have sent him back to Paris.

"Do you know what you want?" said he then, filling his pipe and lighting it, for I made no reply, being too much annoyed; "what you want is not good sense, it is not honesty. All of us peasants, we still possess some good sense and honesty. And we believe, moreover, in the honesty of others, which proves that we ourselves have a little left! No, what you want is education; you have asked for bells, and bells you will get; but all the school you have is a miserable shed, and your only schoolmaster is old Adam Fix, who can teach his children nothing because he knows nothing himself. Well now, if you were to ask for a really good school, there would be no money in the public funds. There is money enough for bells, but for a good

school-master, for a large, well-ventilated room, for
deal benches and tables, for pictures, slates, maps,
and books, there is nothing; for if you had good
schools, your children could read, write, keep accounts; they would soon be able to look into the
Ministers' budgets, and that is exactly what his
Majesty wishes to avoid. You understand now,
cousin; this is the reason why you have no school
and you have bells."

Then he looked knowingly at me:

"And, do you know," said he, after a few moments' thought, "do you know how much all the
schools in France cost? I am not referring to the
great schools of medicine, and law, and chemistry,
the colleges, and the lyceums, which are schools for
wealthy young men, able to keep themselves in
large cities, and to pay for their own maintenance.
I am speaking of schools for the people, elementary
schools, where reading and writing are taught: the
two first things which a man must know, and which
distinguish him from the savages who roam naked
in the American forests? Well, the deputies whom
the people themselves send to protect their interests
in Paris, and whose first thought, if they are not altogether thieves, ought to be to discharge their
duty toward their constituencies—these deputies
have never voted for the schools of the people a
larger sum than seventy-five millions. The state
contributes ten millions as its share; the commune,
the departments, the fathers and mothers do the

rest. Seventy-five millions to educate the people in a great country like ours! it is a disgrace. The United States spends six times the amount. But on the other hand, for the war budget we pay five hundred millions; even that would not be too much if we had five hundred thousand men under arms, according to the calculation which has been made of what it costs per diem for each man; but for an army of two hundred and fifty thousand men, it is too much by half. What becomes of the other three hundred millions? If they were made available to build schools, to pay able masters, to furnish retreats for workmen in their declining days, I should have nothing to say against it; but to jingle in the pockets of MM. the senators and to ring the bells of MM. the curés, I consider that too dear."

As Cousin George bothered my mind with all his arguments, I felt a wish to go to bed, and I said to him:

"All that, cousin, is very fine, but it is getting late: and besides it has nothing to do with the Plébiscite."

I had risen; but he laid his hand upon my arm and said: " Let us talk a little longer—let me finish my pipe. You say that this has nothing to do with the Plébiscite; but that Plébiscite is for all this nice arrangement of things to go on. If the nation believes that all is right, that enough money is left to it, and that it can even spare a little more; that the ministers, the senators, and the princes are not yet

sufficiently fat and flourishing; that the Emperor
has not bought enough in foreign countries; well,
it will say with this Plébiscite, 'Go on, pray go on—
we are quite satisfied.' Does that suit your ideas?"

"Yes. I had rather that than war," said I, in
a very bad temper. "The Empire is peace; I vote
for peace."

Then George himself rose up, emptying his pipe
on the edge of the table, and said: "Christian, you
are right. Let us go to bed. I repent having
bought old Briou's house; decidedly the people in
these parts are too stupid. You quite grieve me."

"Oh, I don't want to grieve you," said I, angrily; "I have quite as much sense as you."

"What!" said he, "you the mayor of Rothalp,
in daily communication with the sous-préfet, you
believe that the object of this Plébiscite is to confirm peace?"

"Yes, I do."

"What, you believe that? Come now. Have
we not peace at the present moment? Do we want
a Plébiscite to preserve it? Do you suppose that
the Germans are taken in by it? Our peasants, to
be sure, are misled; they are indoctrinated at the
curé's house, at the mayoralty-house, at the sous-
préfecture; but not a single workman in Paris is a
dupe of this pernicious scheming. They all know
that the Emperor and the Ministers want war; that
the generals and the superior officers demand it.
Peace is a good thing for tradesmen, for artisans,

for peasants; but the officers are tired of being cramped up in the same rank perpetually without a rise. Already the inferior officers have been disgusted with the profession through the crowds of nobles, Jesuits, and canting hypocrites of all sorts who are thrust into the army. The troops are not animated with a good spirit; they want promotion, or they will end by rousing themselves into a passion: especially when they see the Prussians under our noses helping themselves to everything they please without asking our leave. You don't understand that! There," said he, "I am sleepy. Let us go to bed."

Then I began to understand that my cousin had learned many things in Paris, and that he knew more of politics than I did. But that did not prevent me from being in a great rage with him, for the whole of that day he had done nothing but cause trouble; and I said to myself that it was impossible to live with such a brute.

My wife, at the top of the landing, had heard us disputing; but as we were going upstairs, she came all smiles to meet us, holding the candle, and saying: "Oh, you have had a great deal to tell each other this evening! You must have had enough. Come, cousin, let me take you to your room; there it is. From your window you may see the woods in the moonlight; and here is your bed, the best in the house. You will find your cotton nightcap under the pillow."

" Very nice, Catherine, thank you," said George.

" And I hope you will sleep comfortably," said she, returning to me.

This wise woman, full of excellent good sense, then said to me, while I was undressing: " Christian! what were you thinking of, to contradict your cousin? Such a rich man, and who can do us so much good by and by! What does the Plébiscite signify? What can that bring us in? Whatever your cousin says to you, say ' Amen ' after it. Remember that his wife has relations, and she will want to get everything on her side. Mind you don't quarrel with George. A fine meadow below the mill, and an orchard on the hill-side, are not found every day in the way of a cow."

I saw at once that she was right, and I inwardly resolved never to contradict George again: he might himself alone be worth to us far more than the Emperor, the Ministers, the senators, and all the establishment together; for everyone of those people thought of his own interests alone, without ever casting a thought upon us. Of course we ought to do the same as they did, since they had succeeded so well in sewing gold lace upon all their seams, fattening and living in abundance in this world; not to mention the promises that the bishops made to them for the next.

Thinking upon these things, I lay calmly down, and soon fell asleep.

CHAPTER II

THE next day early, Cousin George, my son Jacob, and myself, after having eaten a crust of bread and taken a glass of wine standing, harnessed our horses, and put them into our two carts to go and fetch my cousin's wife and furniture at the Lützelbourg station.

Before coming into our country, George had ordered his house to be whitewashed and painted from top to bottom; he had laid new floors, and replaced the old shingle roof with tiles. Now the paint was dry, the doors and windows stood open day and night; the house could not be robbed, for there was nothing in it. My cousin, seeing that all was right, had just written to his wife that she might bring their goods and chattels with her.

So we started about six in the morning; upon the road the people of Hangeviller, of Metting, and Véchem, and those who were going to market in the town, were singing and shouting " Vive l'Empereur! "

Everywhere they had voted " Yes," for peace. It was the greatest fraud that had ever been perpetrated: by the way in which the Ministers, the prefects, and the Government newspapers had ex-

plained the Plébiscite, everybody had imagined
that he had really voted peace.

Cousin George hearing this, said, " Oh, you poor
country folks, how I pity you for being such im-
beciles!   How I pity you for believing what these
pickpockets tell you! "

That was how he styled the Emperor's government, and naturally I felt my indignation rise; but
Catherine's sound advice came back into my mind,
and I thought, " Hold your tongue, Christian; don't
say a word—that's your best plan."

All along the road we saw the same spectacle; the
soldiers of the 84th, garrisoned at Phalsbourg,
looked as pleased as men who have won the first
prize in a lottery; the colonel declared that the men
who did not vote " Yes " would be unworthy of being called Frenchmen.   Every man had voted
" Yes; " for a good soldier knows nothing but his
orders.

So having passed before the gate of France, we
came down to the Baraques, and then reached
Lützelbourg.   The train from Paris had passed a
few minutes before; the whistle could yet be heard
under the Saverne tunnel.

My cousin's wife, with whom I was not yet acquainted, was standing by her luggage on the plat-
form; and seeing George coming up, she joyfully
cried, " Ah! is that you? and here is cousin."

She kissed us both heartily, gazing at us, however, with some surprise, perhaps on account of our

blouses and our great wide-brimmed black hats.
But no! it could not be that; for Marie Anne Finck
was a native of Wasselonne, in Alsace, and the Alsacians have always worn the blouse and wide-
brimmed hat as long as I can remember.   But this
tall, thin woman, with her large brown eyes, as bus-
tling, quick, and active as gunpowder, after having
passed thirty years at Paris, having first been cook at
Krantheimer's, at a place called the Barrière de
Montmartre, and then in five or six other inns in
that great city, might well be somewhat astonished
at seeing such simple people as we were; and no
doubt it also gave her pleasure.

    That is my idea.

    " The carts are there, wife," cried George, in
high spirits.   " We will load the biggest with as
much furniture as we can, and put the rest upon the
smaller one.   You will sit in front.   There—look
up there—that's the Castle of Lützelbourg, and that
pretty little wooden house close by, covered all over
with vine, that is a châlet, Father Hoffman-Forty's
châlet, the distiller of cordials, you know the cordial
of Phalsbourg."

    He showed her everything.

    Then we began to load; that big Yéri, who takes
the tickets at the gate and who carries the parcels to
Monsieur André's omnibus, comes to lend us a hand.
The two carts being loaded about twelve o'clock, and
my cousin's wife seated in front of the foremost one
upon a truss of straw, we started at a quiet pace for

the village, where we arrived about three o'clock. But I remember one thing, which I will not omit to mention. As we were coming out of Lützelbourg, a heavy wagon-load of coal was coming down the hill, a lad of sixteen or seventeen leading the horse by the bridle; at the door of the last house, a little child of five years old, sitting on the ground, was looking at our carts passing by; he was out of the road, he could not be in any one's way, and was sitting there perfectly quiet, when the boy, without any reason, gave him a lash with his whip, which made the child cry aloud.

My cousin's wife saw that.

"Why did that boy strike the child?" she inquired.

"That's a coal-heaver," George answered. "He comes from Sarrebrück. He is a Prussian. He struck the child because he is a French child."

Then my cousin's wife wanted to get down to fall upon the Prussian; she cried to him, "You great coward, you lazy dog, you wicked wretch, come and hit me." And the boy would have come to settle her, if we had not been there to receive him; but he would not trust himself to us, and lashed his horses to get out of our reach, making all haste to pass the bridge, and turning his head round toward us, for fear of being followed.

I thought at the time that Cousin George was wrong in saying this boy had a spite against the French because he was a Prussian; but I learned

afterward that he was right, and that the Germans
have borne ill-will against us for years without let-
ting us see it—like a set of sulky fellows waiting for
a good opportunity to make us feel it.

"It is our *good man* that we have to thank for
this," said George. "The Germans fancy that we
have named him Emperor to begin his uncle's tricks
again; and now they look upon our Plébiscite as a
declaration of war. The joy of our sous-préfets,
our mayors, and our curés, and of all those excellent
people who only prosper upon the miseries of mankind, proves that they are not very far out."

"Yes, indeed," cried his wife; "but to beat a
child, that is cowardly."

"Bah! don't let us think about it," said George.
"We shall see much worse things than this; and we
shall have deserved it, through our own folly. God
grant that I may be mistaken!"

Talking so, we arrived home.

My wife had prepared dinner; there was kissing
all round, the acquaintance was made; we all sat
round the table, and dined with excellent appetites.
Marie Anne was gay; she had already seen their
house on her way, and the garden behind it with its
rows of gooseberry bushes and the plum-trees full of
blossom. The two carts, the horses having been
taken out, were standing before their door; and from
our windows might be seen the village people examining the furniture with great interest, hovering
round and gazing with curiosity upon the great

heavy boxes, feeling the bedding, and talking together about this great quantity of goods, just as if it was their own business.

They were remarking no doubt that our cousin George Weber and his wife were rich people, who deserved the respectful consideration of the whole country round; and I myself, before seeing these great chests, should never have dreamed that they could have so much belonging entirely to themselves.

This proved to me that my wife was perfectly right in continuing to pay every respect to my cousin; she had also cautioned our daughter Grédel: as for Jacob, he is a most sensible lad, who thinks of everything and needs not to be told what to do.

But what astonished us a great deal more, was to see arriving about half-past three two other large wagons from the direction of Wéchem, and hearing my cousin cry "Here comes my wine from Barr!"

Before coming to Rothalp he had himself gone to Barr, in Alsace, to taste the wine and to make his own bargains.

"Come, Christian," said he, rising, "we have no time to lose if we mean to unload before nightfall. Take your pincers and your mallet; you will also fetch ropes and a ladder to let the casks down into the cellar."

Jacob ran to fetch what was wanted, and we all came out together—my wife, my daughter, cousin,

and everybody. My man Frantz remained alone at
the mill, and immediately they began to undo the
boxes, to carry the furniture into the house: chests
of drawers, wardrobes, bedsteads, and quantities of
plates, dishes, soup-tureens, etc., which were carried
straight into the kitchen.

My cousin gave his orders: " Put this down in a
corner; set that in another corner."

The neighbors helped us too, out of curiosity.
Everything went on admirably.

And then arrived the wagons from Barr; but
they were obliged to be kept waiting till seven
o'clock. Our wives had already set up the beds and
put away the linen in the wardrobes.

About seven o'clock everything was in order in
the house. We now thought of resting till to-morrow, when George said to us, turning up his sleeves,
" Now, my friend, here comes the biggest part of
the work. I always strike the iron while it's hot.
Let all the men who are willing help me to unload
the casks, for the drivers want to get back to town,
and I believe they are right."

Immediately the cellar was opened, the ladder set
up against the first wagon, the lanterns lighted, the
planks set leaning in their places, and until eleven
o'clock we did nothing but unload wine, roll down
casks, let them down with my ropes, and put them
in their places.

Never had I worked as I did on that day!

Not before eleven o'clock did Cousin George, seeing everything settled to his satisfaction, seem pleased; he tapped the first cask, filled a jug with wine, and said, " Now, mates, come up; we will have a good draught, and then we will get to bed."

The cellar was shut up, so we drank in the large parlor, and then all, one after another, went home to bed, upon the stroke of midnight.

All the villagers were astonished to see how these Parisians worked: they were all the talk. At one time it was how cousin had bought up all the manure at the gendarmerie; then how he had made a contract to have all his land drained in the autumn; and then how he was going to build a stable and a laundry at the back of his house, and a distillery at the end of his yard: he was enlarging his cellars, already the finest in the country. What a quantity of money he must have!

If he had not paid his architect, the carpenters, and the masons cash down, it would have been declared that he was ruining himself. But he never wanted a penny; and his solicitor always addressed him with a smiling face, raising his hat from afar off, and calling him " my dear Monsieur Weber."

One single thing vexed George: he had requested at the préfecture, as soon as he arrived, a license to open his public-house at the sign of " The Pineapple." He had even written three letters to Sarrebourg, but had received no answer. Morning and evening, seeing me pass by with my carts of grain and flour, he called to me through the window, "Hallo, Christian, this way just a minute!"

He never talked of anything else; he even came to tease me at the mayoralty-house, to indorse and seal his letters with attestations as to his good life and character; and yet no answer came.

One evening, as I was busy signing the registration of the reports drawn up in the week by the school-master, he came in and said, "Nothing yet?"

"Cousin, I don't know the meaning of it."

"Very well," said he, sitting before my desk. "Give me some paper. Let me write for once, and then we will see."

He was pale with excitement, and began to write, reading it as he went on:

"MONSIEUR LE SOUS-PRÉFET,—I have requested of you a license to open a public-house at Rothalp. I have even had the honor of writing you three letters upon the subject, and you have given me no answer. Answer me—yes or no! When people are paid, and well paid, they ought to fulfil their duty.

"Monsieur le Sous-préfet, I have the honor to salute you.

"GEORGE WEBER,
"*Late Sergeant of Marines.*"

Hearing this letter, my hair positively stood on end.

"Cousin, don't send that," said I; "the sous-préfet would very likely put you under arrest."

"Pooh!" said he, "you country people, you seem to look upon these folks as if they were demigods; yet they live upon our money. It is we who pay them: they are for our service, and nothing more. Here, Christian, will you put your seal to that?"

Then, in spite of all that my wife might say, I replied, "George, for the love of Heaven, don't ask me that. I should most assuredly lose my place."

"What place? Your place as mayor," said he, "in which you receive the commands of the souspréfet, who receives the commands of the préfet, who receives the orders of a Minister, who does everything that our *honest man* bids him. I had rather be a ragman than fill such a place."

The school-master, who happened to be there, seemed as if he had suddenly dropped from the clouds; his arms hung down the sides of his chair, and he gazed at my cousin with big eyes, just as a man stares at a dangerous lunatic.

I, too, was sitting upon thorns on hearing such words as these in the mayoralty-house; but at last I told him I had rather go myself to Sarrebourg and ask for the permission than seal that letter.

"Then we will go together," said he.

But I felt sure that if he spoke after this fashion to Monsieur le Sous-préfet, he would lay hands upon both of us; and I said that I should go alone, because his presence would put a constraint upon me.

"Very well," he said; "but you will tell me

everything that the sous-préfet has been saying to you."

He tore up his letter, and we went out together.

I don't remember that I ever passed a worse night than that. My wife kept repeating to me that our Cousin George had the precedence over the sous-préfet, who only laughed at us; that the Emperor, too, had cousins, who wanted to inherit everything from him, and that everybody ought to stick to their own belongings.

Next day, when I left for Sarrebourg, my head was in a whirl of confusion, and I thought that my cousin and his wife would have done well to have stayed in Paris rather than come and trouble us when we were at peace, when every man paid his own rates and taxes, when everybody voted as they liked at the préfecture. I could say that never was a loud word spoken at the public-house; that people attended with regularity both mass and vespers; that the gendarmes never visited our village more than once a week to preserve order; and that I myself was treated with consideration and respect: when I spoke but a word, honest men said, "That's the truth; that's the opinion of Monsieur le Maire!"

Yes, all these things and many more passed through my mind, and I should have liked to see Cousin George at Jericho.

This is just how we were in our village, and I don't know even yet by what means other people had made such fools of us. In the end, we have

had to pay dearly for it; and our children ought to
learn wisdom by it.

At Sarrebourg, I had to wait two hours before I
could see Monsieur le Sous-préfet, who was break-
fasting with messieurs the councillors of the arrondissement, in honor of the Plébiscite.   Five or six
mayors of the neighborhood were waiting like myself; we saw filing down the passage great dishes of
fish and game, notwithstanding that the fishing and
shooting seasons were over; and then baskets of
wine; and we could hear our councillors laughing,
"Ha! ha! ha!"   They were enjoying themselves
mightily.

At last Monsieur le Sous-préfet came out; he had
had an excellent breakfast.

"Ha! is that you, gentlemen?" said he; "come
in, come into the office."

And for another quarter of an hour we were left
standing in the office.   Then came Monsieur le
Sous-préfet to get rid of the mayors, who wanted
different things for their villages.   He looked delighted, and granted everything.   At last, having
despatched the rest, he said to me, "Oh! Monsieur
le Maire, I know the object of your coming.   You
are come to ask, for the person called George Weber,
authorization to open a public-house at Rothalp.
Well, it's out of the question.   That George Weber
is a Republican; he has already offered opposition
to the Plébiscite.   You ought to have notified this
to me: you have screened him because he is your

cousin.   Authorizations to keep public-houses are granted to steady men, devoted to his Majesty the Emperor, and who keep a watch over their customers; but they are never granted to men who require watching themselves.   You should be aware of that."

Then I perceived that my rascally deputy, that miserable Placiard, had denounced us.   That old dry-bones did nothing but draw up perpetual petitions, begging for places, pensions, tobacco excise offices, decorations for himself and his honorable family; speaking incessantly of his services, his devotion to the dynasty, and his claims.   His claims were the denunciations, the informations which he, laid before the sous-préfecture ; and, to tell the truth, in those days these were the most valid claims of all.

I was indignant, but I said nothing; I simply added a few words in favor of Cousin George, assuring Monsieur le Sous-préfet that lies had been told about him, that one should not believe everything, etc.   He half concealed a weary yawn; and as the councillors of the arrondissement were laughing in the garden, he rose and said politely, " Monsieur le Maire, you have your answer.   Besides, you already have two public-houses in your village; three would be too many."

It was useless to stay after that, so I made a bow, at which he seemed pleased, and returned quietly to Rothalp.   The same evening I went to repeat to

George, word for word, the answer of the sous-préfet. Instead of getting angry, as I expected, my
cousin listened calmly. His wife only cried out
against that bad lot—she spoke of all the sous-préfets in the most disrespectful manner. But my
cousin, smoking his pipe after supper, took it all very
easily.

"Just listen to me, Christian," said he. "In
the first place, I am much obliged to you for the
trouble you have taken. All that you tell me I
knew beforehand; but I am not sorry to know it for
certain. Yet I could wish that the sous-préfet had
had my letter. As it is, since I am refused a license
to sell a few glasses of wine retail, I will sell wine
wholesale. I have already a stock of white wine,
and no later than to-morrow I am off to Nancy. I
buy a light cart and a good horse; thence I drive to
Thiancourt, where I lay in a stock of red wine. After that I rove right and left all over the country,
and I sell my wine by the cask or the quarter-cask,
according to the solvency of my customers: instead
of having one public-house, I will have twenty. I
must keep moving. With an inn, Marie Anne
would still have been obliged to cook; she has quite
enough to do without that."

"Oh! yes," she said; "for thirty years I have
been cooking dishes of sauerkraut and sausage at
Krantheimer's, at Montmartre, and at Auber's, in
the cloister St. Benoit."

"Exactly so," said George; "and now you shall

cook no longer; but you shall look after the crops, the stacking of the hay, the storage of fruit and potatoes. We shall get in our dividends, and I will trot round the country with my little pony from village to village. Monsieur le Sous-préfet shall know that George Weber can live without him."

Hearing this, I learned that they had money in the funds, besides all the rest; and I reflected that my cousin was quite right to laugh at all the sous-préfets in the world.

He came with me to the door, shaking hands with me; and I said to myself that it was abominable to have refused a publican's license to respectable persons, when they gave it to such men as Nicolas Reiter and Jean Kreps, whom their own wives called their best customers because they dropped under the table every evening and had to be carried to bed.

On the other hand, I saw that it was better for me; for if my cousin had been found infringing the law, I should have had to take depositions, and there would have been a quarrel with Cousin George. So that all was for the best; the wholesale business being only the exciseman's affair.

What George had said, he did next day. At six o'clock he was already at the station, and in five or six days he had returned from Nancy upon his own char-à-banc, drawn by a strong horse, five or six years old, in its prime. The char-à-banc was a new one; a tilt could be put up in wet weather, which could be raised or lowered when necessary to deliver the wine or receive back the empty casks.

The wine from Thiancourt followed. George stored it immediately, after having paid the bill and settled with the carter. I was standing by.

As for telling you how many casks he had then in the house, that would be difficult without examining his books; but not a wine-merchant in the neighborhood, not even in town, could boast of such a vault of wine as he had, for excellence of quality, for variety in price, both red and white, of Alsace and Lorraine.

About that time, my cousin sent for me and Jacob to make a list of safe customers. He wrote on, asking us, "How much may I give to So-and-So?"

"So much."

"How much to that man?"

"So much."

In the course of a single afternoon we had passed in review all the innkeepers and publicans from Droulingen to Quatre Vents, from Quatre Vents to the Dagsberg. Jacob and I knew what they were worth to the last penny; for the man who pays readily for his flour, pays well for his wine; and those who want pulling up by the miller are in no hurry to open their purses to the others.

That was the way Cousin George conducted his business.

He took a lad from our place, the son of the cooper Gros, to drive; and he himself was salesman.

From that day he was only seen passing through Rothalp at a quick trot, his lad loading and unloading.

My cousin, also, had a notion of distilling in the winter. He bought up a quantity of old second-hand barrels to hold the fruits which he hoped to secure at a cheap rate in autumn, and laid up a great store of firewood. Our country people had nothing to do but to look at him to learn something; but the people down our way all think themselves so amazingly clever, and that does not help to make folks richer.

Well, it is plain to you that our cousin's prospects were looking very bright. Every day, returning from his journey to Saverne or to Phalsbourg, he would stop his cart before my door, and come to see me in the mill, crying out: "Hallo! good afternoon, Christian. How are you to-day?"

Then we used to step into the back parlor, on account of the noise and the dust, and we talked about the price of corn, cattle, provender, and everything that is interesting to people in our condition.

What astonished him most of all was the number of Germans to be met with in the mountains and in the plains.

"I see nobody else," said he; "wood-cutters, brewers' men, coopers, tinkers, photographers, contractors. I will lay a wager, Christian, that your young man Frantz is a German, too."

3

"Yes; he comes from the Grand Duchy of Baden."

"How does this happen?" asked George. "What is the meaning of it all?"

"They are good workmen," said I, "and they ask only half the wages."

"And ours—what becomes of them?"

"Ah, you see, Cousin George, that is their business."

"I understand," he said, "that we are making a great mistake. Even in Paris, this crowd of Germans—crossing-sweepers, shop and warehousemen, carters, book-keepers, professors of every kind—astonished me; and since Sadowa, there are twice as many. The more territory they annex, the farther they extend their view. Where is the advantage of our being Frenchmen—paying every year heavier taxes; sending our children to be drawn for the conscription, and paying for their exemption; bearing all the expenses of the State, all the insults of the préfets, the sous-préfets, and the police-inspectors, and the annoyances of common spies and informers, if those fellows, who have nothing at all to bear, enjoy the same advantages with ourselves, and even greater ones; since our own people are sent off to make room for these, who by their great numbers lower the price of hand-labor? This benefits the manufacturers, the contractors, the bourgeois class, but it is misery for the mass of the people. I cannot understand it at all. Our rulers, up there, must be losing their senses. If that goes on, the working-men will cease to care for their country, since it cares so little for them; and the Germans who are favored, and who hate us, will quietly put us out of our own doors."

Thus spoke my cousin, and I knew not what answer to make.

But about this time I had a great trouble, and although this affair is my private business alone, I must tell you about it.

Since the arrival of George, my daughter Grédel, instead of looking after our business as she used to do, washing clothes, milking cows, and so on, was all the blessed day at Marie Anne's. Jacob complained, and said: " What is she about down there? By and by I shall have to prepare the clothes for the wash and hang them upon the hedges to dry, and churn butter. Cannot Grédel do her own work? Does she think we are her servants? "

He was right. But Grédel never troubled herself. She never has thought of any one besides herself. She was down there along with George's wife, who talked to her from morning till night about Paris, the grand squares, the markets, the price of eggs and of meat, what was charged at the barrières; of this, that, and the other: cooking, and what not.

Marie Anne wanted company. But this did not suit me at all; and the less because Grédel had had a lover in the village for some time, and when this is the case, the best thing to be done is always to keep your daughter at home and watch her closely.

It was only a common clerk at a stone-quarry in Wilsberg, a late artillery sergeant, Jean Baptiste Werner, who had taken the liberty to cast his eyes upon our daughter. We had nothing to say against this young man. He was a fine, tall man, thin, with a bold expression and brown mustaches, and who did his duty very well at the quarry by Father Heitz; but he could earn no more than his three francs a day: and any one may see that the daughter of Christian Weber was not to be thrown away upon a man who earns three francs a day. No, that would never do.

Nevertheless, I had often seen this Jean Baptiste Werner going in the morning to his work with his foot-rule under his arm, stopping at the mill-dam, as if to watch the geese and the ducks paddling about the sluice or the hens circling around the cock on the dunghill; and at the same moment Grédel would be slowly combing her hair at her window before the little looking-glass, leaning her head outside. I had also noticed that they said good-morning to each other a good way off, and that that clerk always looked excited and flurried at the sight of my daughter; and I had even been obliged to give Grédel notice to go and comb her hair somewhere else when that man passed, or to shut her window.

This is my case, simply told.

GRÉDEL WOULD BE SLOWLY COMBING HER HAIR AT HER WINDOW.

That young man worried me.   My wife, too, was on her guard.

You may now understand why I should have preferred to have seen our daughter at home; but it was not so easy to forbid her to go to my cousin's. George and his wife might have been angry; and that troubled us.

Fortunately about that time the eldest son of Father Heitz,* the owner of the quarry, asked for Grédel in marriage.

For a long while, Monsieur Mathias Heitz, junior, had come every Sunday from Wilsberg to the " Cruchon d'Or," to amuse himself with Jacob, as young men do when they have intentions with regard to a family.   He was a fine young man, fat, with red cheeks and ears, and always well dressed, with a flowered velvet waistcoat, and seals to his watch-chain; in a word, just such a young man as a girl with any good sense would be glad to have for a husband.

He had property too; he was the eldest of five children.   I reckoned that his own share might be fifteen to twenty thousand francs after the death of his parents.

Well, this young man demanded Grédel in marriage, and at once Jacob, my wife, and myself were agreed to accept him.

Only my wife thought that we ought to consult

---

* It is usual there for fathers of families to be distinguished as Father So-and-So.

Cousin George and Marie Anne. Grédel was just there when I went in with Catherine; but behold! on the first mention of the thing she began to melt into tears, and to say she would rather die than marry Mathias Heitz. You may imagine how angry we were. My wife was going to slap her face or box her ears; but my cousin became angry now, and told us that we ought never to oblige a girl to marry against her will, because this was the way to make miserable households. Then he led us out into the passage, telling us that he took the responsibility of this affair: that he wished to obtain information, and that we were to tell the young man that we required a month for reflection.

We could not refuse him that. Grédel would no longer come home; my cousin's wife begged us not to plague her, and we had to give way to them; but it was one of the greatest troubles of my life. And I thought: "Now you cannot give your daughter to whoever you like; is not this really abominable?"

I felt angry with myself for having listened to my cousin: but, nevertheless, Grédel stayed with them a whole week, in consequence of which we were obliged to hire a charwoman; and Jacob exclaimed that Grédel could not have offered him a worse insult than to refuse his best comrade, a rich fellow, who boldly paid down his money for ten, fifteen, and twenty bottles at the club without winking.

However, he never mentioned it to Cousin

George, for whom he felt the greatest respect on account of his expectations from him, and whose strong language dismayed him.

At last my wife found that Grédel was staying too long away from home; the people of the village would talk about it; so one evening I went to see George, to ask him what he had learned about Heitz's son.

It was after supper. Grédel, seeing me come in, slipped out into the kitchen, and my cousin said to me frankly: " Listen, Christian: here is the matter in two words—Grédel loves another."

" Whom ? "

" Jean Baptiste Werner."

" Father Heitz's clerk? the son of the woodward Werner, who has never had anything but potatoes to eat? Is she in love with him? Let the wretch come—let him come and ask her! I'll kick him down the stairs! And Grédel to grieve me so? Oh! I should never have believed it of her! "

I could have cried.

" Come, Christian," said my cousin, " you must be reasonable."

" Reasonable! she deserves to have her neck wrung! "

I was in a fury; I wanted to lay hold on her. Happily, she had gone into the garden, and George held me back. He obliged me to sit down again, and said: " What is Mathias Heitz? a fat fool who knows nothing but how to play at cards and drink.

He was put to college at Phalsbourg, at M. Verrot's,
like all the other respectable young men in the district; but he now drives about in a char-à-banc in a
flowered waistcoat, with jingling seals: he could
not possibly earn a couple of pence—and the old
man would like to be rid of him by marrying him.
I have obtained information about him. He may
come in for from fifteen to twenty thousand francs
some day; but what are fifteen thousand francs for
an ass? He will eat them, he will drink them—perhaps he has already swallowed half—and if there is
a family, what are fifteen or even twenty thousand
francs between five or six children? Formerly,
when girls used to have an outfit for a marriage portion, and the eldest son succeeded his father, things
went on pretty well. It did not want much talent
to carry on a well-established business, or to follow
up a trade from father to son. But at the present
day, mother-wit and good sense stand in the foremost
rank. Grandfather Heitz was an industrious man;
he made money; but Father Mathias has never
added a sou to his property, and the son has not a
grain of good sense."

"But the other fellow—why he has nothing at
all."

"The other, Jean Baptiste Werner, is a good
man, who has done his duty by Father Heitz; he
knows everything, manages everything, takes in orders, makes all the arrangements for the carriage of
stone by carts or by railway. Heitz puts the money

into his pocket, and Werner has all the work, for want of a little capital to set himself up in business. He has seen foreign service. I have seen his certificates of character in Africa, in Mexico: they are excellent. If I were in your place, I would give Grédel to him."

"Never!" cried I, thumping upon the table; "I had rather drown her."

Half the wine-glasses were shattered on the floor; but my cousin was not angry.

"Well, Christian," said he, "you are wrong. Think it over. Grédel will remain here. I will answer for her. You must not take her away at present. You would be very likely to ill-treat her, and then you would repent of it."

"Let her stay as long as you like!" said I, taking up my hat; "let her never darken my doors again." And I rushed out.

Never in my life had I been so angry and so grieved. At home I did not even dare to say what I had learned; but Jacob suspected it, and one day, as Werner was stopping in front of the mill, he shook his pitchfork at him, shouting: "Come on!" But Werner pretended not to hear him, and went on his way.

I was at last, however, obliged to tell my wife the whole matter. At first she was near fainting; but she soon recovered, and said to me: "Well, if Grédel won't have young Mathias, we shall keep our hundred louis, and we shall have no need to hire a new servant. I should prefer that, for one cannot trust strange servants in a house."

"Yes; but how can we declare to Mathias Heitz that Grédel refuses his son?"

"Oh, don't trouble yourself, Christian," said she; "leave me alone, and don't let us quarrel with Cousin George: that's the principal thing. I will say that Grédel is too young to be married; that is the proper thing to say, and nobody can answer that."

Catherine quieted me in this way. But this business was still racking my brain, when extraordinary things came to pass, which we were far from expecting, and which were to turn our hair gray, and that of many others with us.

CHAPTER III

ONE morning the secretary of the sous-préfet wrote to me to come to Sarrebourg. From time to time we used to receive orders, as magistrates, to go and give an account at the sous-préfecture of what was going on in our district.

I said to myself, immediately on receiving this letter from Secretary Gérard, that it was something about our Agricultural Society, which had not yet delivered the prizes gained by the ducks and the geese a few weeks before.

It was true that the Paris newspapers had for three days past been discussing a Prince of Hohenzollern, who had just been named King of Spain; but what could that signify to us at Rothalp, Illingen, Droulingen, and Henridorf, whether the King of Spain was called Hohenzollern or by any other name?

In my opinion, it could not be about that affair that Monsieur le Sous-préfet wanted to talk to us, but about the old or a new Agricultural Society, or something at least which concerned us in particular. The idea of the parish road and the bells came also into my mind; perhaps that was the object we were sent for.

At last I took up my staff and started for Sarre-bourg.

Arriving there, I found the whole length of the principal street crowded with mayors, police-inspectors, and *juges-de-paix*.* Mother Adler's inn and all the little public-houses were so full that they could not have held another customer.

Then I said to myself, no doubt something quite new is in the wind: as, for instance; a fête like that when her Majesty the Empress and the Prince Imperial, three years before, passed through Nancy to celebrate the union of Lorraine with France. Thereupon I went to the sous-préfecture, where I found already several mayors of the neighborhood talking at the door. They were discussing the price of corn, the high price of cattle food; they were called in one after another.

In half an hour my turn came; Monsieur Christian Weber's name was called, and I entered with my hat in my hand.

Monsieur le Sous-préfet with his secretary Gérard, with his pen stuck behind his ear, were seated there: the secretary began to mend his pen; and Monsieur le Sous-préfet asked me what was going on in my part of the country?

"In our country, Monsieur le Sous-préfet? why, nothing at all. There is a great drought; no rain has fallen for six weeks; the potatoes are very small, and . . ."

* Magistrates.

" I don't mean that, Monsieur le Maire: what
do they think of the Prince Hohenzollern and the
Crown of Spain? "

On hearing this I scratched my head, saying to
myself, " What will you answer to that now?
What must you say? "

Then Monsieur le Sous-préfet asked: " What is
the spirit of your population? "

The spirit of our population? How could I get
out of that?

" You see, Monsieur le Sous-préfet, in our villages the people are no scholars; they don't read
the papers."

" But tell me, what do they think of the war? "

" What war? "

" If, now, we should have war with Germany,
would those people be satisfied? "

Then I began to catch a glimpse of his meaning, and I said: " You know, Monsieur le Sous-
préfet, that we have voted in the Plébiscite to have
peace, because everybody likes trade and business
and quietness at home; we only want to have work
and . . ."

" Of course, of course, that is plain enough; we
all want peace: his Majesty the Emperor, and her
Majesty the Empress, and everybody love peace!
But if we are attacked: if Count Bismarck and the
King of Prussia attack us? "

" Then, Monsieur le Sous-préfet, we shall be
obliged to defend ourselves in the best way we can;

by all sorts of means, with pitchforks, with sticks . . ."

" Put that down, Monsieur Gérard, write down those words. You are right, Monsieur le Maire: I felt sure of you beforehand," said Monsieur le Sous-préfet, shaking hands with me: " You are a worthy man."

Tears came into my eyes. He came with me to the door, saying: " The determination of your people is admirable; tell them so: tell them that we wish for peace; that our only thought is for peace; that his Majesty and their excellencies the Ministers want nothing but peace; but that France cannot endure the insults of an ambitious power. Communicate your own ardor to the village of Roth-alp. Good, very good. *Au revoir*, Monsieur le Maire, farewell."

Then I went out, much astonished; another mayor took my place, and I thought, " What! does that Bismarck mean to attack us! Oh, the villain! "

But as yet I could tell neither why nor how.

I repaired to Mother Adler's, where I ordered bread and cheese and a bottle of white wine, according to custom, before returning home; and there I heard all those gentlemen, the Government officials, the controllers, the tax-collectors, the judges, the receivers, etc., assembled in the public room, telling one another that the Prussians were going to invade us; that they had already taken half of Germany, and that they were wanting now to lay the Spaniards upon our back in order to take the rest: just as they had put Italy upon the back of the Austrians, before Sadowa.

All the mayors present were of the same opinion; they all answered that they would defend themselves, if we were attacked; for the Lorrainers and the Alsacians have never been behindhand in defending themselves: all the world knows that.

I went on listening; at last, having paid my bill, I started to return home.

I went out of Sarrebourg,' and had walked for half an hour in the dust, reflecting upon what had just taken place, when I heard a conveyance coming at a rapid rate behind me. I turned round. It was Cousin George upon his char-à-banc, at which I was much pleased.

" Is that you, cousin? " said he, pulling up.

" Yes; I am just come from Sarrebourg, and I am not sorry to meet with you, for it is terribly warm."

" Well, up with you," said he. " You have had a great gathering to-day; I saw all the public-houses full."

I was up, I took my seat, and the conveyance went off again at a trot.

" Yes," said I; " it is a strange business; you would never guess why we have been sent for to the sous-préfecture."

" What for? "

Then I told him all about it; being much excited against the villain Bismarck, who wanted to invade us, and had just invented this Hohenzollern pretext to drive us to extremities.

George listened. At last he said: " My poor Christian! the sous-préfet was quite right in calling you a worthy fellow; and all those other mayors that I saw down there, with their red noses, are worthy men; but do you know my opinion upon all those matters?"

" What do you think, George?"

" Well, my belief is, that they are leading you like a string of asses by the bridle. That sous-préfet will present his report to the préfet, the préfet to the Minister of the Interior, Monsieur Chevandier de Valdrôme,—the organizer of the Plébiscite—he who told you to vote ' Yes ' to have peace—and that Minister will present his report to the Emperor. They all know that the Emperor desires war, because he needs it for his dynasty."

" What! he wants war?"

" No doubt he does. In spite of all, forty-five thousand soldiers have voted against the Plébiscite. The army is turning round against the dynasty. There is no more promotion: medals, crosses, promotions were distributed in profusion at first, now all that has stopped; the inferior officers have no more hope of passing into the higher ranks, because the army is filled with nobles, with Jesuits from the schools of the Sacred College: in the Court calendars nothing is seen but *de*'s. The soldiers, who spring from the people, begin to discern that they are being gradually extinguished: they are not in a pleasant temper. But war may put everything straight again: a few battles are wanted to throw light upon the malcontents; there must be a victory to crush the Republicans, for the Republicans are gaining confidence: they are lifting up their heads. After a victory, a few thousand of them can be sent to Lambessa and to Cayenne, just as after the Second of December. At the same time, the Jesuits will be placed at the head of the schools, as they were under Charles X., the Pope will be restored, Italy and Germany will be dismembered, and the dynasty will be placed on a strong foundation for twenty years. Every twenty years they will begin again, and the dynasty will strike deep root. But war there must be."

" But what do you mean? It is Bismarck who is beginning it," said I: " it is he who is picking a German quarrel."

" Bismarck," replied my cousin, " is well acquainted with everything that is going on, and so are the very lowest workmen in Paris; but you, you know nothing at all. Your only talk is about potatoes and cabbages: your thoughts never go beyond this. You are kept in ignorance. You are, as it were, the dung of the Empire—the manure to fatten the dynasty. Bismarck is aware that our *honest man* wants war, to temper his army afresh,

4

and shut the mouths of those whose talk is of economy, liberty, honor, and justice; he knows that
never will Prussia be so strong again as she is now
—she already covers three-fourths of Germany; all
the Germans will march at her side to fight against
France: they can put more than a million of men
in the field in fifteen days, and they will be three
or four against one; with such odds there is no need
of genius, the war will go forward of itself—they
are sure of crushing the enemy."

"But the Emperor must know that as well as
you, George," said I; "therefore he will be for
peace." ·

"No, he is relying upon his mitrailleuses: and
then he wants to strengthen his dynasty—what
does the rest matter to him?   To establish his dynasty he took an oath before God and man to the
Republic, and then he trampled upon his oath and
the Republic; he brought destruction upon thousands of good men, who were defending the laws
against him; he has enriched thousands of thieves
who uphold him; he has corrupted our youth by
the evil example of the **prosperity** of brigands,
and the misfortunes of the well-disposed; he has
brought low everything that was worthy of respect,
he has exalted everything which excites disgust and
contempt.   All the men who have approached this
pestilence have been contaminated, to the very
marrow of their bones.   You, Christian, evidently
cannot comprehend these abominable things; but

the worst rogues in this country, the wildest vaga-
bonds among your peasants, could never form an
opinion of the villany of this *honest man:* they
are saints compared with him; at the very sight of
him the heart of every true Frenchman rises up
against him: for the sake of his dynasty he would
sell and sacrifice us all to the last man."

George, in uttering these words, was trembling
with excitement: I saw that he was convinced to
the bottom of his heart of what he said. Fortunately we were alone on the road, far from any
village; no one could hear us.

"But that Hohenzollern," I said, after a few
minutes' silence, "that Leopold Hohenzollern—is
not he the cause of all that is going on?"

"No," said George; "if misfortunes come upon
us, the *honest man* alone will be the cause of it.
If you did but read a newspaper, you would see that
the Spaniards wanted for their king, Montpensier,
a son of Louis Philippe; that could only have
turned out to our good: Montpensier would naturally have become the ally of France. But that
was against the interests of the Napoleon dynasty;
so the *honest man* threatened Spain; then the
Spaniards nominated this Prussian prince in the
place of Montpensier; a prince who could not stand
alone, but whom a million of Germans would support if necessary. They fixed upon him to annoy
our gentleman; of course they had no need to ask
for his advice. Did France consult any one? did

she trouble herself about England, Spain, or Germany, when she proclaimed the Republic, or when she proclaimed Louis Bonaparte Emperor? Has he then a right to thrust his nose into their affairs? No; it is unpleasant for us; but the Spaniards were right; there was no need for them to put themselves out to please our *worthy man* and his fine family. And now—happen what may—I look no longer for peace; the Germans are withdrawing from our country in all directions—they are joining their regiments; the order has been given, and they obey; it is a bad sign. In all the villages that I have been passing through, and upon every road, I have seen these fine fellows, their bundles over their shoulders—they are off home!"

Thus spoke Cousin George to me. I thought this was a little too bad; but, on arriving home, the first thing my wife said to me was, "Do you know that Frantz is going?"

"Our young man?"

"Yes, he wants his wages."

"Ah, indeed. Let him come here at the back, and we will have a talk."

I was much surprised, and I made him come into my room at the bottom of the mill, where I keep my papers and my books. His cow-skin pack was already fastened upon his shoulder.

"Are you going away, Frantz? Have you anything to complain of?"

"No, nothing at all, Monsieur Weber. But I

am obliged to go; for I have received orders to join my regiment."

" Are you a soldier, then? "

" Yes, in the Landwehr. We are all soldiers in Germany."

" But if you liked to stay here, who would come and fetch you? "

" That is an impossibility, M. Weber. I should be declared a deserter. I could never return home again. They would take away all my property, present and to come; my brothers and sisters would come in for it."

" Ah, that is a different thing! Now I understand. There—there's your certificate of character."

I had written a good certificate for him, for he was a good workman. I paid him what I owed him to the last farthing, and wished him a prosperous journey.

Cousin George was right; those Germans were all moving homeward. You would never have thought there were so many in the country; some had passed themselves off for Swiss, some for Luxemburgers; others had quite settled down, and no one would ever have suspected that they owed two or three more years' service to their country. This gave rise to disputes. Those whose situations they had taken, and who bore ill-will against them, fell upon them; the *gendarmerie* beat up the mountains; things were taking an ugly turn.

It was in vain that I affirmed at the mayoralty-
house that the Emperor breathed only peace; for
the Gazettes of the préfecture talked of nothing
but the insults we had had to endure, the ambition of Prussia, revenge for Sadowa, the Catholic
nations who were going to declare *en masse* in our
favor, and all the powers which affirmed the justice of our cause: the enthusiasm for war grew
higher and higher day by day; especially that of
the pedlers, the tinkers, the small dealers, and all
those good fellows who come out of the prisons,
and who are continually seeking for work without
finding any; though they do find walls to get over,
doors to break in, cupboards to plunder. All these
excellent people declared that it was for the honor
of France to make war upon Germany.

And then the Paris newspapers in the pay of
the Government, as we have more recently learned,
continued arriving and were circulated gratis, saying that our ambassador Benedetti had gone to see
Frederick William at the waters of Ems, to entreat
him not to precipitate us into the horrors of war;
that the King had answered that all that was nothing to him, for his Cousin Leopold of Hohenzollern
had only consulted him out of respect, as head of
the family; that he was too good a relation to ad-
vise him not to accept so good a windfall, which was
coming down to him out of the clouds.

Then, indeed, did the indignation of the Gazettes
burst upon the Germans: they must, by all means,

be brought to their senses. Now, fancy the position of a mayor, who only two months before had made all his village vote in the Plébiscite, promising them peace, and who saw clearly at last how they had only made use of him as a tool to dupe his people! I dared no longer look my cousin in the face, for he had warned me of the thing; and now I knew what to think of the honorable members of the Government.

Affairs were going on so badly that war seemed imminent, when one fine morning we learned that Hohenzollern had waived his right to be King of Spain. Ah! now we were out of the mess: now we could breathe more freely. That day my cousin himself was smiling; he came to the mill and said to me: "The Emperor and his Ministers, his préfets and sous-préfets, have not such long noses after all! How well things were going on too! And now they will be obliged to wait for another opportunity to begin. How they must feel sold!"

We both laughed with delight.

More than twenty-five of the principal inhabitants came that day to shake hands with me at the mayoralty-house. It was concluded that his excellency, Monsieur Emile Ollivier, would never be able to tinker this war again, and that peace would be preserved in spite of him: in spite of the Emperor, in spite of Marshal Lebœuf, who had declared to the Senate that *we were ready—five times ready, and that during the whole campaign we*

should never be short of so much as a gaiter but-
ton.

Hohenzollern was praised up to the skies for
having shown such good sense; and as the reserves
had been called out, many young men were glad to
be able to remain in the bosom of their families.

In a word, it was concluded that the whole affair
was at an end; when our *good man* and his honorable Minister informed us that we had begun to
rejoice too soon. All at once, the report ran that
Frederick William had shown our ambassador the
door, saying something so terribly strong against
the honor of his Majesty Napoleon III., that nobody dared repeat it. It appeared that his Majesty
the Emperor, seeing that the King of Prussia had
withdrawn his authorization from the Prince of
Hohenzollern to accept the Crown of Spain, had not
been satisfied with that; and that he had given
orders to his ambassador to demand, furthermore,
his renunciation of any crown whatever that the
Spaniards might offer him in all time to come—for
himself or his family; and that this King, who does
not enjoy at all times the best of tempers, had said
something very strong touching *our honest man.*

That day I was at the mayoralty-house about
eleven o'clock. I had just celebrated the marriage
of André Fix with Kaan's daughter, and the wedding-party had started for church, when the postman Michel comes in and throws down the little
Moniteur upon the table. Then I sat down to read

about the great battle in the Legislative Chambers, fought by Thiers, Gambetta, Jules Favre, Glais-Bizoin and others, against the Ministers, in defence of peace.

It was magnificent. But this had not prevented the majority, appointed to do everything, from declaring war against the Germans, on account of what the King of Prussia had said.

What could he then have said? His excellency Emile Ollivier has never dared to repeat it! My Cousin George declared that he had said something that was right, and naturally very unpleasant: but it is known now, by the reports of our ambassador, that the King of Prussia had said *nothing at all*, and that the indignation of M. Ollivier was nothing but a disgraceful sham to deceive the Chambers, and make them vote for war.

Well, this was the commencement of our calamities; and, for my part, I find that this did not present a cheerful prospect. No! After having endured such miseries, it is not pleasant to remember that we owe them all to M. Emile Ollivier, to Monsieur Lebœuf, to Monsieur Bonaparte, and to other men of that stamp, who are living at this moment comfortably in their country-houses in Italy, in Switzerland, in England; whilst so many unhappy creatures have had their lives sacrificed, or have been utterly ruined; have lost father, children, and friends: but we Alsacians and Lorrainers have lost more than all—our own mother-country.

CHAPTER IV

THE day following this declaration, Cousin George, who could never look upon anything cheerfully, started for Belfort. He had ordered some wine at Dijon, and he wished to stop it from coming. It was the 22d July. George only returned five days later, on the 27th, having had the greatest difficulty in getting there in time.

During these five days I had a hard time. Orders were coming every hour to hurry on the reserves and the Gardes Mobiles, and to cancel renewable furloughs; the gendarmerie had no rest. The Government gazette was telling us of the enthusiasm of the nation for the war. It was pitiable; can you imagine young men sitting quietly at home, thinking: " In five or six months I shall be exempt from service, I may marry, settle, earn money," all at once, without either rhyme or reason, becoming enthusiastic to go and knock over men they know nothing of, and to risk their own bones against them. Is there a shadow of good sense in such notions?

And the Germans! Will any one persuade us that they were coming for their own pleasure—all these thousands of workmen, tradesmen, manufacturers, good citizens, who were living in peace

in their towns and their villages? Will any one
maintain that they came and drew up in lines facing our guns for their private satisfaction, with an
officer behind them, pistol in hand, to shoot them
in the back if they gave way? Do you suppose
they found any amusement in that? Come now,
was not his excellency Monsieur Ollivier the only
man who went into war, as he himself said, " with
a light heart?" He was safe to come back, he was:
he had not much to fear; he is quite well; he made
a fortune in a very short time! But the lads of our
neighborhood, Mathias Heitz, Jean Baptiste Werner, my son Jacob, and hundreds of others, were in
no such hurry: they would much rather have stayed
in their villages.

Later on it was another matter, when you were
fighting for your country; then, of course, many
went off as a matter of duty, without being summoned, whilst Monsieur Ollivier and his friends
were hiding, God knows where! But at that particular moment when all our misfortunes might
have been averted, it is a falsehood to say that we
went enthusiastically to have ourselves cut to pieces
for a pack of intriguers and stage-players, whom
we were just beginning to find out.

When we saw our son Jacob, in his blouse, his
bundle under his arm, come into the mill, saying,
" Now, father, I am going; you must not forget
to pull up the dam in half an hour, for the water
will be up: " when he said this to me, I tell you

my heart trembled; the cries of his mother in the
room behind made my hair stand on end. I could
have wished to say a few words, to cheer up the lad,
but my tongue refused to move; and if I had held
his excellency, M. Ollivier, or his respected master,
by the throat in a corner, they would have made a
queer figure: I should have strangled them in a
moment! At last Jacob went.

All the young men of Sarrebourg, of Château
Salins, and our neighborhood, fifteen or sixteen
hundred in number, were at Phalsbourg to relieve
the 84th, who at any moment might expect to be
called away, and who were complaining of their
colonel for not claiming the foremost rank for his
regiment. The officers were afraid of arriving too
late; they wanted promotion, crosses, medals:
fighting was their trade.

What I have said about enthusiasm is true; it
is equally true of the Germans and the French;
they had no desire to exterminate one another.
Bismarck and our *honest man* alone are responsible: at their door lies all the blood that has been
shed.

Cousin George returned from Belfort on the
27th, in the evening. I fancy I still see him entering our room at nightfall; Grédel had returned
to us the day before, and we were at supper, with
the tin lamp upon the table; from my place, on
the right, near the window, I was able to watch the
mill-dam. George arrived.

I SHOULD HAVE STRANGLED THEM IN A MOMENT.

"Ah! cousin, here you are back again! Did you get on all right?"

"Yes, I have nothing to complain of," said he, taking a chair. "I arrived just in time to countermand my order; but it was only by good luck. What confusion all the way from Belfort to Strasbourg! the troops, the recruits, the guns, the horses, the munitions of war, the barrels of biscuits, all are arriving at the railway in heaps. You would not know the country. Orders are asked for everywhere. The telegraph-wires are no longer for private use. The commissaries don't know where to find their stores, colonels are looking for their regiments, generals for their brigades and divisions. They are seeking for salt, sugar, coffee, bacon, meat, saddles and bridles—and they are getting charts of the Baltic for a campaign in the Vosges! Oh!" cried my cousin, uplifting his hands, "is it possible? Have we come to that—we! we! Now it will be seen how expensive a thing is a government of thieves! I warn you, Christian, it will be a failure! Perhaps there will not even be found rifles in the arsenals, after the hundreds of millions voted to get rifles. You will see; you will see!"

He had begun to stride to and fro excitedly, and we, sitting on our chairs, were looking at him openmouthed, staring first right and then left. His anger rose higher and higher, and he said, "Such is the genius of our honest man, he conducts everything: he is our commander-in-chief! A retired

artillery captain, with whom I travelled from Schle-
stadt to Strasbourg, told me that in consequence of
the bad organization of our forces, we should be unable to place more than two hundred and fifty thousand men in line along our frontier from Luxem-
bourg to Switzerland; and that the Germans, with
their superior and long-prepared organization, could
oppose to us, in eight days, a force of five to six hundred thousand men; so that they will be more than
two to one at the outset, and they will crush us in
spite of the valor of our soldiers. This old officer,
full of good sense, and who has travelled in Germany, told me, besides, that the artillery of the
Prussians carries farther and is worked more rapidly than ours; which would enable the Germans
to dismount our batteries and our mitrailleuses
without getting any harm themselves. It seems
that our great man never thought of that."

Then George began to laugh, and, as we said
nothing, he went on: " And the enemy—the Prussians, Bavarians, Badeners, Wurtembergers, the
Courrier du Bas-Rhin declares that they are coming by regiments and divisions from Frankfort and
Munich to Rastadt, with guns, munitions, and
provisions in abundance; that all the country swarms with them, from Karlsruhe to Baden; that they have blown up the bridge of Kehl,
to prevent us from outflanking them; that we
have not troops enough at Wissembourg. But
what is the use of complaining? Our commander-

in-chief knows better than the *Courrier du Bas-Rhin;* he is an iron-clad fellow, who takes no advice: a man must have some courage to offer him advice!"

And all at once, stopping short, "Christian," he said, "I have come to give you a little advice."

" What?"

" Hide all the money you have got; for, from what I have seen down there, in a few days the enemy will be in Alsace."

Imagine my astonishment at hearing these words. George was not the man to joke about serious matters, nor was he a timid man: on the contrary, you would have to go far to find a braver man. Therefore, fancy my wife's and Grédel's alarm.

" What, George," said I, " do you think that possible?"

" Listen to me," said he. " When on the one side you see nothing but empty beings, without education, without judgment, prudence, or method; and on the other, men who for fifty years have been preparing a mortal blow—anything is possible. Yes, I believe it; in a fortnight the Germans will be in Alsace. Our mountains will check them; the fortresses of Bitche, of Petite Pierre, of Phalsbourg and Lichtenberg; the abatis, and the intrenchments which will be formed in the passes; the ambuscades of every kind which will be set, the bridges and the railway tunnels that they will blow up— all this will prevent them from going farther for three or four months until winter; but, in the meantime, they will send this way reconnoitring parties—Uhlans, hussars, brigands of every kind —who will snap up everything, pillage everywhere —wheat, flour, hay, straw, bacon, cattle, and principally money. War will be made upon our backs. We Alsacians and Lorrainers, we shall have to pay the bill. I know all about it. I have been all over the country-side; believe me. Hide everything; that is what I mean to do; and, if anything happens, at least it will not be our fault. I would not go to bed without giving you this warning; so good-night, Christian; good-night, everybody!"

He left us, and we sat a few moments gazing stupidly at each other. My wife and Grédel wanted to hide everything that very night. Grédel, ever since she had got Jean Baptiste Werner into her head, was thinking of nothing but her marriage-portion. She knew that we had about a hundred louis in cent-sous pieces in a basket at the bottom of the cupboard; she said to herself, "That's my marriage-portion!" And this troubled her more than anything: she even grew bolder, and wanted to keep the keys herself. But her mother is not a woman to be led: every minute she cried: "Take care, Grédel! mind what you are about!"

She looked daggers at her; and I was continually obliged to come to preserve peace between them; for Catherine is not gifted with patience. And so all our troubles came together.

But, in spite of what George had just been saying, I was not afraid. The Germans were less than sixteen leagues from us, it is true, but they would have first to cross the Rhine; then we knew that at Niederbronn the people were complaining of the troops cantoned in the villages: this was a proof that there was no lack of soldiers; and then Mac-Mahon was at Strasbourg; the Turcos, the Zouaves, and the Chasseurs d'Afrique were coming up.

So I said to my wife that there was no hurry yet; that Cousin George had long detested the Emperor; but that all that did not mean much, and it was better to see things for one's self; that I should go to Saverne market, and if things looked bad, then I would sell all our corn and flour, which would come to a hundred louis, and which we would bury directly with the rest.

My wife took courage; and if I had not had a great deal to grind for the bakers in our village, I should have gone next day to Saverne and should have seen what was going on. Unfortunately, ever since Frantz and Jacob had left, the mill was on my hands, and I scarcely had time to turn round.

Jacob was a great trouble to me besides, asking for money by the postman Michel. This man told me that the Mobiles had not yet been called out, and that they were lounging from one public-house to another in gangs to kill time; that they had received no rifles; that they were not quartered in the barracks; and that they did not get a farthing for their food.

This disorder disgusted me; and I reflected that an Emperor who sends for all the young men in harvest-time, ought at least to feed them, and not leave them to be an expense to their parents. For all that I sent money to Jacob: I could not allow him to suffer hunger. But it was a trouble to my mind to keep him down there with my money, sauntering about with his hands in his pockets, whilst I, at my age, was obliged to carry sacks up into the loft, to fetch them down again, to load the carts alone, and, besides, to watch the mill; for no one could be met with now, and the old day-laborer, Donadieu, quite a cripple, was all the help I had. After that, only imagine our anxiety, our fatigue, and our embarrassment to know what to do.

The other people in the village were in no better spirits than ourselves. The old men and women thought of their sons shut up in the town, and the great drought continuing: we could rely upon nothing. The smallpox had broken out, too. Nothing would sell, nothing could be sent by railway: planks, beams, felled timber, building-stone, all lay at the saw-pits or the stone-quarry. The sous-préfet kept on troubling me to search and find out three or four scamps who had not reported themselves, and the consequence of all this was that I did not get to Saverne that week.

Then it was announced that at last the Emperor had just quitted Paris, to place himself at the head of his armies; and five or six days after came the news of his great victory at Sarrebrück, where the mitrailleuses had mown down the Prussians; where the little Prince had picked up bullets, "which made old soldiers shed tears of emotion."

On learning this the people became crazy with joy. On all sides were heard cries of " Vive l'Empereur! " and Monsieur le Curé preached the extermination of the heretic Prussians. Never had the like been seen. That very day, toward evening, just after stopping the mill, all at once I heard in the distance, toward the road, cries of " *Aux armes, citoyens! formez vos bataillons!* "

The dust from the road rose up into the clouds. It was the 84th departing from Phalsbourg; they were going to Metz, and the people who were working in the fields near the road, said, on returning at night, that the poor soldiers, with their knapsacks on their shoulders, could scarcely march for the heat; that the people were treating them with eau-de-vie and wine at all the doors in Metting, and they said, " Good-by! long life to you! " that the officers, too, were shaking hands with everybody, whilst the people shouted, " Vive l'Empereur! "

Yes, this victory of Sarrebrück had changed the face of things in our villages; the love of war was returning. War is always popular when it is successful, and there is a prospect of extending our own territory into other peoples' countries.

That night about nine o'clock I went to caution my cousin to hold his tongue; for after this great victory one word against the dynasty might send him a very long way off. He was alone with his wife, and said to me, " Thank you, Christian, I have seen the despatch. A few brave fellows have been killed, and they have shown the young Prince to the army. That poor little weakly creature has picked up a few bullets on the battle-field. He is the heir of his uncle, the terrible captain of Jena and Austerlitz! Only one officer has been killed; it is not much; but if the heir of the dynasty had had but a scratch, the gazettes would have shed tears, and it would have been our duty to fall fainting."

" Do try to be quiet," said I, looking to see if the windows were all close. " Do take care, George. Don't commit yourself to Placiard and the gendarmes."

" Yes," said he, " the enemies of the dynasty are at this moment in worse danger than the little Prince. If victories go on, they will run the risk of being plucked pretty bare. I am quite aware of that, my cousin; and so I thank you for having come to warn me."

This is all that he said to me, and I returned home full of thoughts.

Next day, Thursday, market-day, I drove my

AND WE HAVE TO PAY THE BILL.

first two wagon-loads of flour to Saverne, and sold them at a good figure. That day I observed the tremendous movement along the railroads, of which Cousin George had spoken; the carriage of mitrailleuses, guns, chests of biscuits, and the enthusiasm of the people, who were pouring out wine for the soldiers.

It was just like a fair in the principal street, from the château to the station—a fair of little white loaves and sausages; but the Turcos, with their blue jackets, their linen trousers, and their scarlet caps, took the place of honor: everybody wanted to treat them.

I had never before seen any of these men; their yellow skins, their thick lips, the conspicuous whites of their eyes, surprised me; and I said to myself, seeing the long strides they took with their thin legs, that the Germans would find them unpleasant neighbors. Their officers, too, with their swords at their sides, and their pointed beards, looked splendid soldiers. At every public-house door, a few Chasseurs d'Afrique had tied their small light horses, all alike and beautifully formed like deer. No one refused them anything; and in all directions, in the inns, the talk was of ambulances and collections for the wounded. Well, seeing all this, George's ideas seemed to me more and more opposed to sound sense, and I felt sure that we were going to crush all resistance.

About two o'clock, having dined at the Bœuf,

I took the way to the village through Phalsbourg, to see Jacob in passing. As I went up the hill, something glittered from time to time on the slope through the woods, when all at once hundreds of cuirassiers came out upon the road by the Alsace fountain. They were advancing at a slow pace by twos, their helmets and their cuirasses threw back flashes of light upon all the trees, and the trampling of their hoofs rolled like the rush of a mighty river.

Then I drew my wagon to one side to see all these men march past me, sitting immovable in their saddles as if they were sleeping, the head inclined forward, and the mustache hanging, riding strong, square-built horses, the canvas bag suspended from the side, and the sabre ringing against the boot. Thus they filed past me for half an hour. They extended their long lines, and stretched on yet to the Schlittenbach. I thought there would be no end to them. Yet these were only two regiments; two others were encamped upon the glacis of Phalsbourg, where I arrived about five in the afternoon. They were driving the pickets into the turf with axes; they were lighting fires for cooking; the horses were neighing, and the townspeople—men, women, and children—were standing gazing at them.

I passed on my way, reflecting upon the strength of such an army, and pitying, by anticipation, the ill-fated Germans whom they were going to encounter. Entering through the gate of Germany,

I saw the officers looking for lodgings, the Gardes
Mobiles, in blouses, mounting guard. They had
received their rifles that morning; and the evening before, Monsieur le Sous-préfet of Sarrebourg
had come himself to appoint the officers of the National Guard. This is what I had learned at the
Vacheron brewery, where I had stopped, leaving my
cart outside at the corner of the " Trois Pigeons."

Everybody was talking about our victory at
Sarrebrück, especially those cuirassiers, who were
emptying bottles by the hundred, to allay the dust
of the road. They looked quite pleased, and were
saying that war on a large scale was beginning
again, and that the heavy cavalry would be in demand. It was quite a pleasure to look on them,
with their red ears, and to hear them rejoicing at
the prospect of meeting the enemy soon.

In the midst of all these swarms of people, of servants running, citizens coming and going, I could
have wished to see Jacob; but where was I to look
for him? At last I recognized a lad of our village—
Nicolas Maïsse—the son of the wood-turner, our
neighbor, who immediately undertook to find him.
He went out, and in a quarter of an hour Jacob appeared.

The poor fellow embraced me. The tears came
into my eyes.

" Well now," said I, " sit down. Are you pretty
well? "

" I had rather be at home," said he.

"Yes, but that is impossible now; you must have patience."

I also invited young Maïsse to take a glass with us, and both complained bitterly that Mathias Heitz, junior, had. been made a lieutenant, who knew no more of the science of war than they did, and who now had ordered of Kuhn, the tailor, an officer's uniform, gold-laced up to the shoulders. Yet Mathias was a friend of Jacob's. But justice is justice.

This piece of news filled me with indignation: what should Mathias Heitz be made an officer for? He had never learned anything at college; he would never have been able to earn a couple of *liards*— whilst our Jacob was a good miller's apprentice.

It was abominable. However, I made no remark; I only asked if Jean Baptiste Werner, who had a few days before joined the artillery of the National Guard, was an officer too?

Then they replied angrily that Jean Baptiste Wernér, in spite of his African and Mexican campaigns, was only a gunner in the Mariet battery, behind the powder magazines. Those who knew nothing became officers; those who knew something of war, like Mariet and Werner, were privates, or at the most sergeants. All this showed me that Cousin George was right in saying that we should be driven like beasts, and that our chiefs were void of common-sense.

Looking at all these people coming and going,

the time passed away. About eight o'clock, as we were hungry, and I wished to keep my boy with me as long as I could, I sent for a good salad and sausages, and we were eating together, with full hearts, to be sure, but with a good appetite. But a few moments after the retreat, just when the cuirassiers were going to camp out, and their officers, heavy and weary, were going to rest in their lodgings, a few bugle notes were sounded in the *place d'armes*, and we heard a cry—"To horse! to horse!"

Immediately all was excitement. A despatch had arrived; the officers put on their helmets, fastened on their swords, and came running out through the gate of Germany. Countenances changed; every one asked, "What is the meaning of this?"

At the same time the police inspector came up; he had seen my cart, and cried, "Strangers must leave the place—the gates are going to be closed."

Then I had only just time to embrace my son, to press Nicolas's hand, and to start at a sharp gallop for the gate of France. The drawbridge was just on the rise as I passed it; five minutes after I was galloping along the white high-road by moonlight, on the way to Metting. Outside on the glacis, there was not a sound; the pickets had been drawn, and the two regiments of cavalry were on the road to Saverne.

I arrived home late: everybody was asleep in our village. Nobody suspected what was about to happen within a week.

CHAPTER V

THE whole way I thought of nothing but the cuirassiers. This order to march immediately appeared to me to betoken no good: something serious must have occurred; and as, upon the stroke of eleven, I was putting my horses up, after having put my cart under its shed, the idea came into my head that it was time now to hide my money. I was bringing back from Saverne sixteen hundred livres: this heavy leathern purse in my pocket was perhaps what reminded me. I remembered what Cousin George had said about Uhlans and other scamps of that sort, and I felt a cold shiver come over me.

Having, then, gone upstairs very softly, I awoke my wife: " Get up, Catherine."

" What is the matter? "

" Get up: it is time to hide our money."

" But what is going on? "

" Nothing. Be quiet—make no noise—Grédel is asleep. You will carry the basket: put into it your ring and your ear-rings, everything that we have got. You hear me! I am going to empty the ditch, and we will bury everything at the bottom of it."

Then, without answering, she arose.

I went down to the mill, opened the back-door softly, and listened. Nothing was stirring in the village; you might have heard a cat moving. The mill had stopped, and the water was pretty high. I lifted the mill-dam, the water began to rush, boiling, down the gulley; but our neighbors were used to this noise even in their sleep, so all remained quiet.,

Then I went in again, and I was busy emptying into a corner the little box of oak in which I kept my tools—the pincers, the hammer, the screw-driver, and the nails, when my wife, in her slippers, came downstairs. She had the basket under her arm, and was carrying the lighted lantern. I blew it out in a moment, thinking: Never was a woman such a fool.

Downstairs I asked Catherine if everything was in the basket.

"Yes."

"Right. But I have brought from Saverne sixteen hundred francs: the wheat and the flour sold well."

I had put some bran into the box; everything was carefully laid in the bottom; and then I put on a padlock, and we went out, after having looked to see if all was quiet in the neighborhood. The sluice was already almost empty; there was only one or two feet of water. I cleared away the few stones which kept the rest of the water from running out, and went into it with my spade and pickaxe as far as just beneath the dam, where I began to make a deep hole; the water was hindering me, but it was flowing still.

Catherine, above, was keeping watch: sometimes she gave a low " Hush! "

Then we listened, but it was nothing—the mewing of a cat, the noise of the running water—and I went on digging. If any one had had the misfortune to surprise us, I should have been capable of doing him a mischief. Happily no one came; and about two o'clock in the morning the hole was three or four feet deep. I let down the box, and laid it down level, first stamping soil down upon it with my heavy shoes, then gravel, then large stones, then sand; the mud would cover all over of itself: there is always plenty of mud in a millstream.

After this I came out again covered with mud. I shut down the dam, and the water began to rise. About three o'clock, at the dawn of day, the sluice was almost full. I could have begun grinding again; and nobody would ever have imagined that in this great whirling stream, nine feet under water and three feet under ground, lay a snug little square box of oak, clamped with iron, with a good padlock on it, and more than four thousand livres inside. I chuckled inwardly, and said: " Now let the rascals come! "

And Catherine was well pleased too. But about four, just as I was going up to bed again, comes

Grédel, pale with alarm, crying: " Where is the money ? "

She had seen the cupboard open and the basket empty. Never had she had such a fright in her life before. Thinking that her marriage-portion was gone, her ragged hair stood upon end; she was as pale as a sheet. " Be quiet," I said, " the money is in a safe place."

" Where ? "

" It is hidden."

" Where ? "

She looked as if she was going to seize me by the collar, but her mother said to her: " That is no business of yours."

Then she became furious, and said, that if we came to die, she would not know where to find her marriage-portion.

This quarrelling annoyed me, and I said to her: " We are not going to die; on the contrary, we shall live a long while yet, to prevent you and your Jean Baptiste from inheriting our goods."

And thereupon I went to bed, leaving Grédel and her mother to come to a settlement together.

All I can say is that girls, when they have got anything into their heads, become too bold with their parents, and all the excellent training they have had ends in nothing. Thank God, I had nothing to reproach myself with on that score, nor her mother either. Grédel had had four times as many blows as Jacob, because she deserved it, on account of her wanting to keep everything, putting it all into her own cupboard, and saying, " There, that's mine! "

Yes, indeed, she had had plenty of correction of that kind: but you cannot beat a girl of twenty: you cannot correct girls at that age; and that was just my misfortune: it ought to go on forever!

Well, it can't be helped.

She upset the house and rummaged the mill from top to bottom, she visited the garden, and her mother said to her, " You see, we have got it in a safe place; since you cannot find it, the Uhlans won't."

I remember that just as we were going up to sleep, that day, the 5th of August, early in the morning, Catherine and I had seen Cousin George in his char-à-banc coming down the valley of Dosenheim, and it seemed to us that he was out very early.   The village was waking up; other people, too, were going to work: I lay down, and about eight o'clock my wife woke me to tell me that the postman, Michel, was there.   I came down, and saw Michel standing in our parlor with his letter-bag under his arm.   He was thoughtful, and told me that the worst reports were abroad; that they were speaking of the great battle near Wissembourg, where we had been defeated; that several maintained that we had lost ten thousand men, and the Germans seventeen thousand; but that there was nothing certain, because it was not known whence these rumors proceeded, only that the commanding officer of Phalsbourg, Tail-

lant, had proclaimed that morning that the inhabitants would be obliged to lay in provisions for six
weeks.   Naturally, such a proclamation set people
a-thinking, and they said: " Have we a siege before
us?   Have **we** gone back to the times of the great
retreat and downfall of the first Emperor?   Ought
things forever to end in the same fashion? "

My wife, Grédel, and I, stood listening to Michel,
with lips compressed, without interrupting him.

" And you, Michel," said I, when he had done,
" what do you think of it all? "

" Monsieur le Maire, I am a poor postman; I want
my place; and if my five hundred francs a year were
taken from me, what would become of my wife and
children? "

Then I saw that he considered our prospects were
not good.   He handed me a letter from Monsieur le
Sous-préfet—it was the last—telling me to watch
false reports; that false news should be severely
punished, by order of our préfet, Monsieur Podevin.

We could have wished no better than that the
news had been false!   But at that time, everything
that displeased the sous-préfets, the préfets, the Ministers, and the Emperor, was false, and everything
that pleased them, everything that helped to deceive
people—like that peaceful Plébiscite—was truth!

Let us change the subject: the thought of these
things turns me sick!

Michel went away, and all that day might be
noticed a stir of excitement in our village; men com-

ing and going, women watching, people going into
the wood, each with a bag, spade, and pickaxe;
stables clearing out; a great movement, and all faces
full of care: I have always thought that at that moment every one was hiding, burying anything he
could hide or bury.   I was sorry I had not begun
to sell my corn sooner, when my cousin had cautioned me a week before; but my duties as mayor
had prevented me: we must pay for our honors.   I
had still four cart-loads of corn in my barn—now
where could I put them?   And the cattle, and the
furniture, the bedding, provisions of every sort?
Never will our people forget those days, when every
one was expecting, listening, and saying: " We are
like the bird upon the twig.   We have toiled, and
sweated, and saved for fifty years, to get a little
property of our own; to-morrow shall we have anything left?   And next week, next month—shall we
not be starving to death?   And in those days of distress, shall we be able to borrow a couple of liards
upon our land, or our house?   Who will lend to us?
And all this on account of whom?   Scoundrels who
have taken us in."

Ah! if there is any justice above, as every honest
man believes, these abominable fellows will have a
heavy reckoning to pay.   So many miserable men,
women, children await them there; they are there
to demand satisfaction for all their sufferings. Yes, I
believe it.   But they—oh! they believe in nothing!
There are, indeed, dreadful brigands in this world!

All that day was spent thus, in weariness and anxiety. Nothing was known. We questioned the people who were coming from Dosenheim, Neuviller, or from farther still, but they gave no answer but this: " Make your preparations! The enemy is advancing! "

And then my stupid fool of a deputy, Placiard, who for fifteen years did nothing but cry for tobacco licenses, stamp offices, promotion for his sons, for his son-in-law, and even for himself—a sort of beggar, who spent his life in drawing up petitions and denunciations—he came into the mill, saying, " Monsieur le Maire, everything is going on well— çamarche—the enemy are being drawn into the plain: they are coming into the net. To-morrow we shall hear that they are all exterminated, every one! "

And the municipal councillors, Arnold, Frantz, Sépel, Baptiste Dida, the wood-monger, came crowding in, saying that the enemy must be exterminated; that fire must be set to the forest of Haguenau to roast them, and so on! Every one had his own plan. What fools men can be!

But the worst of it was when my wife, having learned from Michel the proclamations in the town, went up into our bacon stores, to send a few provisions to Jacob; and she perceived our two best hams were missing, with a pig's cheek, and some sausages which had been smoked weeks.

Then you should have seen her flying down the
6

stairs, declaring that the house was full of thieves; that there was no trusting anybody; and Grédel, crying louder than she, that surely Frantz, that thief of a Badener, had made off with them.   But mother had visited the bacon-room a couple of days after Frantz had left; she had seen that everything was straight; and her wrath redoubled.

Then said Grédel that perhaps Jacob, before leaving home, had put the hams into his bag with all the rest; but mother screamed, " It is a falsehood!   I should have seen it.   Jacob has never taken anything without asking for it.   He is an honest lad."

The clatter of the mill was music compared to this uproar: I could have wished to take to flight.

About seven my cousin came back upon his char-à-banc.   He was returning from Alsace; and I immediately ran into his house to hear what news he had.   George, in his large parlor, was pulling off his boots and putting on his blouse when I entered.

" Is that you, Christian? " said he.   " Is your money safe? "

" Yes."

" Very well.   I have just heard fine news at Bouxviller.   Our affairs are in splendid order!   We have famous generals!   Oh, yes! here is rather a queer beginning; and, if matters go on in this way, we shall come to a remarkable end."

His wife, Marie Anne, was coming in from the kitchen: she set upon the table a leg of mutton, bread, and wine.   George sat down, and whilst eating, told me that two regiments of the line, a regiment of Turcos, a battalion of light infantry, and a regiment of light horse, with three guns, had been posted in advance of Wissembourg, and that they were there quietly bathing in the Lauter, and washing their clothes, right in front of fifty thousand Germans, hidden in the woods; not to mention eighty thousand more on our right, who were only waiting for a good opportunity to cross the Rhine. They had been posted, as it were, in the very jaws of a wolf, which had only to give a snap to catch them, every one—and this had not failed to take place!

The Germans had surprised our small army corps the morning before; fierce encounters had taken place in the vines around Wissembourg; our men were short of artillery; the Turcos, the light-armed men, and the line had fought like lions, one to six: they had even taken eight guns in the beginning of the action; but German supports coming up in heavy masses had at last cut them to pieces; they had bombarded Wissembourg, and set fire to the town; only a few of our men had been able to retreat to the cover of the woods of Bitche going up the Vosse. It was said that a general had been killed, and that villages were lying in ruins.

It was at Bouxviller that my cousin had heard of this disaster, some of the light horsemen having arrived the same evening. There was also a talk of deserters; as if soldiers, after being routed, without knowledge of a woody country full of mountains,

going straight before them to escape from the
enemy, should be denounced as deserters. This is
one of the abominations that we have seen since that
time. Many heartless people preferred crying out
that these poor soldiers had deserted rather than give
them bread and wine: it was more convenient, and
cheaper.

"Now," said George, "all the army of Strasbourg, and that of the interior, who should have
been in perfect order, fresh, rested, and provided
with everything at Haguenau, but the rear of which
is still lagging behind on the railways as far as Lune-
ville; all these are running down there, to check
the invasion. Fourteen regiments of cavalry, principally cuirassiers and chasseurs, are assembling at
Brumath. Something is expected there; Mac-
Mahon is already on the heights of Reichshoffen,
with the commander of engineers, Mohl, of Haguenau, and other staff officers, to select his position.
As fast as the troops arrive they extend before Niederbronn. I heard this from some people who were
flying with wives and children, their beds and other
chattels on carts, as I was leaving Bouxviller about
three o'clock. They wanted to reach the fort of
Petite Pierre; but hearing that the fort is occupied
by a company, they have moved toward Strasbourg.
I think they were right. A great city, like Strasbourg, has always more resources than a small place,
where they have only a few palisades stuck up to
hide fifty men."

This was what Cousin George had learned that very day.

Hearing him speak, my first thought was to run to the mill, load as much furniture as I could upon two wagons, and drive at once to Phalsbourg; but my cousin told me that the gates would be closed; that we should have to wait outside until the reopening of the barriers, and that we must hope that it would be time enough to-morrow.

According to him, the great battle would not be fought for two or three days yet, because a great number of Germans had yet to cross the river, and they would, no doubt, be opposed. It is true that the fifty thousand men who had made themselves masters of Wissembourg might descend the Sauer; but then we should be nearly equal, and it was to the interest of the Germans only to fight when they were three to one. George had heard some officers discussing this point at the inn, in the presence of many listeners, and he believed, according to this, that the 5th army corps, which was extending in the direction of Metz, by Bitche and Sarreguemines, under the orders of General de Failly, would have time to arrive and support MacMahon. I thought so, too: it seemed a matter of course.

We talked over these miseries till nine o'clock. My wife and Grédel had come to carry their quarrels even to my Cousin Marie Anne's, who said to them: " Oh! do try to be reasonable. What matter two or three hams, Catherine? Perhaps you

will soon be glad to know that they have done good
to Jacob, instead of seeing them eaten up by Uhlans
under your own eyes."

You may be sure that my wife did not agree with
this. But at ten o'clock, Cousin Marie Anne, full of
thought, having said that her husband was tired and
that he had need of rest, we left, after having wished
him good-evening, and we returned home.

That night—if my wife had not awoke from time
to time, to tell me that we were robbed, that the
thieves were taking everything from us, and that we
should be ruined at last—I should have slept very
well; but there seemed no end to her worrying, and
I saw that she suspected Grédel of having given the
hams to Michel for Jean Baptiste Werner, without,
however, daring to say so much. I was thinking of
other things, and was glad to see her go down in the
morning to attend to her kitchen; not till then did I
get an hour or two of sleep.

The next day all was quiet in the village; everybody had hid his valuables, and they only feared one
thing, and that was a sortie from Phalsbourg to
carry off our cattle. All the children were set to
watch in the direction of Wechem; and if anything
had stirred in that quarter, all the cattle would have
been driven into the woods in ten minutes.

But there was no movement. All the soldiers of
the line had gone, and the commanding officer, Taillant, could not send the lads of our village to carry
away their own parents' cattle.

So all this day, the 10th of August, was quiet enough in our mountains.

About twelve o'clock some wood-cutters of Krappenfelz came to tell us that they could hear cannon on the heights of the Falberg, in the direction of Alsace; but they were not believed, and it was said:

"These are inventions to frighten us." For many people take a pleasure in frightening others.

All was quiet until about ten o'clock at night. It was very warm; I was sitting on a bench before my mill, in my shirt-sleeves, thinking of all my troubles. From time to time a thick cloud overshadowed the moon, which had not happened for a long time, and rain was hoped for. Grédel was washing the plates and dishes in the kitchen; my wife was trotting up and down, peeping into the cupboards to see if anything else had been stolen besides her hams; in the village, windows and shutters were closing one after another; and I was going up to bed too, when a kind of a rumor rose from the wood and attracted my attention; it was a distant murmuring; something was galloping there, carts were rolling, a gust of wind was passing. What could it be? My wife and Grédel had gone out, and were listening too. At that moment, from the other end of the village, arose a dispute which prevented us from making out this noise any longer, which was approaching from the mountain, and I said to Catherine: " The drunk-

ards at the ' Cruchon d'Or ' begin these disturbances
every night.   I must put an end to that, for it is a
disgrace to the parish."

But I had scarcely said this when a crowd of people appeared in the street opposite the mill, shouting, " A deserter! a deserter! "

And the shrill voice of my deputy Placiard rose
above all the rest, crying: " Take care of the horse!
Mind you don't let him escape! "

A tall cuirassier was moving quietly in the midst
of all this mob, every man in which wanted to lay
hold of him—one by the arm, another by the collar.
He was making no resistance, and his horse followed
him limping, and hanging his head; the *bangard*
was leading him by the bridle.

Placiard then seeing me at the door, cried: " Monsieur le Maire, I bring you a deserter, one of those
who fled from Wissembourg, and who are now
prowling about the country to live and glut at the
expense of the country people.   He is drunk even
now.   I caught him myself."   All the rest, men
and women, shouted: " Shut him up in a stable !
Send for the gendarmes to fetch him away!   Do
this—do that "—and so on.

I was much astonished to see this fine tall fellow,
with his helmet and his cuirass, who could have
shouldered his way in a minute through all these
people, going with them like a lamb.   Cousin
George had come up at the same moment.   We
hardly knew what to do about this business, for man

and horse were standing there perfectly still, as if stupefied.

At last I felt I must say something, and I said : " Come in."

The *bangard* tied up the horse to the ring in the barn, and we all burst in a great crowd into my large parlor downstairs, slamming the door in the face of all those brawlers who had nothing to do in the house; but they remained outside, never ceasing for a moment to shout: " A deserter! "   And half the village was coming: in all directions you could hear the wooden clogs clattering.

Once in the room, my wife fetched a candle from the kitchen.   Then, catching sight of this strong and square-built man, with his thick mustaches, his tall figure, his sword at his side, his sleeves and his cuirass stained with blood, and the skin on one side of his face torn away and bruised all round to the back of the head, we saw at once that he was not a deserter, and that something terrible had happened in our neighborhood; and Placiard having again begun to tell us how he had himself caught this soldier in his garden, where the poor wretch was going to hide, George cried indignantly: " Come now, does a man like that hide himself?   I tell you, M. Placiard, that it would have taken twenty like you to hold him, if he had chosen to resist."

The cuirassier then turned his head and gazed at George; but he spoke not a word.   He seemed to be mute with stupefaction.

" You have come from a fight, my friend, haven't you? " said my cousin, gently.

" Yes, sir."

" So they have been fighting to-day? "

" Yes."

" Where? "

The cuirassier pointed in the direction of the Falberg, on the left by the saw-mills. " Down there." he said, " behind the mountains."

" At Reichshoffen? "

" Yes, that is it: at Reichshoffen."

" This man is exhausted," said George: " Catherine, bring some wine." My wife took the bottle out of the cupboard and filled a glass; but the cuirassier would not drink: he looked on the ground before him, as if something was before his eyes. What he had just told us made us turn pale.

" And," said George, " the cuirassiers charged? "

" Yes," said the soldier, " all of them."

" Where is your regiment now? " He raised his head.

" My regiment? it is down there in the vineyards, amongst the hops, in the river. . . ."

" What! in the river? "

" Yes: there are no more cuirassiers! "

" No more cuirassiers? " cried my cousin; " the six regiments? "

" Yes, it is all over! " said the soldier, in a low voice: " the grapeshot has mown them down. There are none left! "

"THE GRAPESHOT HAS MOWN THEM DOWN. THERE ARE NONE LEFT!"

"Oh!" cried Placiard, "now you see: what did I say? He is one of those villains who propagate false reports. Can six regiments be mown down? Did you not yourself say, Monsieur le Maire, that those six regiments alone would bear down everything before them?"

I could answer nothing; but the perspiration ran down my face.

"You must lock him up somewhere, and let the gendarmes know," continued Placiard. "Such are the orders of Monsieur le Sous-préfet."

The cuirassier wiped with his sleeves the blood which was trickling upon his cheek; he appeared to hear nothing.

Out of all the open windows were leaning the forms of the village people, with attentive ears.

George and I looked at each other in alarm.

"You have blood upon you," said my cousin, pointing to the soldier's cuirass, who started and answered:

"Yes; that is the blood of a white lancer: I killed him!"

"And that wound upon your cheek?"

"That was given me with a sword handle. I got that from a Bavarian officer—it stunned me—I could no longer see—my horse galloped away with me."

"So you were hand-to-hand?"

"Yes, twice; we could not use our swords: the

men caught hold of one another, fought and killed one another with sword hilts."

Placiard was again going to begin his exclamations, when George became furious: "Hold your tongue, you abominable toady! Are you not ashamed of insulting a brave soldier, who has fought for his country?"

"Monsieur le Maire," cried Placiard, "will you suffer me to be insulted under your roof while I am fulfilling my duties as deputy?"

I was much puzzled: but George, looking angrily at him, was going to answer for me; when a loud cry arose outside in the midst of a furious clattering of horses: a terrible cry, which pierced to the very marrow of our bones.

"The Prussians!   The Prussians!"

At the same moment a troop of disbanded horsemen were flying past our windows at full speed: they flashed past us like lightning; the crowd fell back; the women screamed: "Lord have mercy upon us! we are all lost!"

After these cries, and the passage of these men, I stood as if rooted to the floor, listening to what was going on outside; but in another minute all was silence.   Turning round, I saw that everybody, neighbors, men and women, Placiard, the rural policeman, all had slipped out behind.   Grédel, my wife, George, the cuirassier, and myself, stood alone in the room.   My cousin said to me: "This man has told you the truth; the great battle has been fought and lost to-day! These are the first fugitives who have just passed. Now is the time for calmness and courage; let everybody be prepared: we are going to witness terrible things."

And turning to the soldier: " You may go, my friend," he said, " your horse is there; but if you had rather stay——"

" No; I will not be made prisoner! "

" Then come, I will put you on the way."

We went out together. The horse before the barn had not moved; I helped the cuirassier to mount: George said to him: " Here, on the right, is the road to Metz; on the left to Phalsbourg; at Phalsbourg, by going to the right, you will be on the road to Paris."

And the horse began to walk, dragging itself painfully. Then only did we see that a shred of flesh was hanging down its leg, and that it had lost a great deal of blood. My cousin followed, forgetting to say good-night. Was it possible to sleep after that?

From time to time during the night horsemen rode past at the gallop. Once, at daybreak, I went to the mill-dam, to look down the valley; they were coming out of the woods by fives, sixes, and tens, leaping out of the hedges, smashing the young trees; instead of following the road, they passed through the fields, crossed the river, and rode up the hill in front, without troubling about the corps. There seemed no end of them!

About six the bells began to ring for matins. It

was Sunday, the 7th August, 1870; the weather was magnificent.   Monsieur le Curé crossed the street at nine, to go to church, but only a few old women attended the service to pray.

Then commenced the endless passage of the defeated army retreating upon Sarrebourg, down the valley; a spectacle of desolation such as I shall never forget in my life.   Hundreds of men who could scarcely be recognized as Frenchmen were coming up in disordered bands; cavalry, infantry, cuirassiers without cuirasses, horsemen on foot, foot soldiers on horseback, three-fourths unarmed!   Crowds of men without officers, all going straight on in silence.

What has always surprised me is that no officers were to be seen.   What had become of them?   I cannot say.

No more singing.   No more cries of " Vive l'Empereur! "   " À Berlin! à Berlin! "

Dismay and discouragement were manifest in every countenance.

Those who shall come after will see worse things than this: since men are wolves, foxes, hawks, owls, all this must come round again: a hundred times, a thousand times; from age to age, until the consummation of time: it is the glory of kings and emperors passing by!

They all cry, " Jesus, have pity upon us, miserable sinners!   Jesus, Saviour, bless us! "

But all this time they are hard at work with the

hooked bill and the sharp claws upon the unhappy carcass of mankind. Each tears away his morsel! And yet they all have faith, Lutherans and Catholics: they are all worthy people! And so on forever.

Thus passed our army after the battle of Reichshoffen; and the others the Germans were following: they were at Haguenau, at Tugwiller, at Bouxviller; they were advancing from Dosenheim, to enter our valley; very soon we were to see them!

CHAPTER VI

ALL that day we were in a state of fear, Grédel alone was afraid of nothing; she came in and out, bringing us the news of Rothalp.

Many people from Tugwiller, Neuwiller, Dosenheim, passed through the village with carts full of furniture, bedding, mattresses, all in confusion, shouting, calling to each other, whipping their horses, turning round to see if the Uhlans were not at their heels; it was the general flight before the deluge. These unhappy beings had lost their heads. They said that the Prussians were taking possession of all the boys of fifteen or sixteen to lead their horses or carry their bags.

Two soldiers of the line who passed about twelve were still carrying their rifles; they were white with dust. I called them in, through the window, and gave them a glass of wine. They belonged to the 18th, and told us that their regiment no longer existed; that all their officers were killed or wounded; that another regiment, I cannot remember which, had fired upon them for a long time; that at last ammunition was wanting; that at the fort of La Petite Pierre the garrison had refused to receive them; and that the 5th army corps, commanded by General de Failly, posted in the neighborhood of Bitche, might have come in time to fall into position; and a good deal more besides.

These were brave men, whose hearts had not failed them. They started again in the direction of Phalsbourg, and we wished them good luck.

In the afternoon Marie Anne came to see us. Her husband had started for the town early, saying that nothing positive could be learned in our place; that the soldiers saw nothing but their own little corner of the battle-field, without troubling themselves about the rest, and that he would learn exactly down there if we had any hope left.

George was to return for dinner; but at seven o'clock he was not home yet. His wife was uneasy. Bad news kept coming in; peasants were arriving from Neuwiller, who said that the Prussians were already marching upon Saverne, and were making requisitions as they went. The peasants were flying to Dabo in the mountains; the women, through force of habit, were telling their beads as they walked; whilst the men, great consumers of eau-de-vie, were flourishing their sticks, and looking in their rear with threatening gestures, which did not hinder them from stepping out rapidly.

One of these men, whom I asked if he had seen the battle, told me that the dead were heaped up in the fields like sacks of flour in my mill. I think he was inventing that, or he had heard it from others.

Night was coming on, and Cousin Marie Anne was going home, when all at once George came in.

" Is my wife here, Christian? " he asked.

" Yes; you will sup with us? "

" No; I have had something to eat down there. But what sights I have seen! It is enough to drive one mad."

" And Jacob? " asked my wife.

" Jacob is learning drill. He got a rifle the day before yesterday, and to-morrow he will have to fight."

George sat down in the window-corner while we were at supper, and he told us that on his arrival at Phalsbourg, about six in the morning, the gate of France had just been opened, but that that of Germany, facing Saverne, remained closed; that in that direction from the outposts to Quatre Vents, nothing was to be seen but fugitives, calling, and firing pistol-shots to get themselves admitted; that he had had time to put up his horse and cart at the Ville de Bâle, and to go upon the ramparts to witness this spectacle, when at the same instant the drawbridge fell, and the crowd of Turcos, Zouaves, foot-soldiers, officers, generals, all in a confused mass, had rushed through the gate; in the whole number, he had seen but one flag, surrounded by about sixty men of the 55th, commanded by a lieutenant; the rest were mingled together, in hopeless confusion, the most part without arms, and under no sort of discipline;

they had lost all respect for their chiefs. It was a rout—a complete rout.

He had seen superior officers invaded at their own tables under the tent of the Café Meyer, by private soldiers, and veterans throwing themselves back in their chairs with elbows squared in the presence of their officers, looking defiantly upon them, and shouting, " A bottle! " The waiters came obsequiously to wait upon them for fear of a scene, whilst the officers pretending to hear and see nothing, seemed to him the worst thing he had seen yet. Yet it was deserved; for these officers—officers of rank— knew no more about the roads, paths, streams and rivers of the country than their soldiers, who knew nothing at all. They did not even know the way from Phalsbourg to Sarrebourg by the high-road, which a child of eight might know.

He had heard a staff-officer ask if Sarrebourg was an open town; he had seen whole battalions halting upon that road, not knowing whether they were right.

We should ourselves see these deplorable things next day, for our retreating soldiers did nothing but turn and turn again ten times upon the same roads, around the same mountains, and ended by returning to the same spot again so tired, exhausted, and starved, that the Prussians, if they had come, would only have had to pick them up at their leisure.

Yet George had one moment's satisfaction in this melancholy disorganization; it was to see, as he told us, those sixty men of the 56th halt in good order upon the *place*, and there rest their flag against a tree. The lieutenant who commanded them made them lie on the ground, near their rifles, and almost immediately they fell asleep in the midst of the seething crowd. The young officer himself went quietly to sit alone at a small table at the café.

"He," said my cousin, "had a map cut into squares, which he began to study in detail. It gave me pleasure to look at him; he reminded me of our naval officers. He knew something! And whilst his men were asleep, and his rescued flag was standing there, he watched, after all this terrible defeat. Colonels, commanders, were arriving depressed and wearied; the lieutenant did not stir. At last he folded up his map and put it back into his pocket, then he went to lie down in the midst of his men, and soon fell asleep too. He," said my cousin, "*was* an officer! As for the rest, I look upon them as the cause of our ruin: they have never commanded, they have never learned. There is no want of able men in the artillery and engineers; but they are only there to do their part: they command only their own arm, and are compelled to obey superior orders, even when those orders have no sense in them."

One thing which made my cousin tremble with anger, was to learn that the Emperor had the supreme command, and that nothing might be done without taking his Majesty's instructions at head-quarters: not a bridge might be blown up, not a tunnel, before receiving his Majesty's permission!

"What is the use of sending or receiving despatches?" said George. "I only hope our *honest man* will be found to have given orders to blow up the Archeviller tunnel, or the Prussians will overrun the whole of France; they will convey their guns, their munitions of war, their provisions, and their men by railway, whilst our poor soldiers will drag along on foot and perish miserably!"

Listening to him our distress increased more and more.

He had seen in the place a few guns saved from capture, with their horses fearfully mangled, and already so thin with overwork, that one might have thought they had come from the farthest end of Russia. And all these men, coming and going, laid themselves down in a line under the walls to sleep, at the risk of being run over a hundred times.

The doors and windows of all the houses were open; the soldiers might be seen densely crowded in the side streets, the passages, the rooms, the vestibules and yards, busily eating. The townspeople gave them all they had; the poorest shed tears that they had nothing to give, so many poor wretches inspired pity; they were so commiserated that they had been beaten. In richer houses they were cooking from morning till night; when one troop was satisfied another took their place.

George, relating these things, had his eyes filled with tears.

" Well, there are a good many kind people in the world yet," said he.   " Very soon those poor Phals-bourgers, when they are blockaded, will have nothing to put into their own mouths; their six weeks' victuals are already consumed, without mentioning their other provisions.   Compared with these poor townspeople, we peasants are selfish monsters."

He fixed his eyes upon us, and we answered nothing.   I had already driven our cows into the wood, with the flocks of the village.   Doubtless he knew of it!   But surely we must keep something to eat! George was right; but one cannot help thinking of the morrow: those who do not are sure to repent sooner or later.

Well, well—all the same, it was very fine of these townspeople; but they have suffered heavily for it: during four months the officer in command kept everything for his soldiers, and took away from the inhabitants all that they had whether they were willing or not.

I do affirm these things.   People will take them for what they are worth; but it is only the simple truth!   What afflicted us still more was to hear what George had to tell us of the battle.

In the midst of that great crowd he had long sought for some one to tell him all about it.   At last the sight of an old sergeant of *chasseurs-à-pied,* thin and tough as whip-cord, his sleeve covered with stripes, and with a bright eye, made him think : "There's my man! I am sure he has had a clear insight into things; if he will talk to me, I shall get at the bottom of the story."

So he had invited him into the inn, to take a glass of wine. The sergeant examined him for a moment, accepted, and they entered together the Ville de Bâle at the end of the court, for all the rooms were full of people; and there, eating a slice of ham and drinking a couple of bottles of Lironcourt, the sergeant having his heart opened, and receiving, moreover, a cent-sous piece, had declared that all our misfortunes arose from two causes: first, that a height on the right had not been occupied, whence the Germans had made their appearance only about twelve o'clock, and from which they could not be dislodged because they commanded the whole field of battle; and because their artillery, more numerous and better than ours, searched us through and through with shell and grape; their practice was so admirable that it was no use falling back, or bearing to the right or the left: at the first shot their balls fell into the midst of our ranks. We have since heard that the heights to which the sergeant referred were those of Gunstedt.

He then told George that the 5th corps, commanded by De Failly, which was expected from hour to hour, never appeared at all; that even if he had come, we probably should not have won the battle, for the Germans were three or four to one—but that we might have effected a retreat in good order by Niederbronn upon Saverne.

This old sergeant was from the Nièvre; George has often spoken to me of him since, and told me that, in his opinion, he knew much more than many of MacMahon's officers; that he possessed good sense, and had a clear perception of things. George was of opinion that, with a little training, many Frenchmen of the lower ranks would be found to possess military genius, and that they might be confidently relied upon; but that our love of dancing and plays had done us harm, since it was supposed that good dancers and good actors would be able men: which would be the cause of our ruin if we did not abandon such notions.

My cousin told me many other things that evening which have escaped my memory; our terrible anxiety for the future prevented me from listening properly. But all the misfortunes in the world have not the power of depriving a man of sleep ; though for the last two days we had never slept. George and his wife went home about ten, and we went to bed.

Next day I had to celebrate the marriage of Chrétien Richi with his first cousin Lisbette; notice had been given for a week, and when invitations are sent out such things cannot be postponed. I should have liked to be carrying my hay and straw into the wood, for cattle cannot live upon air; and as I was pressed for time, I sent for Placiard to take my place. But he could nowhere be found; he had gone into hiding like all the functionaries of the Empire, who are always ready to receive their salaries and to denounce people in quiet times, and very sharp in taking themselves off the moment they ought to be at their posts.

At ten o'clock, then, I was obliged to put on my sash and go; the wedding party were waiting, and I went up into the hall with them.   I sat in the armchair, telling the bridegroom and bride to draw near, which of course they did.

I was beginning to read the chapter on the duties of husband and wife, when in a moment a great shouting arose outside: "The Prussians! the Prussians!"   One of the groomsmen, with his bunch of roses, left; Chrétien Richi turned round, the bride and the rest looked at the door; and I stood there, all alone, stuck fast with the clerk, Adam Fix.   In a moment the groomsman returned, crying out that the people of Phalsbourg were making a sortie into the wood to lift our cattle; and that they were coming too to search our houses.   Then I could have sent all the wedding-party to Patagonia, when I fancied the position of my wife and Grédel in such a predicament; but a mayor is obliged to keep his dignity, and I cried out: "Do you want to be married?   Yes or no?"

They returned in a moment, and answered "Yes!"

"Well, you *are* married!"

And I went out while the witnesses signed, and
ran to the mill.

Happily this report of a sortie from Phalsbourg
was false.   A gendarme had just passed through the
village, bearing orders from MacMahon, and hence
came all this alarm.

Nothing new happened until seven in the
evening.   A few fugitives were still gaining the
town; but at nightfall began the passage of the
5th army corps, commanded by General de
Failly.

So, then, these thirty thousand men, instead of
descending into Alsace by Niederbronn, were now
coming behind us by the road to Metz, on this side
of the mountains.   They were not even thinking of
defending our passes, but were taking flight into
Lorraine!

Half our village had turned out, astonished to see
this army moving in a compact mass, upon Sarrebourg and Fénétrange.   Until then it had been
thought that a second battle would be fought at
Saverne.   People had been speaking of defending
the Falberg, the Vachberg, and all the narrow, rock-
strewn passes; the roads through which might have
been broken up and defended with abatis, from
which a few good shots might have kept whole regiments in check; but the sight of these thousands of
men who were forsaking us without having fought
—their guns, their mitrailleuses, and the cavalry
galloping and rolling in a cloud along the highway,

to get farther out of the enemy's reach—made our hearts bleed.   Nobody could understand it.

Then a poor disabled soldier, lying on the grass, told me that they had been ordered from Bitche to Niederbronn, from Niederbronn to Bitche, and then from Bitche to Petersbach and Ottwiller, by dreadful roads, and that now they could hold on no longer: they were all exhausted!   And in spite of myself, I thought that if men worn out to this degree were obliged to fight against fresh troops continually reinforced, they would be beaten before they could strike a blow!   Yes, indeed, the want of knowledge of the country is one of the causes of our miseries.

Grédel, Catherine, and I, returned to the mill in the greatest distress.

It had at last begun to rain, after two months' drought.   It was a heavy rain, which lasted all the night.

My wife and Grédel had gone to bed, but I could not close my eyes.   I walked up and down in the mill, listening to this down-pour, the heavy rumbling of the guns, the pattering of endless footsteps in the mud.   It was march, march—marching without a pause.

How melancholy ! and how I pitied these unhappy soldiers, spent with hunger and fatigue, and compelled to retreat thus.

Now and then I looked at them through the window-panes, down which the rain was streaming. They were marching on foot, on horseback, one by

one, by companies, in troops, like shadows. And
every time that I opened the window to let in fresh
air, in the midst of this vast trampling of feet, those
neighings, and sometimes the curses of the soldiers
of the artillery-train, or the horseman whose horse
had dropped from fatigue or refused to move farther, I could hear in the far distance, across the
plain two or three leagues from us, the whistle of the
trains still coming and going in the passes.

Then noticing upon the wall one of those maps of
the theatre of war which the Government had sent
us three weeks ago, and which extended from Alsace as far as Poland, I tore it down, crumpled it up
in my hand, and flung it out. Everything came
back to me full of disgust. Those maps, those fine
maps, were part of the play; just like the conspira-
cies devised by the police, and the explanations of
the sous-préfets to make us vote " Yes " in the Plébiscite. Oh, you play-actors! you gang of swin-
dlers! Have you done enough yet to lead astray
your imbecile people? Have you made them miserable enough with your ill-contrived plays?

And it is said that the whole affair is going to be
played over again: that they mean to put a ring
through our noses to lead us along; that many
rogues are reckoning upon it to settle their little
affairs, to slip back into their old shoes and get fat
again by slow degrees, humping their backs just like
our curé's cat when she has found her saucer again
after having taken a turn in the woods or the gar-

den: it is possible, indeed!   But then France will be
an object of contempt; and if those fellows succeed,
she will be worse than contemptible, and honorable
men will blush to be called Frenchmen!

At daybreak I went to raise the mill-dam, for this
heavy rain had overflowed the sluice.   The last
stragglers were passing.   As I was looking up the
village, my neighbor Ritter, the publican, was coming out from under the cart-shed with his lantern; a
stranger was following him—a young man in a gray
overcoat, tight trousers, a kind of leather portfolio
hanging at his side, a small felt hat turned up over
his ears, and a red ribbon at his button-hole.

This I concluded was a Parisian; for all the Parisians are alike, just as the English are: you may
tell them among a thousand.

I looked and listened.

" So," said this man, " you have no horse? "

" No, sir; all our beasts are in the wood, and at
such a time as this we cannot leave the village."

" But twenty francs are pretty good pay for four
or five hours."

" Yes, at ordinary times; but not now."

Then I advanced, asking: " Monsieur offers
twenty francs to go what distance? "

" To Sarrebourg," said the stranger, astonished
to see me.

" If you will say thirty, I will undertake to convey you there.   I am a miller; I always want my
horses; there are no others in the village."

" Well, do; put in your horses."

These thirty francs for eight leagues had flashed upon me. My wife had just come down into the kitchen, and I told her of it; she thought I was doing right.

Having then eaten a mouthful, with a glass of wine, I went out to harness my horses to my light cart. The Parisian was already there waiting for me, his leather portmanteau in his hand. I threw into the cart a bundle of straw; he sat down near me, and we went off at a trot.

This stranger seeing my dappled grays galloping through the mud, seemed pleased. First he asked me the news of our part of the country, which I told him from the beginning. Then in his turn he began to tell me a good deal that was not yet known by us. He composed gazettes; he was one of those who followed the Emperor to record his victories. He was coming from Metz, and told me that General Frossard had just lost a great battle at Forbach, through his own fault in not being in the field while his troops were fighting, but being engaged at billiards instead.

You may be sure I felt that to be impossible; it would be too abominable; but the Parisian said so it was, and so have many repeated since.

" So that the Prussians," said he, " broke through us, and I have had to lose a horse to get out of the confusion: the Uhlans were pursuing; they followed nearly to a place called Droulingen."

" That is only four leagues from this place," said
I. " Are they already there? "

" Yes; but they fell back immediately to rejoin
the main body, which is advancing upon Toul. I
had hoped to recover lost ground by telling of our
victories in Alsace; unfortunately at Droulingen,
the sad news of Reichshoffen,* and the alarm of
the flying inhabitants, have informed me that we
are driven in along our whole line; there is no
doubt these Prussians are strong; they are very
strong.   But the Emperor will arrange all that with
Bismarck! "

Then he told me there was an understanding between the Emperor and Bismarck; that the Prussians would take Alsace; that they would give us
Belgium in exchange; that we should pay the expenses of the war, and then things would all return
into their old routine.

" His Majesty is indisposed," said he, " and has
need of rest; we shall soon have Napoleon IV., with
the regency of her Majesty the Empress, the French
are fond of change."

Thus spoke this newspaper-writer, who had been
decorated, who can tell why? He thought of nothing but of getting safe into Sarrebourg, to catch the
train, and send a letter to his paper; nothing else
mattered to him.   It is well that I had taken a pair
of horses, for it went on raining.   Suddenly we
came upon the rear of De Failly's army; his guns,

* Called generally by us, the Battle of Woerth.

powder-wagons, and his regiments so crowded the road, that I had to take to the fields, my wheels sinking in up to the axle-trees.

Nearing Sarrebourg, we saw also on our left the rear of the other routed army, the Turcos, the Zouaves, the chasseurs, the long trains of MacMahon's guns; so that we were between the two fugitive routs: De Failly's troops, by their disorder, looked just as if they had been defeated, like the other army. All the people who have seen this in our country can confirm my account, though it seems incredible.

At last, I arrived at the Sarrebourg station, when the Parisian paid me thirty francs, which my horses had fairly earned. The families of all the railway *employés* were just getting into the train for Paris; and you may be sure that this Government newspaper-writer was delighted to find himself there. He had his free pass: but for that the unlucky man would have had to stay against his will; like many others who at the present time are boasting loudly of having made a firm stand, waiting for the enemy.

I quickly started home again by cross-roads, and about twelve I reached Rothalp. The artillery was thundering amongst the mountains; crowds of people were climbing and running down the little hill near the church to listen to the distant roar. Cousin George was calmly smoking his pipe at the window, looking at all these people coming and going.

THE ARTILLERY WAS THUNDERING AMONGST THE MOUNTAINS.

"What is going on?" said I, stopping my cart before his door.

"Nothing," said he; "only the Prussians attacking the little fort of Lichtenberg. But where are you coming from?"

"From Sarrebourg."

And I related to him in a few words what the Parisian had told me.

"Ah! now it is all plain," said he. "I could not understand why the 5th corps was filing off into Lorraine, without making one day's stand in our mountains, which are so easily defended: it did really seem too cowardly. But now that Frossard is beaten at Forbach, the thing is explained: our flank is turned. De Failly is afraid of being taken between two victorious armies. He has only to gain ground, for the cattle-dealer David has just told me that he has seen Uhlans behind Fénétrange. The line of the Vosges is surrendered; and we owe this misfortune to Monsieur Frossard, tutor to the Prince Imperial!"

The school-master, Adam Fix, was then coming down from the hill with his wife, and cried that a battle was going on near Bitche. He did not stop, on account of the rain. George told me to listen a few minutes. We could hear deep and distant reports of heavy guns, and others not so loud.

"Those heavy reports," said George, "come from the great siege-guns of the fort; the others are the

8

enemy's lighter artillery. At this moment, the German army, at six leagues from us, victorious in Alsace, is on the road from Woerth to Siewettler, to unite with the army that is moving on Metz; it is defiling past the guns of the fort. To-morrow we shall see their advanced guard march past us. It is a melancholy story, to be defeated through the fault of an imbecile and his courtiers; but we must always remember, as a small consolation, to every man his turn." He began again to smoke, and I went on my way home, where I put up my horses. I had earned my thirty francs in six hours; but this did not give me complete satisfaction. My wife and Grédel were also on the hill listening to the firing; half the village were up there; and all at once I saw Placiard, who could not be found the day before, jumping through the gardens, puffing and panting for breath.

"You hear, Monsieur le Maire," he cried—" you hear the battle? It is King Victor Emmanuel coming to our help with a hundred and fifty thousand men!"

At this I could no longer contain myself, and I cried, " Monsieur Placiard, if you take me for a fool, you are quite mistaken; and if you are one, you had better hold your tongue. It is no use any longer telling these poor people false news, as you have been doing for eighteen years, to keep up their hopes to the last moment. This will never more bring tobacco-excise to you, and stamp-offices

to your sons. The time for play-acting is over.
You are telling me this through love of lying; but
I have had enough of all these abominable tricks; I
now see things clearly. We have been plundered
from end to end by fellows of your sort, and now
we are going to pay for you, without having had
any benefit ourselves. If the Prussians become our
masters, if they bestow places and salaries, you will
be their best friend; you will denounce the patriots
in the commune, and you will have them to vote
plébiscites for Bismarck! What does it matter to
you whether you are a Frenchman or a German?
Your true lord, your true king, your true emperor,
is the man who pays! "

As fast as I spoke my wrath increased, and all
at once I shouted: " Wait, Monsieur l'Adjoint,
wait till I come out; I will pay you off for the Emperor, for his Ministers, and all the infamous crew
of your sort who have brought the Prussians into
France! " But I had scarcely reached the door,
when he had already turned the corner.

CHAPTER VII

On that day we had yet more alarms.

Between one and two o'clock, standing before my mill, I fancied I could hear a drum beating up the valley. All the village was lamenting, and crying, " Here are the Prussians! "

All along the street, people were coming out, gazing, listening; boys ran into the woods, mothers screamed. A few men more fearful than the rest went off too, each with a loaf under his arm; women raised their hands to Heaven, calling them back and declaring they would go with them. And whilst I was gazing upon this sad spectacle, suddenly two carts came up, full gallop, from the valley of Graufthal.

It was the noise of these two vehicles that I had mistaken for drums approaching. A week later I should not have made this mistake, for the Germans steal along like wolves: there is no drumming or bugling, as with us; and you have twenty thousand men on your hands before you know it.

The people riding in the carts were crying, " The Prussians are at the back of the saw-mills! "

They could be heard afar off; especially the women, who were raising themselves in the cart, throwing up their hands.

At a hundred yards from the mill the cart stopped, and recognizing Father Diemer, municipal councillor, who was driving, I cried to him, " Hallo, Diemer! pull up a moment.   What is going on down there? "

" The Prussians are coming, Monsieur le Maire," he said.

" Oh, well, well, if they must come sooner or later, what does it signify?   Do come down."

He came down, and told me that he had been that morning to the forest-house of Domenthal in his conveyance, to fetch away his wife and daughter who had been staying there with relations for a few days; and that on his way back he had seen in a little valley, the Fischbachel, Prussian infantry, their arms stacked, resting on the edge of the wood, making themselves at home; which had made him gallop away in a hurry.

That was what he had seen.

Then other men came up, woodmen, who said that they were some of our own light infantry, and that Diemer had made a mistake; then more arrived, declaring that they *were* Prussians; and so it went on till night.

About seven o'clock I saw an old French soldier, the last who came through our village; his leg was bandaged with a handkerchief, and he sat upon the bench before my house asking me for a piece of bread and a glass of water, for the love of God!   I went directly and told Grédel to fetch him bread and wine. She poured out the wine herself for this poor fellow, who was suffering great pain. He had a ball in his leg; and, in truth, the wound smelt badly, for he had not been able to dress it, and he had dragged himself through the woods from Woerth.

He had eaten nothing for twenty-four hours, and told us that the colonel of his regiment had fallen, crying, "Friends, you are badly commanded! Cease to obey your generals!"

He only rested for a few minutes, not to let his leg grow stiff, and went on his weary way to Phalsbourg.

He was the last French soldier that I saw after the battle of Reichshoffen.

At night we were told that the peasants of Graufthal had found a gun stuck fast in the valley; and two hours later, whilst we were supping, our neighbor Katel came in pale as death, crying, "The Prussians are at your door!"

Then I went out. Ten or fifteen Uhlans were standing there smoking their short wooden pipes, and watering their horses at the mill-stream.

Imagine my surprise, especially when one of these Uhlans began to greet me in bad Prussian-German: "Oho! good-evening, Monsieur le Maire! I hope you have been pretty well, Monsieur le Maire, since I last had not the pleasure of seeing you?"

He was the officer of the troop. My wife, and

Grédel, too, were looking from the door. As I made
no answer, he said, " And Mademoiselle Grédel!
here you are, as fresh and as happy as ever. I suppose you still sing morning and evening, while you
are washing up? "

Then Grédel, who has good eyes, cried, " It is that
great knave who came to take views in our country
last year with his little box on four long legs! "

And, even in the dusk, I could recognize one of
those German photographers who had been travelling about the mountains a few months before, taking the likenesses of all our village folks. This
man's name was Otto Krell; he was tall, pale, and
thin, his nose was like a razor back, and he had a way
of winking with his left eye while paying you com-
pliments. Ah! the scoundrel! it was he, indeed,
and now he was an Uhlan officer: when Grédel had
spoken, I recognized him perfectly.

" Exactly so, Mademoiselle Grédel," said he,
from his tall horse. " It is I myself. You would
have made a good gendarme; you would have
known a rogue from an honest man in a moment."

He burst out laughing, and Grédel said, " Speak
in a language I can understand; I cannot make
out your patois."

" But you understand very well the patois of
Monsieur Jean Baptiste Werner," answered this
gallows-bird, making a grimace. " How is good
Monsieur Jean Baptiste? Is he in as good spirits as
ever? Have you still got your little likeness of him,

you know, close to your heart—that young gentleman, I mean, that I had to take three times, because he never came out handsome enough?"

Then Grédel, ashamed, ran into the house, and
my wife took refuge in her room.

Then he said to me, " I am glad to see you, Monsieur le Maire, in such excellent health. I came
to you, first of all, to wish you good-morning; but
then, I must acknowledge, my visit has another
object."

And as I still answered nothing, being too full of
indignation, he asked me:

" Have you still got those nice Swiss cows? splendid animals? and the twenty-five sheep you had last
year?"

I understood in a moment what he was driving
at, and I cried: " We have nothing at all; there is
nothing in this village; we are all ruined; we cannot furnish you a single thing."

" Oh! come now, please don't be angry, Monsieur
Weber. I took your likeness, with your scarlet
waistcoat and your great square-cut coat; I know
you very well, indeed! you are a fine fellow! I have
orders to inform you that to-morrow morning 15,000
men will call here for refreshments; that they are
fond of good beef and mutton, and not above enjoying good white bread, and wine of Alsace, also vegetables, and coffee, and French cigars. On this paper
you will find a list of what they want. So you had
better make the necessary arrangements to satisfy

them; or else, Monsieur le Maire, they will help
themselves to your cows, even if they have to go and
look for them in the woods of the Biechelberg,
where you have sent them; they will help themselves to your sacks of flour, and your wine, that
nice, light wine of Rikevir; they will take everything, and then they will burn down your house.
Take my advice, welcome them as German brothers,
coming to deliver you from French bondage: for
you are Germans, Monsieur Weber, in this part of
the country.   Therefore prepare this requisition
yourself. If you want a thing done well, do it yourself; you will find this plan most advantageous. It
is out of friendship to you, as a German brother, and
in return for the good dinner you gave me last year
that I say this. And now, good-night."

He turned round to his men, and all together
filed off in the darkness, going up by the left toward
Berlingen.

Then, without even going into my own house,
I ran to my cousin's, to tell him what had happened.
He was going to bed.

" Well, what is the matter? " said he.

Completely upset, I told him the visit I had had
from these robbers, and what demands they had
made. My cousin and his wife listened attentively;
then George, after a minute's thought, said:
" Christian, force is force! If 15,000 men are to
pass here, it means that 15,000 will pass by Metting,
15,000 by Quatre Vents, 15,000 by Lützelbourg,

and so forth. We are invaded; Phalsbourg will be blockaded, and if we stir, we shall be knocked on the head without notice before we can count ten. What would you have? It's war! Those who lose must pay the bill. The good men who have been plunder- ing us for eighteen years have lost for us, and we are going to pay for them; that is plain enough. Only, if we make grimaces while we pay, they ask more; and if we go to work without much grumbling, they will shave us not quite so close: they will pretend to treat us with consideration and indulgence; they won't rob quite so roughly; they will be a little more gentle, and strip you with more civility. I have seen that in my campaigns. Here is the advice which I give, for your own and everybody else's in- terest. First of all, this very evening, you must send for your cows from the Biechelberg; you will tell David Hertz to drive the two best to his slaughter- house; and when the Prussians come and they have seen these two fine animals, David will kill them be- fore their eyes. He will distribute the pieces under the orders of the commanders. That will just make broth in the morning for the 15,000 men, and if that is not enough, send for my best cow. All the village will be pleased, and they will say, ' The mayor and his cousin are sacrificing themselves for the com- mune.'

" That will be a very good beginning; but then as we shall have begun with ourselves, and nobody can make any objection after that, you had better put an ox of Placiard's under requisition, then a cow of Jean Adam's, then another of Father Diemer's, and so on, in proportion to their wants; and that will go on till the end of the cows, the oxen, the pigs, the sheep and the goats. And you must do the same with the bread, the flour, the vegetables, the wine; always beginning at you and me. It is sad; it is a great trouble; but his Majesty the Emperor, his Ministers, his relations, his friends and acquaintances have gambled away our hay, our straw, our cattle, our money, our meadows, our houses, our sons, and ourselves, pretending all the while to consult us; they have lost like fools: they never kept their eye on the game, because their own little provision was already laid by, somewhere in Switzerland, in Italy, in England, or elsewhere; and they risked nothing but that vast flock which they were always accustomed to shear, and which they call the people. Well, my poor Christian, that flock is ourselves—we peasants! If I were younger; if I could make forced marches as I did at thirty, I should join the army and fight; but in the present state of things, all I can do is, like you, to bow down my back, with a heart full of wrath, until the nation has more sense, and appoints other chiefs to command."

The advice of George met with my approbation, and I sent the herdsmen to fetch my cows at the Biechelberg. I told him, besides, to give notice to the principal inhabitants that if they did not bring back their beasts to the village, the **Prussians would** go themselves and fetch them, because they knew the country roads better than ourselves; and that they would put into the pot first of all the cattle of those who did not come forward willingly.

My wife and Grédel were standing by as I gave this order to Martin Kopp: they exclaimed against it, saying that I was losing my senses; but I had more sense than they had, and I followed the advice of George, who had never misled me.

It was on the night of the 9th to the 10th of August that the small fortress of Lichtenberg, defended by a few veterans without ammunition, opened its gates to the Prussians; that MacMahon left Sarrebourg with the remainder of his forces, without blowing up the tunnel at Archeviller, because his Majesty's orders had not arrived; that the Germans, concentrated at Saverne, after extending right and left from Phalsbourg, sent first their Uhlans by the valley of Lützelbourg to inspect the railway, supposing that it would be blown up, then sent an engine through the tunnel, then ventured a train laden with stones, and were much astonished to find it arriving in Lorraine without difficulty; that MacMahon made his retreat on foot, whilst they advanced on trucks and carriages: and that they were able to send on their guns, their stores, their provisions, their horses and their men toward Paris; maintaining their troops by exhausting the provisions of Alsace and the other side of the Vosges. These things we learned afterward.

That same night the Prussians put their first guns into battery at the Quatre Vents to bombard the town, whilst they went completely round to the other side, by the fine road over the Falberg, which seemed to have been constructed through the forest expressly for their convenience.

They lost no time, examined and inspected everything, and found everything in perfect order to suit their convenience.

That night passed away quietly; they had too many things to look after to trouble themselves about our little village hidden in the woods, knowing well that we could neither run away nor defend ourselves; for all our young men were in the town, and we were unarmed and without any material of war. They left us to be gobbled up whenever they liked.

Many have asserted, and still believe, that we have been delivered up to the Germans in exchange for Belgium; because Alsace, according to the Emperor, was a German and Lutheran country, and Belgium, French and Catholic. But Cousin George has always said that these conjectures were erroneous, and that our misfortunes arose entirely from the thievishness of the Government; and chiefly of those who, under color of upholding the dynasty, were making a good bag, granted themselves pensions, enriched themselves by sweeping strokes of cunning, and became great men at a cheap rate: and also from the folly of the people, who were kept steeped in ignorance, to make them praise the tricks and the robberies of the rest.

My opinion is the same.

It was the cupidity of some in depriving the country of a powerful and numerous army, able to defend us; whilst, on the other hand, they deprived what army there was of provisions, arms, and munitions of war: surely this was enough! There is no need to go further to seek for the causes of our shame and our miseries.

Therefore our cattle returned from the Biechelberg in obedience to my orders; and my two best cows waited in the stable, eating a few handfuls of hay, until the first requisition of the Prussians should arrive.

The village people who saw this highly approved of my conduct, never imagining that their turn would come so soon.

Time passed away, and it was supposed that this quiet might last a good while, when a squadron of Prussian lancers, and, a little farther on, a squadron of hussars, appeared at the bottom of our valley.

For an advanced guard they had a few Uhlans —an order which we have since noticed they observed constantly; three hundred paces to the front rode two horsemen, each with a pistol in his hand resting on the thigh, and who halted from time to time to question people, threatening to kill them if they did not give plain answers to their questions;

and behind them came the main body, always at
the same distance.

We, standing under our projecting eaves, or
leaning out of our windows, men, women, and children, gazed upon the men who were coming to devour us, to ruin us, and strip the very flesh off our
bones. It was, as it were, the Plébiscite advancing
upon us under our own eyes, armed with pistol and
sword, the guns and the bayonets behind.

First, the cavalry extended from the hill at Berlingen to the Graufthal, to Wechem, to Mittelbronn, and farther still; then marched up several
regiments of infantry, their black and white stand-
ards flying.

We were watching all this without stirring.
The officers, in spiked helmets, were galloping to
and fro, carrying orders; the curé Daniel, in his
presbytery, had lifted his little white blinds, and
our neighbor Katel exclaimed, "Dear, dear, one
would never have thought there could be so many
heretics in the world."

This is exactly the state of ignorance that had
been kept up amongst us from generation to generation: making people believe that there was nobody in the universe besides themselves; that we
were a thousand to one, and that our religion was
universal. Pure and simple folly, upheld by lies!

It was a great help to us to have such grand
notions about ourselves! It made us feel enor-
mously strong!

But hypocrites can always get out of their scrapes: they vanish in the distance with well-lined pockets, and their victims are left behind sticking in the mud up to the chin!

Since our reverend fathers the Jesuits have so many spies posted about in the world, they should have told us how strong the heretics were, and not suffered us to believe until the last that we were the only masters of the earth. But they considered: " These French fools will allow themselves to be hacked down to the very last man for our honor; they will drive back the Lutherans; and then we shall make a great figure: the Holy Father will be infallible, and we shall rule under his name."

These things are so evident now, that one is almost ashamed to mention them.

As soon as the cavalry were posted on the heights of the place, at the rear of the hills, the infantry regiments, standing with ordered arms, began to march off.

I could hear from my door the loud voices of the officers, the neighing of the horses, and the departure of the battalions, which filed off, keeping step in admirable order. Ah! if our officers had been as highly trained, and our soldiers as firmly disciplined as the Germans, Alsace and Lorraine would still have been French.

I may be told that a good patriot ought to refrain from saying such things; but what is the use of hiding facts? Would hiding them prevent them

from being true? I say these things on purpose
to open people's eyes. If we want to recover what
we have lost, everything must be changed; our officers must be educated, our soldiers disciplined, our
contractors must supply stores, clothing, and provisions without blunders and deficiencies, or if they
fail they must be shot; the life of a brave and generous nation is better worth than that of a knave,
whose ignorance, laziness, or cupidity may cause
the loss of provinces.

We must have a large, national army, like that
of the Germans, and, to possess this army, every
man must serve; the cripples and deformed in offices; every man besides, in the ranks. Full permission must be given to wear spectacles, which do
not hinder a man from fighting; and citizens, as
well as workmen and peasants, must come under
fire. Unless we do this, we shall be beaten—beaten
again, and utterly ruined!

And above all, as Cousin George said, we must
place at the head of affairs a man with a cool head,
a warm heart, and great experience; in whose eyes
the honor of the nation shall be above his own interest, and on whose word all men may rely, because he has already proved that his confidence in
himself will not desert him, even in the most peril-
ous times.

But we are yet very far from this; and one would
really believe, in looking at the conceited countenances of the fugitives who are returning from Eng-

o

land, Belgium, Switzerland, and farther yet, that they have won important victories, and that the country does them injustice in not hailing them as deliverers.

And now I will quietly pursue this history of our village; whoever wants to come round me again with hypocritical pretences of honesty, will have to get up very early in the morning indeed.

After the Germans had posted their infantry within the squares formed by the cavalry, they dragged guns and ammunition up the height of Wechem, in the rear of our hills. Then the thoughts of Jacob, and all our poor lads, whom they were going to shell, came upon us, and mother began to cry bitterly. Grédel, too, thinking of her Jean Baptiste, had become furious; if, by misfortune, we had had a gun in the house, she would have been quite capable of firing upon the Prussians, and so getting us all exterminated; she ran upstairs and downstairs, put her head out at the window, and a German having raised his head, saying, " Oh! what a pretty girl! " she shouted, " Be sure always to come out ten against one, or it will be all up with you! "

I was downstairs, and you may imagine my alarm. I went up to beg her to be quiet, if she did not want the whole village to be destroyed; but she answered rudely, " I don't care—let them burn us all out! I wish I was in the town, and not with all these thieves."

"TRY TO BE ALWAYS TEN AGAINST ONE!"

I went down quickly, not to hear more.

The rain had begun to fall again, and these Prussians kept pouring in, by regiments, by squadrons: more than forty thousand men covered the plain; some formed in the fields, in the meadows, trampling down the second crop of grass and the potatoes —all our hopes were there under their feet! others went on their way; their wheels sunk into the clay, but they had such excellent horses that all went on under the lashes of their long whips, as the Germans use them. They climbed up all the slopes; the hedges and young trees were bent and broken everywhere.

When might is right, and you feel yourself the weakest, silence is wisdom.

The report ran that they were going to attack Phalsbourg in the afternoon; and our poor Mobiles, and our sixty artillery recruits pressed to serve the guns, were about to have a dreadful storm falling upon them, as a beginning to their experience. Those heaps of shells they were hurrying up to Wechem forced from us all cries of " Poor town! poor townspeople! poor women! poor children! "

The rain increased, and the river overflowed its banks down all the valley from Graufthal to Metting. A few officers were walking down the street to look for shelter; I saw a good number go into Cousin George's, principally hussars, and at the same moment a gentleman in a round hat, black cloak and trousers, stepped before the mill and asked me: " Monsieur le Maire?"

" I am the mayor."

" Very good.   I am the army chaplain, and I am come to lodge with you."

I thought that better than having ten or fifteen scoundrels in my house; but he had scarcely closed his lips when another came, an officer of light horse, who cried: " His highness has chosen this house to lodge in."

Very good—what could I reply?

A brigadier, who was following this officer, springs off his horse, goes under the shed, and peeps into the stable. " Turn out all that," said he.

" Turn out my horses, my cattle? " I exclaimed.

" Yes—and quickly too. His highness has twelve horses: he must have room."

I was going to answer, but the officer began to swear and storm so loudly, without listening to anything I could plead, shouting at me that every one of my beasts would be driven to be slaughtered immediately if I made any difficulty, that without saying another word, I drove them all out, my heart swelling, and my head bowed with despair. Grédel, watching from her window, saw this, and coming down, red with anger, said to the officer: " You must be a great coward to behave so roughly to an old man who cannot defend himself."

My hair stood on end with horror; but the officer vouchsafed not a word, and went off instantly.

Then the chaplain whispered in my ear: " You are going to have the honor of entertaining Monseigneur, the reigning Duke of Saxe-Meiningen, and you must call him ' Your highness.' "

I thought with myself: " You, and your highness, and all the highnesses in the world, I wish you were all of you five hundred thousand feet in the bowels of the earth. You are a bad lot. You came into the world for the misery of mankind. Thieves! rogues! "

I only thought these things: I would not have said them for the world. Several persons had been shot in our mountains the last two days—fathers of families—and the remembrance of these things makes one prudent.

As I was reflecting upon our misfortunes, his highness arrived, with his aides-de-camp and his servants. They alighted, entered the house, hung up their wet clothes against the wall, and filled the kitchen. My wife ran upstairs, I stood in a corner behind the stove: we had nothing left to call our own.

This Duke of Saxe was so tall that he could scarcely walk upright under my roof. He was a handsome man, covered with gold-lace ornaments; and so were the two great villains who followed him—Colonel Egloffstein and Major Baron d'Engel. Yes, I could find no fault with them on account of their height or their appetites; nor did they seem to mind us in the least. They laughed, they chatted, they swung themselves round in my room, jingling their swords on the stone floor, on the stairs, everywhere, without paying the smallest attention to me—I seemed to be in *their* house.

From their arrival until their departure, the fire never once went out in my kitchen; my wood blazed; my pans and kettles, my roasting-jack, went on with their business; they twisted the necks of my fowls, my ducks, my geese, plucked them, and roasted them: they fetched splendid pieces of beef, which they minced to make rissoles, and sliced to make what they called " biftecks " ; then they opened my drawers and cupboards, spread my table-cloths on my table, rinsed out my glasses and my bottles, and fetched my wine out of my cellar.

They waited upon his highness and his officers; the doors and windows stood open, the rain poured in; orderlies came on horseback to receive orders, and darted away; and about five o'clock the guns began to thunder and roar at Quatre Vents. The bombardment was beginning in that direction; the two bastions of the arsenal and the bakery answered.

That was the bombardment of the 11th, in which Thibaut's house was delivered to the flames. It would be long before we should see the last of it; but as we had never before heard the like, and these rolling thunders filled our valley between the woods and the rocks of Biechelberg, we trembled.

Grédel, every time that our heavy guns replied,

said: "Those are ours; we are not all dead yet! Do you hear that?"

I pushed her out, and his highness asked, "What is that?"

"Nothing," said I; "it is only my daughter: she is crazy."

About a quarter to seven the firing ceased.

The Baron d'Engel, who had gone out a few minutes before, came back to say that a flag of truce had gone to summon the place to surrender; and that on its refusal the bombardment would re-open at once.

There was a short silence. His highness was eating.

Suddenly entered a colonel of hussars—a hideous being, with a retreating forehead, a squint in his eye, and red hair—decorated all over with ribbons and crosses, like a North American Indian. He walks in. Salutations, hand-shaking all round, and a good deal of laughing. They seat themselves again, they devour—they swallow everything! And that hussar begins telling that he has taken MacMahon's tent—a magnificent tent, with mirrors, china, ladies' hats and crinolines. He laughed, grinning up to his ears; and his highness was highly delighted, ·saying that MacMahon would have given a representation of his victory to the great ladies of Paris.

Of course this was an abominable lie; but the Prussians are not afraid of lying.

That hussar—whose name I cannot remember, although I have often heard it from others—said besides, that, after having ridden a couple of hours through the forest of Elsashausen, he had fallen upon the village of Gundershoffen, where a few companies of French infantry had established themselves, and that he had surprised and massacred them all to the last man, without the loss of a single horseman!

Then he began to laugh again, saying that in war you often might have an agreeable time of it, and that this would be among his most cheerful reminiscences.

Hearing him from my seat behind the stove, I said: " And are these men called Christians? Why, they are worse than wolves! They would drink human blood out of skulls, and boast of it! "

They went on talking in this fashion, when a very young officer came to say that the defenders of Phalsbourg refused to surrender, and that they were going to shell the town, to set fire to it.

I could listen no longer. Grédel and my wife went to shut themselves in upstairs, and I went out to breathe a different air from these wild monsters.

It was raining still. I wanted fresh air—I should have liked to throw myself into the river with all my clothes on.

Fresh regiments were passing. Now it was white cuirassiers; they extended along the meadows below Metting; other regiments in dense masses advanced on Sarrebourg. Down there the bayonets and the helmets sparkled and glistened in the setting sun, in spite of the torrents of rain. It was easy to see that our unfortunate army of two hundred thousand men could not resist such a deluge.

But the three hundred thousand other soldiers that we should have had, and which we had been paying for the last eighteen years, where then were they? They were in the reports presented by the Ministers of War to the Legislative Assembly; and the money which should have paid for their complete equipment and their armament, that was in London, put down to his Majesty's account : the *honest man*, he had laid up savings.

All these Germans, encamped as far as the eye could see under the rain, were beginning to cut down our fruit-trees to warm themselves; in all directions our beautiful apple-trees, our pear-trees, still laden with fruit, came to the ground; then they were stripped bare, chopped to pieces, and burnt with the sap in them: the falling rain did not prevent the wood from lighting, on account of the quantity underneath which the fire dried at last.

The whole plain and the table-land above were in a blaze with these fires.

What a loss for the country!

It had taken fifty-six years, since 1814, to grow these trees; they were in full bearing; for fifty years our children and grand-children will not see their equals around our village; the whole are destroyed!

With this spectacle before my eyes, indignation stifled my voice; I turned my eyes away, and went to Cousin George's, hoping to hear there a few words of encouragement.

I was right; the house was full; Cousin Marie Anne, a bold and unceremonious woman, was busy cooking for all her lodgers. Amongst the number were two of her old customers at the Rue Mouffetard; a Jew, who had come to Paris to learn gardening at the Jardin des Plantes, and a saddler, both seated near the hearth with an appearance of shame and melancholy in their countenances. The soldiers, who were crowding even the passage, smoked, and examined now and then to see if the meat and potatoes looked promising in the big copper in the washhouse: there was no other in the house large enough to boil such a large quantity of provisions.

Every soldier had an enormous slice of beef, a loaf, a portion of wine, and even some ground coffee; some had under their arms a rope of onions, turnips, a head of cabbage, stolen right and left. These were the hussars.

In the large parlor were the officers, who had just returned in succession from their reconnaissances; as they went up into the room, you could hear the clanking of their swords and their huge boots making the staircase shake.

As I was coming in by the back door, not having been able to make way through the passage, George was coming out of the room; he saw me above the helmets of all these people, and cried to me: " Christian! stay outside; I am stifled here! I am coming! "

Room was made for him, and we went down together into the garden, under the shelter of his stack of wood.   Then he lighted a pipe, and asked me: " Well, how are you going on down there? "

I told him all.

" I," said he, " have already had to receive the colonel of the hussars last night.   An hour after the visit of the Uhlans, there is a tap on the shutters; I open.   Two squadrons of hussars were standing there, round the house; there was no way of escape."

" ' Open! '

" I obey.   The colonel, a sort of a wolf, whom I saw just now going to your house, enters the first, pistol in hand; he examines all round: ' You are alone? '

" ' Yes; with my wife.'

" ' Very well! '

" Then he went into the passage, and called an aide-de-camp.   Three or four soldiers came in; they carry chairs and a table into the kitchen.   The colonel unfolds a large map upon the floor; he takes off his boots, and lays himself upon it.   Then he calls: ' Such a one, are you here? '

" ' Present, colonel.'

" Then six or seven captains and lieutenants enter.

" ' Such an one, do you see the road to Metting! '

" They had all taken small maps out of their pockets.

" ' Yes, colonel.'

" ' And from Metting to Sarrebourg? '

" ' Yes, colonel.'

" ' Tell me the names.'

" And the officer named the villages, the farms, the streams, the rivers, the clumps of wood, the curves in the road, and even the intersection of foot-paths.

" The colonel followed with his nail.

" ' That will do!   Now go and take twenty men and push on as far as St. Jean, by such a road. You will see!   In case of resistance, you will inform me. Come, sharp! '

" And the officer goes off.

" The colonel, still lying upon his map, calls another.

" ' Present, colonel.'

" ' You see Lixheim? '

" ' Yes, colonel.'

" And so on.

" In half an hour's time, he had sent off a whole squadron on reconnaissances to Sarrebourg, Lix-heim, Diemeringen, Lützelbourg, Fénétrange, everywhere in that direction.   And when they had all started, except twenty or thirty horses left behind, he got up from the floor, and said to me: ' You will give me a good bed, and you will prepare breakfast for to-morrow at seven o'clock; all those officers

will breakfast with me: they will have good appetites. You have poultry and bacon. Your wife is
a good cook, I know; and you have good wine. I
require that everything shall be good. You hear
me!'

"I made no answer, and I went out to tell my
wife, who had just dressed and was coming downstairs. She had heard what was said, and answered,
'Yes, we will obey, since the robbers have the power
on their side.'

"That knave of a colonel could hear perfectly
well; but it was no matter to him: his business was
to get what he wanted.

"My wife took him upstairs and showed him his
bed. He looked underneath it, into all the cupboards, the closet; then he opened the two windows
in the corner to see his men below at their posts; and
then he lay down.

"Until morning all was quiet.

"Then the others came back. The colonel listened to them; he immediately sent some of the men
who had stayed behind to Dosenheim, in the direction of Saverne; and about a couple of hours after
these same hussars returned with the advanced
guard of the army corps. The colonel had ascer-
tained that all the mountain passes were abandoned,
and that Lorraine might be entered without danger;
that MacMahon and De Failly had arrived in the
open plain, and that there would be no battle in our
neighborhood."

This is all that Cousin George told me, smoking his pipe.

They had just thrown open the door which opens into the garden, to let air into the kitchen, and we looked from our retreat upon all those Germans with their helmets, their wet clothes, their strings of vegetables, and their joints of meat under their arms. As fast as it was cooked Marie Anne served out the broth, the meat, and the vegetables to those who presented themselves with their basins; when they went out, others came. Never could fresher meat be seen, and in such quantities: one of their pieces would have sufficed four or five Frenchmen.

How sad to think that our own men had suffered hunger in our own country, both before and after the battle! How it makes the heart sink!

Without having said a word, George and I had thought the same thing, for all at once he said: " Yes, those people have managed matters better than we have. That meat is not from this country, since they have not yet requisitioned the cattle. It has come by rail; I saw that this morning on the arrival of the gun-carriages. They have also received for the officers large puddings, bullocks' paunches stuffed with minced meats, and other eatables that I am not acquainted with; only their bread is black, but they seem to enjoy it. Their contractors don't come from the clouds, like ours; they may not set rows of figures quite so straight even as ours; but their soldiers get meat, bread, wine, and coffee, whilst ours are starving, as we ourselves have seen. If they had received half the rations of these men, the peasants of Niederbronn would never have complained of them: they could still have fed the unfortunate men upon their retreat."

About eleven at night I returned to the mill a little calmer. The sentinels knew me already. His highness was asleep; so were also his two aides-de-camp and the chaplain: they had taken possession of our beds without ceremony. The servants had gone to sleep in the barn upon my straw; and as for me, I did not know where to go. Still, I was a little more composed in thinking upon what my cousin had told me. If these Germans received their provisions by railway, all might be well; I hoped we might yet keep our cattle, and that then these people would proceed farther. With this hope I lay on the flour-sacks in the mill and fell fast asleep.

But next day I saw how completely mistaken George was in the matter of provisions. I am not speaking only of all that was stolen in our village; every moment people came to me with complaints, as if I was responsible for everything.

"Monsieur le Maire, they have taken the bacon out of my chimney."

"Monsieur le Maire, they have stolen the boots from under my bed."

"Monsieur le Maire, they have given my hay to their horses. What must I do to feed my cow?"

And so on.

The Prussians are the worst thieves in the world; they have no shame; they would take the bread out of your very mouth to swallow it.

These complaints made me so angry that I took courage to speak to his highness, who listened very kindly, and said it was very unfortunate, but that I should remember the French proverb, " À la guerre, comme à la guerre; " and that this proverb applied to peasants as well as to soldiers.

I could have borne all this if the requisitions had not begun; but now the quartermasters were making their appearance, to settle with me, as they said.

It was of no use to urge that we were poor people, already three-fourths ruined; they answered: " Settle your own business.   We must have so many tons of hay; so many bushels of oats, barley, flour; so much of meat, both beef and mutton, of good quality; or else, Monsieur le Maire, we will burn down your village."

His highness the Duke of Saxe and his officers had just gone to inspect the camp around the place; I was left alone.   I wanted to ring the church bells to assemble the municipal council, but all bell-ringing was forbidden.   Then I sent round the rural policeman to summon each councillor, one after the other; but the councillors did not stir: they thought that by remaining at home they would prevent the Prussians from doing anything.

In this extremity I made Martin Kopp publish by

beat of drum the list of all that the village had to supply in provisions and articles of every kind, before eleven in the morning; entreating all honest people to make haste, if they did not want to see their houses in flames from one end of the village to the other.

Scarcely had this notice been given out, when everybody made haste to bring all they could.

The quartermasters made out an inventory; they carried away my best cow, and gave me a receipt for everything in the name of his Majesty the King of Prussia.

The general indignation was terrible.

Such was the robbery and violence, in those earlier days, that not so much as a pound of salt meat could have been bought by us in the whole country; and as for fresh meat, it was no use thinking of it. Well, when the Prussians resorted to requisition, everything was obtained, by means of that threat of *fire!* It was known what they had done in Alsace, and, of course, they were supposed easily capable of beginning again.

After these requisitions, which might be regarded as a little bouquet for his highness, the Prussians raised their camp, announcing to us the arrival of new-comers. I also heard M. le Baron d'Engel command one of his orderlies to order at Sarrebourg six thousand rations of bread and of coffee. Then I saw clearly that it was intended we should feed all these fellows till the end of the campaign, and my sad reflections may easily be imagined. The German commissariat no longer seemed to me so admirable. I could see that it was simply organized robbery and pillage.

The Duke and his followers had scarcely departed, when a captain of blue hussars, Monsieur Collomb, came to take his place, with six horses, and his adjutant, the Count Bernhardy, with three more horses. They came from Saverne wet through, having spent the night in the open air, and this gave them a terrible appetite.

I explained that everything had been taken from us—that we had nothing left to eat for ourselves; but they would not believe me, and my wife was obliged to turn the house topsy-turvy to find something for them to eat.

While eating and drinking enough for four, these two gentlemen found time to tell us that they had hung eleven peasants of Gunstedt on the day of the battle of Reichshoffen! They also told us, what was quite true, that next day provisions would arrive in our village. Unhappily, this long train of provisions, which seemed endless, passed on direct to Sarrebourg.

This was the 12th of August.

We had, then, this captain, his adjutant, their servants, and their horses on our shoulders; all of whom we had to feed to the full until the day of their departure.

The batteries of Phalsbourg had dismounted the

German guns at the Quatre Vents. Sick and wounded in great numbers had been sent to the great military hospital at Saverne; there were a few left in the school-room of Pfalsweyer: this annoyed the Prussians.   One would have thought that it was our duty to let them come and rob, pillage, and bombard and burn us, without defending ourselves; that we were guilty of crimes against them, and that they had rights over us, as a nation of valets.

They actually thought this.

And I have always heard these Germans making such complaints: whether they took us for fools, or were fools themselves, I do not know exactly which; but I think there was something of both.

After the passage of a convoy of provisions, which went past us for two hours, came cannon, powder-wagons, and shells.   Never had our poor village heard such a noise; it was like a torrent roaring over the rocks.

The 11th corps was passing.   There were twelve like it, each from eighty to ninety thousand men.

We now knew nothing whatever about our own troops, nor our relations and friends in the town. We were shut up as in an island, in the midst of this deluge of Prussians, Bavarians, Wurtemburgers, Badeners, who streamed through in long, interminable columns, and seemed to have no end.

It appears that the requisitions which had been made the night before, and that immense convoy of provisions, were not enough for their army, so they no longer cared to address themselves to Monsieur le Maire; for the officers whom we lodged having left us early in the morning, all at once, about seven o'clock, loud cries arose in the village: the Prussians were coming to carry off all our remaining cattle at one swoop.   But this time they had not taken their measures so cleverly; they had not guarded the backs of our houses, and every one began to drive his beasts into the wood—oxen, cows, goats, all were clambering up the hill, the women and the girls, the old men and children behind.

Thus they caught scarcely anything.

From that hour, in spite of their threats, our cattle remained in the woods; and it was also known that we had *francs-tireurs* traversing the country. Some said that they were Turcos escaped from Woerth, others that they were French chasseurs; but the Prussians no longer ventured out of the high-roads in small parties; and this is, no doubt, the reason why they did not go to find our cattle in the Krapenfelz.

The next day, the 13th of August, the Prussians were seen in motion in the direction of Wechem. A Prussian prince, advanced in years, with long nose and chin, and always on horseback, was at Metting; and the rumor ran that the great bombardment of Phalsbourg was going to begin, and that more than sixty guns were in position above the mill at Wechem: that they were throwing up earthworks to

cover the guns, and that it was going to be very
serious.

That very day, when I was least expecting it, the
quartermasters came back to requisition meat. But
I told them that all the beasts were in the wood,
through their own fault; that they had insisted on
taking everything at once, and now they would get
nothing.

On hearing these perfectly correct observations
of mine, they tried threats. Then I said to them:
" Take me—eat me—I am old and lean. You will
not get much out of me."

However, as they threatened us with fire, I gave
public notice that the Prussians still claimed, in the
name of the King of Prussia, ten hundred-weight of
oats and of barley, three thousand of straw, and as
much of hay; and that if the whole was not delivered
in the market square on the stroke of twelve, they
would set fire to the place without compassion.

And this time, too, it all came.

These Germans had found out the way to compel
people to strip themselves even of their very shirts!
Fire! fire! There lies the true genius of the Prussians. No one had imagined *fire*—the power
of *fire*, like these brigands. God alone had brought
down fire hitherto upon His miserable creatures to
punish heavy crimes, as at Sodom and Gomorrah;
they resorted to it to rob and plunder us! It was
the punishment of our folly.

But let us hope that nations will not always be

so wicked.   God will take pity upon us.   I do not
say the God of the Jesuits, nor of the Prussians, who
are Protestant Jesuits!   But He whom every man
feels in his own heart; He who draws from us the
tears of pity and compassion, which we drop upon
our brothers unjustly slain; He is the God of whom
I speak, and it is to Him that I cry when I say:
" Look upon our sufferings!   Have we deserved
them? are we accountable for our ignorance?   If
so, then punish us!   But if others are to blame: if
they have refused us schools; if they have never
taught us anything that we ought to know; if they
have profited by our credulity to impose upon us,
oh! God, pardon us, and restore to us our country,
our dear country, Alsace and Lorraine!   Let us not
be reduced to receiving blows like the German soldiers!   Degrade not our children, our poor children, to become servants and beasts of burden to the
German nobles!   My God! we have been verily
guilty in believing our ' honest man,' who swore to
Thee with full intent to break his oath: and his
Ministers, who plunged into war ' with a light
heart!' after having promised us peace, and who
first secured their own safety and well-lined pockets!   Nevertheless, we of Alsace and Lorraine, the
most faithful children of the Great Revolution, have
not deserved that we should become Germans and
Prussians!   Alas! what a calamity! . . ."

I have just been weeping!   After such a flood of
miseries and abominable acts my heart overflows!

Now I pursue my sad story; and I will try never to forget that I am relating a true history, which everybody knows; which all the world has seen.

That same day, toward evening, several vans full of Alsacians, returning from Blamont, passed through our village to return home. The Prussians had obliged them to walk; their horses were nothing but bags of bones; and the people, emaciated, yellow-looking, had been so battered with blows, so famished with hunger, that they staggered at every step.

They had not received so much as a ration of bread on the whole journey; the Germans devoured everything! They would have seen our poor fellows—whom they had compelled to bear the burden of their baggage—they would have seen them drop with weariness and starvation before their eyes, without giving them a drop of water! But for our unhappy invaded Lorraine brothers, who fed them out of their own poverty, they would have perished, every one.

This is the truth! We experienced it ourselves not long afterward; for the same fate was reserved to us.

After the passage of these miserable creatures, to whom I gave a little bread—though we had scarcely any left, since the Germans, only two days before, had robbed us of twenty-seven loaves just fresh out of the oven—after this melancholy sight, we saw coming with a terrible clatter and ringing of sabres, one after the other, three Prussian aides-de-camp, who were announced to us; the first as a colonel, the second a general, and the third I cannot remember what—a duke, a prince, something of that kind!

It was the colonel whom I had the honor, as they called it, to entertain, Colonel Waller, of the 10th regiment of Silesian grenadiers; and then followed the general, who did me the honor to sup at my house at my expense.   This man's name was Macha-Cowsky.   They had the pleasure of informing us that that very night Phalsbourg was going to be thoroughly shelled.   Those gentlemen are full of the greatest delicacy; they imagined that this good news was going to delight me, my wife, and my daughter!

The flag of the Silesian grenadiers was brought into the colonel's apartment.   This regiment was arriving from the Austrian frontier; it had waited for the declaration of neutrality of the good Catholics down there, to come by rail and unite with the twelve army corps which were invading us with so much glory.

I learned this by overhearing their conversation.

That was a very bad night for us.   The officers wanted to be waited on separately, one after the other; my poor wife was obliged to cook for them, to bring them plates—in a word, to be their servant; and Grédel, in spite of her indignation, was helping her mother, pale with passion and biting her lips to keep it down.

The general and the colonel took their supper at nine, the aide-de-camp at ten; and so forth all the night through, without giving a thought to the exhaustion and trouble of the poor women.

They were laughing a good deal over what Monsieur le Curé of Wilsberg had said the night before; who had told them that the misfortunes of Napoleon had arisen from his withdrawing his troops from Rome, and that " whoever ate of the Pope would burst asunder! "

They enjoyed these words and had great fun over them.

I, in my corner, came to the conclusion that from a fool you must expect nothing but folly.

At last I dropped off to sleep, with my head upon my knees; but scarcely had daylight appeared when the house was filled with the ringing of spurs and steel scabbards, and above all rose the loud voice of the aide-de-camp: " Where are you, you scoundrel! will you come, ass! fool! brute! come this way, will you! "

This is the way he called his servant! This is exactly the way they treat their soldiers, who listen to them gravely, the hand raised beside the ear, eyes looking right before them, without uttering a sound! He is lucky, too, if the speech finishes without a smart box on the ears or a kick in the rear! This is what they hope to see us coming to some day; this is what they call " instructing us in the noble virtues of the Germans."

The colonel breakfasted at about five in the morning; a company came for the flag, and the regiments marched off. We were rejoicing, when about seven, the bombardment opened with an awful crashing noise. Sixty guns at Wechem were firing at the same time.

The town replied; but at half-past eight a heavy cloud of smoke was already overhanging Phalsbourg; the heavy guns of the fortress only replied with the more spirit; the shells whizzed, the bombs burst upon the hill-side, and the thunders of the bastion of Wilsenberg roared and rolled in echoing claps to the remotest ends of Alsace.

My wife and Grédel, seated opposite each other, looked silently in each other's faces; I paced up and down with my head bowed, thinking of Jacob, and of all those good people who at that moment had before their eyes the spectacle of their burning houses and furniture, the fruit of their fifty years of labor.

At ten I came out; the dense column of smoke had spread wider and wider; it extended toward the hospital and the church; it seemed like a vast black flag which drooped low from time to time and rose again to meet the clouds.

A squadron of cuirassiers, and behind them another of hussars, dashed past up the face of the hill; but they came down again with lightning speed in the direction of Metting, where the Prussian prince had his head-quarters.

The shells of the sixty guns went on their way rising through the air and falling into the smoke; the bombs and the shells from the town dropped behind the Prussian batteries, and exploded in the fields.

The echoes could be heard from the Lützelbourg, thundering from one moment to another. The old castle down below must have shaken and trembled upon its rock.

In the midst of all this terrible din the pillage was beginning afresh; bands of robbers were breaking from their ranks, and whilst the officers were admiring the burning town through their field-glasses, *they* were running from house to house, pointing their bayonets at the women and demanding eau-de-vie, butter, eggs, cheese, anything that they expected to find according to the inspector's reports. If you kept bees, they must have honey; if you kept poultry, it must be fowls or eggs. And these brigands, in bands of five or six, rummaged and plundered everywhere. They committed other horrible deeds, which it is not fit even to mention.

These are your good old German manners!

And they reproach us with our Turcos; but the Turcos are saints compared with these filthy vagabonds, who are still polluting our hospitals.

Coming nearer to us, these robbers found a man awaiting them firmly at his door; I had grasped a pitchfork, Grédel stood behind with an axe. Then, having, I suppose, no written order to rob, and fearful lest my neighbors should come to my side, they sneaked away farther.

But about eleven, a lieutenant, with a canteen woman, came to order me to give up to him a few pints of wine; saying that he would pay me every sou, by and by. This was a polite way of robbing; for who would be such a fool as to refuse credit to a man who has you by the throat. I took them down to the cellar, the woman filled her two little barrels, and then they departed.

About one the colonel returned at the head of his regiment, and advanced as far as the door without alighting from his horse, asking for a glass of wine and a piece of bread, which my wife presented him. He could not stop another moment.

Scarcely had he left us, when again the canteen woman's barrels had to be replenished. This time it was an ensign, who swore that the debt should be fully paid that very night. He emptied my cask, and went off with a conceited strut.

Whilst all this was going on, the cannon were thundering, the smoke rising higher and thicker. The bombs from Phalsbourg burst on the plateau of Berlingen. At half-past four half the town was blazing; at five the flames seemed spreading farther yet; and the church steeple, which was built of stone, seemed still to be standing erect, but as hollow as a cage; the bells had melted, the solid beams and the roof fallen in; from a distance of five miles you could see right through it. About ten, the people in our village, standing before their houses with clasped hands, suddenly saw the flames pierce to an immense height through the dense smoke into the sky.

The cannon ceased to roar. A flag of truce had just gone forward once more to summon the place to surrender. But our lads are not of the sort who give themselves up; nor the people of Phalsbourg either: on the contrary, the more the fire consumed, the less they had to lose; and fortunately, the biscuit and the flour which had been intended for Metz, since the battle of Reichshoffen had remained at the storehouses, so that there were provisions enough for a long while. Only meat and salt were failing: as if people with any sense ought not to have a stock of salt in every fortified town, kept safe in cellars, enough to last ten years. Salt is not expensive; it never spoils; at the end of a century it is found as good as at first. But our commissaries of stores are so perfect! A poor miller could not presume to offer this simple piece of advice. Yet the want of salt was the cause of the worst sufferings of the inhabitants during the last two months of the siege.

The flag of truce returned at night, and we learned that there was no surrender.

Then a few more shells were fired, which killed some of those who had already left the shelter of the casemates—some women, and other poor creatures. At last the firing ceased on both sides. It was about nine. The profound silence after all this uproar seemed strange. I was standing at my own door looking round, when suddenly, in the dark street, my cousin appeared.

"Is anybody there?"

"No."

And we entered the room, where were Grédel and my wife.

"Well," said he, laughing and winking, "our boys won't give in. The commanding officer is a brave fellow."

"Yes," said my wife, "but what has become of Jacob?"

"Pooh!" said George, "he is perfectly well. I have seen very different bombardments from these; at Saint Jean d'Ulloa they fired upon us with shells of a hundred-and-twenty pounds; these are only sixes and twelves. Well, after all when a man has seen his thirtieth or fortieth year, it is a good deal to say. Don't be uneasy; I assure you that your boy is quite well: besides, are not the ramparts the best place?"

Then he sat down and lighted his pipe. The blazing town sent out such a glow of light that the shadows of our casements were quivering on the illumined bed-curtains.

"It is burning fiercely," said my cousin. "How hot they must be down there! But how unfortunate that the Archeviller tunnel should not have been blown up! and that the orders of his Majesty did not arrive to apply the match to the train that was ready laid. What a misfortune for France to have such an incompetent man at her head! The town holds out; if the tunnel had only been blown up, the Germans would have been obliged to take the town! The bombardment makes no impression; they would have been obliged to proceed by regular approaches, by digging trenches, and then make two or three assaults. This would have detained them a fortnight, three weeks, or a month; and during this interval, the country might have taken breath. I know that the Prussians have a road by Forbach and Sarre Union to hold the railway at Nancy; but Toul is there! And then there is a wide difference between marching on foot one day's march, and then another day's march with guns, and ammunition, and all sorts of provisions dragging after you, convoys to be escorted and watched for fear of sudden attacks; and holding a perfect railroad which brings everything quietly under your hands! Yes, it is indeed a misfortune to be ruled by an idiot, who has people around him declaring he is an eagle."

Thus spoke my cousin; and my wife informed him that it would please her much better to see the Germans pass by than to have to entertain them.

"You speak just like a woman," answered George. "No doubt we are suffering losses; but do you suppose that France will not indemnify us?

Do you think we shall always be having idiots **and** sycophants for our deputies? If we are not paid for this, who, in future, will think of defending his country? We should all open our doors to the enemy: this would be the destruction of France. Get these notions out of your head, Catherine, and be sure that the interest of the individual is identical with that of the nation. Ah! if that tunnel had been blown up the Germans would have been **in a** very different position!"

Thereupon, my cousin fixed his eyes upon that unhappy town, which resembled a sea of fire; out of two hundred houses, fifty-two, besides the church, were a prey to the flames. No noise could be heard on account of the distance, but sometimes a red glare shot even to us, and the moon, sailing through the clouds on our left peacefully went on her way as she has done since the beginning of the world. All the hateful passions, all the fearful crimes of men never disturb the stars of heaven in their silent paths! George, having gazed with teeth set and lips compressed, left us without another word.

We sat up all that night. You may be sure that no one slept in the whole village; for every one had there a son, a brother, or a friend.

The next day, the 15th of August, when the morning mists had cleared away, the smoke was rising still, but it was not so thick. Then the main body of the German army proceeded on their march to Nancy; and the lieutenant, who, the night before, had promised to pay me for my wine, had stepped out left foot foremost, having forgotten to say good-by to me. If the rest of the German officers are at all like that fellow, I would strongly recommend no one ever to trust them even with a single *liard* on their mere word.

After the departure of this second army, came the 6th corps; the next day, Sunday, and the day after there passed cavalry regiments: chasseurs, lancers, hussars, brown, green, and black, without number. They all marched past us down our valley, and their faces were toward the interior of France. Yet there remained a force of infantry and artillery around Phalsbourg, at Wechem, Wilsberg, at Biechelberg, the Quatre Vents, the Baraques, etc. The rumor ran that they were to be reinforced with heavier artillery, to lay regular siege to the place; but what they had was just sufficient to secure the railroad, the Archeviller tunnel, and in our direction the pass of the Graufthal.

The provisions, the stores, the spare horses, and the infantry followed the valley of Lützelbourg; their cavalry were in part following after ours.

Since that time we have seen no bombardments, except on a small scale. Sorties might easily have been made by the townspeople, for all right-minded people would rather have given their cattle to the town than see them requisitioned by the Prussians.

Yes, indeed, it was those requisitions which tormented us the most. Oh, these requisitions! The

11

seven or eight thousand men who were blockading the town lived at our expense, and denied themselves nothing.

But a little later, during the blockade of Metz, we were to experience worse miseries yet.

CHAPTER VIII

A FEW days after the passage of the last squadrons of hussars, we learned that the Phalsbourgers had made a sortie to carry off cattle from the Biechelberg. That night we might have captured the whole of the garrison of our village; but the officer in command of the party was a poor creature. Instead of approaching in silence, he had ordered guns to be fired at two hundred paces from the enemy's advanced posts, to frighten the Prussians! But they, in great alarm, had sprung out of their beds, where they lay fast asleep, and had all decamped, firing back at our men; and the peasants lost no time in driving their cattle into the woods.

From this you may see what notions our officers had about war.

"The men of 1814," said our old forester, Martin Kopp, "set to work in a different way; they were sure to fetch back bullocks, cows, and prisoners into the town."

When Cousin George was spoken to of these matters, he shrugged his shoulders and made no remark.

Worse than all, the Prussians made fun of us unlucky villagers of Rothalp, calling us " *la grande nation!* " But was it our fault if our officers, who had almost all been brought up by the Jesuits, knew nothing of their profession? If our lads had been drilled, if every man had been compelled to serve, as they are in Germany; and if every man had been given the post for which he was best fitted, according to his acquirements and his spirit, I don't think the Prussians would have got so much fun out of " *la grande nation.*"

This was the only sortie attempted during the siege. The commander, Talliant, who had plenty of sense, was quite aware that with officers of this stamp, and soldiers who knew nothing of drill, it was better to keep behind the ramparts and try to live without meat.

About the same time the officer in command of the post of the Landwehr at Wechem, the greatest drunkard and the worst bully we have ever seen in our part of the country, came to pay me his first visit, along with fifteen men with fixed bayonets.

His object was to requisition in our village three hundred loaves of bread, some hay, straw, and oats in proportion.

In the first place he walked into my mill, crying, " Hallo! good-morning, M. le Maire! "

Seeing those bayonets at my door, a fidgety feeling came over me.

" I am come to bring you a proclamation from his Majesty the King of Prussia. Read that! "

And I read the following proclamation:

"We, William, King of Prussia, make known
to the inhabitants of the French territory that the
Emperor Napoleon III., having attacked the German nation by sea and by land, whose desire was
and is to live at peace with France, has compelled
us to assume the command of our armies, and, con-
sequently upon the events of war, to cross the
French frontier; but that I make war upon soldiers and not upon French citizens, who shall continue to enjoy perfect security, both as regards
their persons and their property, as long as they
shall not themselves compel me, by hostile measures against the German troops, to withdraw my
protection from them."

"You will post up this proclamation," said the
lieutenant to me, "upon your door, upon that of
the mayoralty-office, and upon the church-door.
Well! are you glad?"

"Of course," said I.

"Then," he replied, "we are good friends; and
good friends must help one another. Come, my
boys," he cried to his soldiers, with a loud laugh,
"come on—let us all go in. Here you may fancy
yourselves at home. You will be refused nothing.
Come in!"

And these robbers first entered the mill; then they
passed on into the kitchen; from the kitchen into the
house, and then they went down into the cellar.

My wife and Grédel had sought safety in flight.

Then commenced a regular organized pillage.

They cleared out my chimney of its last hams and flitches of bacon, they broke in my last barrel of wine; they opened my wardrobe—scenting down to the very bottom like a pack of hounds. I saw one of these soldiers lay hands even upon the candle out of the candlestick and stuff it into his boot.

One of my lambs having begun to bleat:

"Hallo!" cried the lieutenant. "Sheep! we want mutton."

And the infamous rascals went off to the stable to seize upon my sheep.

When there was nothing left to rob, this gallant officer handed me the list of regular requisitions, saying, "We require these articles. You will bring the whole of them this very evening to Wechem, or we shall be obliged to repeat our visit: you comprehend, Monsieur le Maire? And, especially, do not forget the proclamations, his Majesty's proclamations; that is of the first importance: it was our principal object in coming. Now, Monsieur le Maire, *au revoir, au revoir!*"

The abominable brute held out his hand to me in its coarse leather glove—I turned my back upon him; he pretended not to see it, and marched off in the midst of his soldiers, all loaded like pack-horses, laughing, munching, tippling; for every man had filled his tin flask and stuffed his canvas bag full.

Farther on they visited several of the other principal houses—my cousin's, the curé Daniel's.

They were so loaded with plunder that, after their last visit, they halted to lay under requisition a horse and cart, which seemed to them handier than carrying all that they had stolen.

War is a famous school for thieves and brigands; by the end of twenty years mankind would be a vast pack of villains.

Perhaps this may yet be our fate; for I remember that the old school-master at Bouxviller told us that there had been once in ancient times populous nations, richer than we are, who might have prospered for thousands of years by means of commerce and industry, but who had been so madly bent upon their own extermination by means of war, that their country became at last sandy wastes, where not a blade of grass grows now and nothing is found but scattered rocks.

This is our impending fate; and I fear I may see it before I die, if such men as Bismarck, Bonaparte, William, De Moltke, and all those creatures of blood and rapine do not swiftly meet with their deserved retribution.

The pillaging lieutenant that I told you of just now was made a captain at the end of the war— the reward of his merit. I cannot just now recollect his name; but when I mention that he used to roam from village to village, from one public-house to another, soaking in, like a sand-bank, wine, beer, and ardent spirits; that he bellowed out songs like a bull-calf; that he used in a maudlin way to prate about little birds; that he levied requisitions at random; and that he used to return to his quarters about one, or two, or three o'clock in the morning, so intoxicated that it was incredible that a human being in such a state could keep his seat on horseback, and yet was ready to begin again next morning; yes, I need but mention these circumstances, and everybody will recognize in a minute the big German brute!

The other Landwehr officers, in command at Wilsberg, Quatre Vents, Mittelbronn, and elsewhere, were scarcely better. After the departure of the princes, the dukes, and the barons, these men looked upon themselves as the lords of the land. Every day we used to hear of fresh crimes committed by them upon poor defenceless creatures. One day, at Mittelbronn, they shot a poor idiot who had been running barefoot in the woods for ten years, hurting nobody; the next day, at Wilsberg, they stripped naked a poor boy who unfortunately had come too near their batteries, and the officer himself, with his heavy boots kicked him till the blood ran; and then, at the Quatre Vents, they pulled out of the cellar two feeble old men, and exposed them two days and nights to the rain and the cold, threatening to kill them if they did but stir; they pillaged oxen, sheep, hay, straw, smashed furniture, burst in windows, day after day, for the mere pleasure of killing and destroying.

Sometimes they found amusement in threaten-

THEY DREW TWO POOR OLD MEN FROM THEIR CELLAR.

ing to make the curés and the maires drive the
cattle which they themselves had lifted. And as
the Germans enjoy the reputation with us of being
very learned, I feel bound to declare that I have
never seen one, whether officer or private, with a
book in his hand.

Cousin George said, with good reason, that all
their learning bears upon their military profession:
the spy system, and the study of maps for officers,
and discipline under corporal punishment for the
rest. The only clear notion they have in their
heads is that they must obey their chiefs and calmly
receive slaps in the face.

The young men employed in trade are great
travellers. They get information in other countries; they are sly; they never answer questions;
they are good servants, and cheap; but at the first
signal, back they go to get kicked; and they think
nothing of shooting their old shopmates, and those
whose bread they have been eating for years.

In their country some are born to slap, others to
be slapped. They regard this as a law of nature;
a man is honorable or not according as he may be
the son of a nobleman or a tradesman, a baron or
a workman. With them, the less honorable the
man the better the soldier; he is only expected to
obey, to black boots, and to rub down the officer's
horse when he is ordered: a banker's, or a rich
citizen's son obeys just like any one else! Hence
there is no doubt that their armies are well disci-

plined. George said that their superior officers handled a hundred thousand men with greater ease than ours could manage ten thousand, and that, for that purpose, less talent was needed. No doubt! If I, who am only a miller, had by chance been born King of Prussia, I should lead them all by the bridle, like my horses, and better. I should simply be careful, on the eve of any difficult enterprise, to consult two or three clever fellows who should clear up my ideas for me, and engage in my service highly educated young men to look after affairs. Then the machine would act of itself, just like my mill, where the cogs work into each other without troubling me. The machinery does everything; genius, good sense, and good feeling are not wanted.

These ideas have come into my mind, thinking upon what I have observed since the opening of this campaign; and this is why I say we must have discipline to play this game over again; only, as the French possess the sentiment of honor, they must be made to understand that he who has no discipline is wanting in honor, and betrays his country. Then, without kicking and slapping, we shall obtain discipline; we may handle vast masses, and shall beat the Germans, as we have done hundreds of times before.

These things should be taught in every school, and the schools should be numberless; at the very head of the catechism should be written: "The first virtue of the citizen under arms is obedience; the man who disobeys is a coward, a traitor to the Republic."

These were my thoughts; and now I continue my story.

After the passage of the German armies, our unhappy country was, as it were, walled round with a rampart of silence; for all the men who were blockading Phalsbourg, and the few detachments which were still passing with provisions, stores, flocks of sheep, and herds of oxen through the valley, were under orders not to speak to us, but leave us to the influence of fear. We received no more newspapers, no more letters, nor the least fragment of intelligence from the interior. We could hear the bombardment of Strasbourg when the wind blew from the Rhine. All was in flames down there; but, as no one dared to come and go, on account of the enemy's posts placed at every point, nothing was known. Melancholy and grief were killing us. No one worked. What was the use of working, when the bravest, the most industrious, the most thrifty saw the fruit of their labor devoured by innumerable brigands? Men almost regretted having done their duty by their children, in depriving themselves of necessaries, to feed in the end such base wretches as these. They would say: " Is there any justice left in the world? Are not upright men, tender mothers of families, and dutiful children, fools? Would it not be better to

become thieves and rogues at once? Do not all the
rewards fall to the brutish? Are not those hypocrites who preach religion and mercy? Our only
duty is to become the strongest. Well, let us be
the strongest; let us pass over the bodies of our
fellow-creatures, who have done us no harm; let us
spy, cheat, and pillage: if we are the strongest, we
shall be in the right."

Here is the list of the requisitions, made in the
poorest cabins, for every Prussian who lodged
there: judge what must have been our misery.

" For every man lodging with you, you will have
to furnish daily 750 grammes of bread, 500
grammes of meat, 250 grammes of coffee, 60
grammes of tobacco, or five cigars, a half litre of
wine, or a litre of beer, or a tenth part of a litre
of eau-de-vie. Besides, for every horse, twelve
kilos of oats, five kilos of hay, and two and a half
kilos of straw."*

Every one will say, " How was it possible for unfortunate peasants to supply all that? It is impossible."

Well, no. The Prussians did get it, in this wise:
They made excursions to the very farthest farms,
they carried off everything, hay, straw; elsewhere
they carried off the cattle; elsewhere, corn; elsewhere, again, wine, eau-de-vie, beer; elsewhere
they demanded contributions in money. Every

* Bread, about 2 lbs.; meat, 1½ lbs.; coffee, 8 oz.; tobacco,
2 oz.; wine, ¾ pint; or beer, 1½ pints; oats, 26 lbs., etc.

man gave up what he had to give, so that by the end
of the campaign there was nothing left.

Yes, indeed! We were comfortable before this
war; we were rich without knowing it. Never had
I supposed that we had in our country such quantities of hay, so many head of cattle.

It is true that, at the last, they gave us bonds;
but not until three-quarters and more of our provisions had been consumed. And now they make
a pretence of indemnifying us; but in thirty years,
supposing there is peace—in thirty years our village will not possess what it had last year.

Ah! vote, vote in plébiscites, you poor, miserable
peasants! Vote for bonds for hay, straw, and meat,
milliards and provinces for the Prussians! Our
honest man promises peace; he who has broken his
oath—trust in his word!

Whenever I think on these things, my hair
stands on end. And those who voted against the
Plébiscite, they have had to pay just as dearly.
How bitterly they must feel our folly; and how
anxious they must be to educate us!

Imagine the condition of my wife and of my
daughter seeing us so denuded! for women cleave
to their savings much more closely than men; and
then mother was only thinking of Jacob, and Grédel of her Jean Baptiste.

Cousin George knew this. He tried several
times to get news of the town. A few Turcos,
who had escaped from the carnage of Froeschwiller,

had remained in town, and every day a few got
through the postern to have a shot at the Germans.
On the other hand, as the attack on the place had
been sudden and unforeseen, there had been no
time to throw down the trees, the hedges, the cottages, and the tombstones in the cemetery. So this
work began afresh: everything within cannon-shot
was razed without mercy.

George tried to reach these men, but the enemy's
posts were still too close. At last he got news, but
in a way which can scarcely be told—by an abandoned woman, who was allowed in the German
lines. This creditable person told us that Jacob was
well; and, no doubt, she also brought some kind of
good news to Grédel, who from that moment was
another woman. The very next day she began to
talk to us about her marriage-portion, and insisted
upon knowing where we had hidden it. I told her
that it was in the wood, at the foot of a tree. Then
she was in alarm lest the Prussians should have discovered it, for they searched everywhere; they had
exact inventories of what was owned by every
householder. They had gone even to the very end
of our cellars to discover choice wines: for instance,
at Mathis's, at the saw-mills, and at Frantz Sépel's,
at Metting. Nothing could escape them, having
had for years our own German servants to give
them every information, who privately kept an account of our cattle, hay, corn, wine, and everything
every house could supply. These Germans are the

most perfect spies in the world; they come into
the world to spy, as birds do to thieve: it is part of
their nature. Let the Americans and all the people
who are kind enough to receive them think of this.
Their imprudence may some day cost them dearly.
I am not inventing. I am not saying a word too
much. We are an example. Let the world profit
by it.

So Grédel feared for our hoard. I told her I
had been to see, and that nothing in the neighborhood had been disturbed.

But, after having quieted her, I myself had a
great fright.

One Sunday evening, about thirty Prussians,
commanded by their famous lieutenant, came to
the mill, striking the floor with the butt-ends of
their muskets, and shouting that they must have
wine and eau-de-vie.

I gave them the keys of the cellar.

" That is not what I want," said the lieutenant.
" You took sixteen hundred livres at Saverne last
month; where are they? "

Then I saw that I had been denounced. It was
Placiard, or some of that rabble; for denunciations
were beginning. *All who have since declared for
the Germans were already beginning this business.*
I could not deny it, and I said: " It is true. As I
was owing money at Phalsbourg, I paid what I
owed, and I placed the rest in safety under the care
of lawyer Fingado."

" Where is that lawyer? "

" In the town guarded by the sixty big guns that you know of."

Then the lieutenant paced up and down, growling, " You are an old fox. I don't believe you. You have hid your money somewhere. You shall send in your contribution in money."

" I will furnish, like others, my contribution for six men with what I have got. Here are my hay, my wheat, my straw, my flour. Whatever is left you may have; when there is nothing left, you may seek elsewhere. You may kill the people; you may burn towns and villages; but you cannot take money from those who have none."

He stared at me, and one of the soldiers, mad with rage, seized me by the collar, roaring, " Show us your hoard, old rascal! "

Several others were pushing me out of doors; my wife came crying and sobbing; but Grédel darted in, armed with a hatchet, crying to these robbers, " Pack of cowards! You have no courage—you are all like Schinderhannes! "

She was going to fall upon them; but I bade her: " Grédel, go in again."

At the same time I threw open my waistcoat, and told the brute who was pointing his bayonet at my breast: " Now thrust, wretch; let it be over! "

It seems that there was something at that moment in my attitude which awed them; for the lieutenant, who did nothing but scour the country

with his band, exclaimed: " Come, let us leave
monsieur le maire alone. When we have taken the
place, we shall find his money at the lawyer's.
Come, my lads, come on; let us go and look elsewhere. His Majesty wants crown-pieces: we will
find them. Good-by, Monsieur le Maire. Let us
bear no malice."

He was laughing; but I was as pale as death, and
went in trembling.

I fell ill.

Many people in the country were suffering from
dysentery, which we owe again to these gormandiz-
ers, for they devoured everything; honey, butter,
cheese, green fruit, beef, mutton, everything was
ingulfed anyhow down their huge swallows. At
Pfalsweyer they had even swallowed vinegar for
wine. I cannot tell what they ate at home, but the
voracity of these people would make you suppose
that at home they knew no food but potatoes and
cold water.

In their sanitary regulations there was plenty of
room for improvement; health and decency were
alike disregarded.

That year the crows came early; they swept
down to earth in great clouds. But for this help,
a plague would have fallen upon us.

I cannot relate all the other torments these Prussians inflicted upon us; such as compelling us to
cut down wood for them in the forest, to split it, to
pile it up in front of their advanced posts; threat-

12

ening the peasants with having to go to the front
and dig in the trenches. On account of this, whole
villages fled without a minute's warning, and the
Landwehr took the opportunity to pillage the
houses without resistance. Worse than all, they
polluted and desecrated the churches—to the great
distress of all right-minded people, whether Catholics, Protestants, or Jews. This proved that these
fellows respected nothing; that they took a pleasure in humiliating the souls of men in their tender-
est and holiest feelings; for even with ungodly men
a church, a temple, a synagogue are venerable
places. There our mothers carried us to receive the
blessing of God; there we called God to witness our
love for her with whom we had chosen to travel together the journey of life; thither we bore father
and mother to commend their souls to the mercy of
God after they had ceased to suffer in this world.

These wretched men dared do this; therefore
shall they be execrated from generation to generation, and our hatred shall be inextinguishable!

Whilst all these miseries were overwhelming us,
rumors of all sorts ran through the country. One
day Cousin George came to tell us that he had
heard from an innkeeper from Sarrebourg that a
great battle had been fought near Metz; that we
might have been victorious, but that the Emperor,
not knowing where to find his proper place, got in
everybody's way; that he would first fly to the
right, then to the left, carrying with him his escort

of three or four thousand men, to guard his person and his ammunition-wagons; that it had been found absolutely necessary to declare his command vacant, and to send him to Verdun to get rid of him; for he durst not return to Paris, where indignation against his dynasty broke out louder and louder.

"Now," said my cousin, "Bazaine is at the head of our best army. It is a sad thing to be obliged to intrust the destinies of our country to the hands of the man who made himself too well known in Mexico; whilst the Minister of War, old De Montauban, has distinguished himself in China, and in Africa in that Doineau affair. Yes, these are three men worthy to lay their heads close together—the Emperor, Bazaine, and Palikao! Well, let us hope on: hope costs nothing!"

Thus passed away the month of August—the most miserable month of August in all our lives!

On the first of September, about ten o'clock at night, everybody was asleep in the village, when the cannon of Phalsbourg began to roar: it was the heavy guns on the bastion of Wilschberg, and those of the infantry barracks. Our little houses shook.

All rose from their beds and got lights. At every report our windows rattled. I went out; a crowd of other peasants, men and women, were listening and gazing. The night was dark, and the red lightning flashes from the two bastions lighted up the hills second after second.

Then curiosity carried me away. I wished to know what it was, and in spite of all my wife could say, I started with three or four neighbors for Berlingen. As fast as we ascended amongst the bushes, the din became louder; on reaching the brow of this hill, we heard a great stir all round us. The people of Berlingen had fled into the wood: two shells had fallen in the village. It was from this height that I observed the effect of the heavy guns, the bombs and shells rushing in the direction where we stood, hissing and roaring just like the noise of a steam-engine, and making such dreadful sounds that one could not help shrinking.

At the same time we could hear a distant rolling of carriages at full gallop; they were driving from Quatre Vents to Wilschberg: no doubt it was a convoy of provisions and stores, which the Phalsbourgers had observed a long way off: the moon was clouded; but young people have sharp eyes. After seeing this, we came down again, and I recognized my cousin, who was walking near me.

" Good-evening, Christian," said he, " what do you think of that? "

" I am thinking that men have invented dreadful engines to destroy each other."

" Yes, but this is nothing as yet, Christian; it is but the small beginning of the story: in a year or two peace will be signed between the King of Prussia and France; but eternal hatred has arisen between the two nations—just, fearful, unforgiv-

ing hatred. What did we want of the Germans?
Did we want any of their provinces? No, the majority of Frenchmen cared for no such thing.
Did we covet their glory? No, we had military
glory enough, and to spare. So that they had no
inducement to treat us as enemies. Well, whilst
we were trying, in the presence of all Europe, the
experiment of universal suffrage at our own risk
and peril—and this step so fair, so equitable, but
still so dangerous with an ignorant people, had
placed a bad man at the helm—these *good Christians* took advantage of our weakness to strike the
blow they had been fifty-four years in preparing.
They have succeeded! But woe to us! woe to
them! This war will cost more blood and tears
than the Zinzel could carry to the Rhine!"

Thus spoke Cousin George: and, unhappily,
from that day I have had reason to acknowledge
that he was right. Those who were far from the
enemy are now close, and those who are farther
off will be forced to take a part. Let the men of
the south of France remember that they are French
as well as we, and if they don't want to feel the
sharp claw of the Prussian upon their shoulders, let
them rise in time: next to Lorraine comes Champagne; next to Alsace comes Franche Comté and
Burgundy; these are fertile lands, and the Germans are fond of good wine. Clear-sighted men had
long forewarned us that the Germans wanted Alsace and Lorraine: we could not believe it; now

the same men tell us, " The Germans want the whole of France! This race of slappers and slapped want to govern all Europe! Hearken! The day of the Chambords, upheld by the Jesuits, and of the Bonapartes, supported by spies and fools, has gone by forever! Let us be united under the Republic, or the Germans will devour us! " I think the men who tender this advice have a claim to be heard.

The day after the cannonade we learned that some carts had been upset and pillaged near Berlingen. Then the Prussian major declared that the commune was responsible for the loss, and that it would have to pay up five hundred francs damages.

Five hundred francs! Alas! where could they be found after this pillage?

Happily, the Mayor of Berlingen succeeded in making the discovery that the sentinels who had the charge of the carts had themselves committed the robbery, to make presents to the depraved creatures who infested the camp, and the general contributions went on as before.

Early in September the weather was fine; and I shall always remember that the oats dropped by the German convoys began to grow all along the road they had taken. No doubt there was a similar green track all the way from Bavaria far into the interior of France.

What a loss for our country! for it always fell to our share to replace anything that was lost or

stolen. Of course the Prussians are too honorable
to pick or steal anywhere!

In that comparatively quiet time by night we
could hear the bombardment of Strasbourg. About
one in the morning, while the village was asleep,
and all else in the distance was wrapped in silence,
then those deep and loud reports were heard one by
one. The citadel alone received five shells and one
bomb per minute. Sometimes the fire increased in
intensity; the din became terrible; the earth
seemed to be trembling far away down there: it
sounded like the heavy strokes of the gravedigger
at the bottom of a grave.

And this went on forty-two days and forty-two
nights without intermission: the new Church, the
Library, and hundreds of houses were burned to
the ground; the Cathedral was riddled with shot;
a shell even carried away the iron cross at its summit. The unhappy Strasbourgers cast longing eyes
westward; none came to help. The men who have
told me of these things when all was over could not
refrain from tears.

Of Metz we heard nothing; rumors of battles,
combats in Lorraine, ran through the country: rumors of whose authenticity we knew nothing.

The silence of the Germans was maintained;
but one evening they burst into loud hurrahs from
Wechem to Biechelberg, from Biechelberg to
Quatre Vents. George and his wife came with
pale faces.

" Well, you know the despatch? "

" No; what is it? "

" The *honest man* has just surrendered at Sedan
with eighty thousand Frenchmen! From the beginning of the world the like of it has never been
seen. He has given up his sword to the King of Prussia—his famous sword of the 2d December. He
thought more of his own safety and his ammunition-
wagons than of the honor of his name and of the
honor of France! Oh, the arch-deceiver! he has
deceived me even in this: I did think he was brave!"

George lost all command over himself.

" There," said he, " that was to be the end of
it! His own army was those ten or fifteen thousand Decemberlings supplied by the Préfecture of
Police, armed with loaded staves and life-preserv-
ers to break the heads of the defenders of the laws.
He thought himself able to lead a French army to
victory, as if they were his gang of thieves; he has
let them into a sort of a sink, and there, in spite of
the valor of our soldiers, he has delivered them up
to the King of Prussia: in exchange for what? We
shall know by and by. Our unhappy sons refused
to surrender: they would have preferred to die
sword in hand, trying to fight their way out; it was
his Majesty who, three times, gave orders to hoist
the white flag! "

Thus spoke my cousin, and we, more dead than
alive, could hear nothing but the shouts and re-
joicings outside.

A flag of truce had just been despatched to the town. The Landwehr, who for some time had been occupying the place of the troops of the line with us—men of mature age, more devoted to peace than to the glory of King William—thought that all was over; that the King of Prussia would keep his word; that he would not continue against the nation the war begun against Bonaparte, and that the town would be sure to surrender now.

But the commander, Taillant, merely replied that the gates of Phalsbourg would be opened whenever he should receive his Majesty's written commands; that the fact of Napoleon's having given up his sword was no reason why he should abandon his post; and that every man ought to be on his guard, in readiness for whatever might happen.

The flag of truce returned, and the joy of the Landwehr was calmed down.

At this time I saw something which gave me infinite pleasure, and which I still enjoy thinking of.

I had taken a short turn to Saverne by way of the Falberg, behind the German posts, hoping to learn news. Besides, I had some small debts to get in; money was wanted every day, and no one knew where to find it.

About five o'clock in the evening, I was returning home; the weather was fine; business had prospered, and I was stepping into the wayside inn at Tzise to take a glass of wine. In the parlor were seated a dozen Bavarians, quarrelling with

as many Prussians seated round the deal tables.
They had laid their helmets on the window-seats,
and were enjoying themselves away from their officers; no doubt on their return from some maraud-
ing expedition.

A Bavarian was exclaiming: "We are always
put in the front, we are. The victory of Woerth
is ours; but for us you would have been beaten.
And it is we who have just taken the Emperor and
all his army. You other fellows, you do nothing
but wait in the rear for the honor and glory, and the
profit, too!"

"Well, now," answered the Prussian, "what
would you have done but for us? Have you got
a general to show? Tell me your men. You are
in the front line, true enough. You bear your
broken bones with patience—I don't deny that.
But who commands you? The Prince Royal of
Prussia, Prince Frederick Charles of Prussia, our
old General de Moltke, and his Majesty King William! Don't tell us of your victories. Victories belong to the chiefs. Even if you were every one
killed to the last man, what difference would that
make? Does an architect owe his fame to his materials? What have picks, and spades, and trowels
to do with victory?"

"What! the spades!" cried a Bavarian; "do
you call us spades?"

"Yes, we do!" shouted the Prussian, arrogantly
thumping the table.

Then, bang, bang went the pots and the bottles; and I only just had time to escape, laughing, and thinking: "After all, these poor Bavarians are right—they get the blows, and the others get the glory. Bismarck must be sly to have got them to accept such an arrangement. It is rather strong. And, then, what is the use of saying that the King of Bavaria is led by the Jesuits."

About the 8th or 10th of September, the report ran that the Republic had been proclaimed at Paris; that the Empress, the Princess Mathilde, Palikao, and all the rest had fled; that a Government of National Defence had been proclaimed; that every Frenchman from twenty to forty years of age had been summoned to arms. But we were sure of nothing, except the bombardment of Strasbourg and the battles round Metz.

Justice compels me to say that everybody looked upon the conduct of Bazaine as admirable—that he was looked upon as the saviour of France. It was thought that he was bearing the weight of all the Germans upon his shoulders, and that, finally, he would break out, and deliver Toul, Phalsbourg, Bitche, Strasbourg, and crush all the investing armies.

Often at that time George said to me: "It will soon be our turn. We shall all have to march. My plans are already made; my rifle and cartridge-box are ready. You must have the alarm-bell sounded as soon as we hear the cannon about Sarreguemines and Fénétrange. We shall take the Germans between two fires."

He said this to me in the evening, when we were alone, and I am sure I could have wished no better; but prudence was essential: the Landwehr kept increasing in number from day to day. They used to come and sit in our midst around the stove; they smoked their long porcelain pipes, with their heads down, in silence. As a certain number understood French, without telling us so, there was no talking together in their presence: every one kept his thoughts to himself.

All these Landwehr from Baden, Wurtemberg, and Bavaria, were commanded by Prussian officers, so that Prussia supplied the officers, and the German States the soldiers: by these means they learn obedience to their true lords and masters. The Prussians were made to command, the others humbly to obey: thus they gained the victory. And now it must remain so for ages; for the Alsacians and Lorrainers might revolt, France might rise, and troubles might come in all directions. Yes, all these good Landwehr will remain under arms from father to son; and the more numerous their victories, the higher the Prussians will climb upon their backs, and keep them firmly down.

One thing annoyed them considerable; this was a stir in the Vosges, and a talk of francs-tireurs, and of revolted villages about Epinal. Of course this stirred us up too. These Landwehr treated the

francs-tireurs as brigands in ambush to shoot down
respectable fathers of families, to rob convoys, and
threatened to hang them.

. For all that, many thought—" If only a few
came our way with powder and muskets, we would
join them and try to get rid of our troubles ourselves."

Hope rose with these francs-tireurs; but the requisitions harassed us all the more.

The pillage was not quite so bad, but it went
on still.   When our Landwehr, whom we were
obliged to lodge and keep, went off to mount guard
at Phalsbourg, others came in troops from the
neighboring villages, shouting, storming, and bawl-
ing for oxen, sheep, bacon!   And when they had
terribly frightened the women, these fellows, after
all, were satisfied with a few eggs, a cheese, or a
rope of onions; and then they would take their departure quite delighted.

Our own Landwehr no doubt did the same, for
they never seemed short of vegetables to cook; and
these good fathers of families conscientiously divided it with all the abominable creatures who followed them and had no other way of living.   How
else could it be?   It takes time to turn a man into
a beast, but a few months of war soon bring men
back into the savage state.

CHAPTER IX

On the 29th of September, a Prussian vague-mestre* brought me some proclamations with orders to make them public.

These proclamations declared that we were now part of the department of La Moselle, and that we were under a Prussian prefect, the Count Henkel de Bonnermark, who was himself under the orders of the Governor-General of Alsace and Lorraine, the Count Bismarck-Bohlen, provisionally residing at Haguenau.

I cannot tell what evil spirit then laid hold of me; the Landwehr had brought us the day before the news of the capitulation of Strasbourg; I had been worried past all endurance by all the requisitions which I was ordered to call for, and I boldly declared my refusal to post that proclamation: that it was against my conscience; that I looked upon myself as a Frenchman still, and they need not expect an honest man to perform such an errand as that.

The vaguemestre seemed astonished to hear me. He was a stout man, with thick brown mustaches, and prominent eyes.

* The person in command of a wagon train—also an Army letter-carrier.

190

" Will you be good enough to write that down,
M. le Maire? " he said.

" Why not? I am tired out with all these vexa-
tious acts. Let my place be given to your friend,
M. Placiard: I should be thankful. Let him order
these requisitions. I look upon them as mere robbery."

" Well, write that down," said he. " I obey orders: I have nothing to do with the rest."

Then, without another thought, I opened my
desk, and wrote that Christian Weber, Mayor of
Rothalp, considered it against his conscience to proclaim Bismarck-Bohlen Governor of a French prov-
ince, and that he refused absolutely.

I signed my name to it, with the date, 29th September, 1870; and it was the greatest folly I ever
committed in my life: it has cost me dear.

The vaguemestre took the paper, put it in his
pocket, and went away. Two or three hours after,
when I had thought it over a little, I began to repent, and I wished I could have the paper back
again.

That evening, after supper, I went to tell George
the whole affair; he was quite pleased.

" Very good, indeed, Christian," said he. " Now
your position is clear. I have often felt sorry that
you should be obliged, for the interest of the commune and to avoid pillage, to give bonds to the Prussians. People are so absurd! Seeing the signa-
ture of the mayor, they make him, in a way, respon-

sible for everything; every one fancies he is bearing
more than his share.   Now you are rid of your
burden; you could not go so far as to requisition in
the name of Henkel de Bonnermark, self-styled prefect of La Moselle; let some one else do that work;
they will have no difficulty in finding as many ill-
conditioned idiots as they want for that purpose."

My cousin's approbation gave me satisfaction, and
I was going home, when the same vaguemestre, in
whose hands I had placed my resignation in the
morning, entered, followed by three or four Landwehr.

"Here is something for you," said he, handing
me a note, which I read aloud:

"The persons called Christian Weber, miller, and
George Weber, wine-merchant, in the village of
Rothalp, will, to-morrow, drive to Droulingen, four
thousand kilos of hay and ten thousand kilos of
straw, without fail.   By order—FLOEGEL."

"Very well," I replied.   For although this requisition appeared to me to be rather heavy, I would
not betray my indignation before our enemies; they
would have been too much delighted.   "Very well,
I will drive my hay and my straw to Droulingen."

"You will drive it yourself," said the vaguemestre, brutally.   "All the horses and carts in the village have been put into requisition; you have too
often forgotten your own."

"I can prove that my horses and my carts have

been worked oftener than any one's," I replied, with rising wrath. "There are your receipts; I hope you won't deny them!"

"Well, it doesn't matter," said he. "The horses, the carts, the hay and straw are demanded; that is plain."

"Quite plain," said Cousin George. "The strongest may always command."

"Exactly so," said the vaguemestre.

He went out with his men, and George, without anger, said, "This is war! Let us be calm. Perhaps our turn will come now that the *honest man* is no longer in command of our armies. In the meantime the best thing we can do, if we do not want to lose our horses and our carts besides, will be to load to-night, and to start very early in the morning. We shall return before seven o'clock to supper; and then they won't be able to take any more of our hay and straw, because we shall have none left."

For my part, I was near bursting with rage; but, as he set the example, by stripping off his coat and putting on his blouse, I went to wake up old Father Offran to help me to load.

My wife and Grédel were expecting me: for the vaguemestre and his men had called at the mill, before coming to George's house, and they were trembling with apprehension. I told them to be calm; that it was only taking some hay and straw to Droulingen, where I should get a receipt for future payment.

13

Whether they believed it or not, they went in again.

I lighted the lantern, Offran mounted up into the loft and threw me down the trusses, which I caught upon a fork. About two in the morning, the two carts being loaded, I fed the horses and rested a few minutes.

At five o'clock, George, outside, was already calling " Christian, I am here! "

I got up, put on my hat and my blouse, opened the stable from the inside, put the horses in, and we started in the fresh and early morning, supposing we should return at night.

In all the villages that we passed through, troops of Landwehr were sitting before their huts, ragged, with patched knees and filthy beards, like the description of the Cossacks of former days, smoking their pipes; and the cavalry and infantry were coming and going.

Those who remained in garrison in the villages were obliged by their orders to give up their good walking-boots to the others, and to wear their old shoes.

Mounted officers, with their low, flat caps pulled down upon their noses, were skimming along the paths by the road-side like the wind. In the old wayside inns, in the corners of the yards the dung-hills were heaped up with entrails and skins of beasts: hides, stuffed with straw, were hanging also from the banisters of the old galleries, where we used to see washed linen hanging out to dry.   Misery, unspeakable misery, and gnawing anxiety were marked upon the countenances of the people.   The Germans alone looked fat and sleek in their broken boots; they had good white bread, good red wine, good meat, and smoked good tobacco or cigars: they were living like fighting-cocks.

At a certain former time, these people had complained bitterly of our invasion of their country, without remembering that they had begun by invading ourselves.   And yet they were right.   At the close of the First Empire, the French were only fighting for one man; but the Germans had since had their revenge twice, in 1814 and 1815, and for fifty years they had always been coming to us as friends, and were received like brothers: we bore no malice against them, and they seemed to bear none against us; peace had softened us.   We only wished for their prosperity, as well as for our own; for nations are really happy only when their neighbors are prospering: then business and industry all move hand in hand together.   That was our position! We said nothing more of our victories; we talked of our defeats, so as to do full justice to their courage and their patriotism; we acknowledged our faults; they pretended to acknowledge theirs, and talked of fraternity.   We believed in their uprightness, in their candor and frankness: we were really fond of them.

Now hatred has arisen between us.

Whose the fault?

First, our stupidity, our ignorance. We all believed that the Plébiscite was for peace; the Ministers, the préfets, the sous-préfets, the magistrates,
the commissioners of police, everybody in authority
confirmed this. A villain has used it to declare
war! But the Germans were glad of the war; they
were full of hatred, and malice, and envy, without
betraying it: they had long watched us and studied
us; they endured everlasting drill and perpetual
fatigue to become the strongest, and sought with
pains for an opportunity to get war declared against
themselves, and so set themselves right in the eyes
of Europe. The Spanish complication was but a
trap laid by Bismarck for Bonaparte. The Germans said to one another: "We have twelve hundred thousand men under arms; we are four to one.
Let us seize the opportunity! If the French Government take it into their heads to organize and discipline the Garde Mobile, all might be lost. . . .
Quick, quick!"

This is the uprightness, frankness, and fraternity
of the Germans!

Our idiot fell into the trap. The Germans overwhelmed us with their multitudes. They are our
masters; they hold our country; we are paying them
milliards! and now they are coming back, just as before, into our towns and cities in troops, smiling
upon us, extending the right hand: "Ha! ha! how
are you now? Have you been pretty well all this

long while? What! don't you know me? You look angry! Ah! but you really shouldn't. Such friends, such good old friends! Come, now! give me a small order, only a small one; and don't let us think of that unhappy war!"

Faugh! Let us look another way; it is too horrible.

To excuse them, I say (for one must always seek excuses for everything) man is not by nature so debased; there must be causes to explain so great a want of natural pride; and I say to myself—that these are poor creatures trained to submission, and that these unfortunate beings do as the birds do that the birdcatcher holds captives in his net; they sing, they chirp, to decoy others.

"Ah! how jolly it is here! how delightful here in Old Germany, with an Emperor, kings, princes, German dukes, grand-dukes, counts, and barons! What an honor to fight and die for the German Fatherland! The German is the foremost man in the world."

Yes. Yes. Poor devils! We know all about that. That is the song your masters taught you at school! For the King of Prussia and his nobility you work, you spy, you have your bones broken on the battle-field! They pay you with hollow phrases about the noble German, the German Fatherland, the German sky, the German Rhine; and when you sing false, with rough German slaps upon your German faces.

No; no! it is of no use; the Alsacians and the Lorrainers will never whistle like you: they have learned another tune.

Well! all this did not save us from being nipped, George and me, and from being made aware that at the least resistance they would wring our necks like chickens. So we put a good face upon a bad game, observing the desolation of all this country, where the cattle plague had just broken out. At Lohre, at Ottviller, in a score of places, this terrible disease, the most ruinous for the peasantry, was already beginning its ravages; and the Prussians, who eat more than four times the quantity of meat that we do—when it belongs to other people—were afraid of coming short.

Their veterinary doctors knew but one remedy; when a beast fell ill, refused its fodder, and became low-spirited, they slaughtered it, and buried it with hide and horns, six feet under ground. This was not much cleverer than the bombardment of towns to force them to surrender, or the firing of villages to compel people to pay their requisitions. But then it answered the purpose!

The Germans in this campaign have taught us their best inventions! They had thought them over for years, whilst our school-masters and our gazettes were telling us that they were passing away their time in dreaming of philosophy, and other things of so extraordinary a kind that the French could not understand the thing at all.

About eleven we were at Droulingen, where was a Silesian battalion ready to march to Metz. It seems that some cavalry were to follow us, and that the requisitions had exhausted the fodder in the country, for our hay and straw were immediately housed in a barn at the end of the village, and the major gave us a receipt. He was a gray-bearded Prussian, and he examined us with wrinkled eyes, just like an old gendarme who is about to take your description.

This business concluded, George and I thought we might return at once; when, looking through the window, we saw them loading our carts with the baggage of the battalion. Then I came out, exclaiming: "Hallo! those carts are ours! We only came to make a delivery of hay and straw!"

The Silesian commander, a tall, stiff, and uncompromising-looking fellow, who was standing at the door, just turned his head, and, as the soldiers were stopping, quietly said: "Go on!"

"But, captain," said I, "here is my receipt from the major!"

"Nothing to me," said he, walking into the mess-room, where the table was laid for the officers.

We stood outside in a state of indignation, as you may believe. The soldiers were enjoying the joke. I was very near giving them a rap with my whip-handle; but a couple of sentinels marching up and down with arms shouldered, would certainly have passed their bayonets through me. I turned pale, and went into Finck's public-house, where George had turned in before me. The small parlor was full of soldiers, who were eating and drinking as none but Prussians can eat and drink; almost putting it into their noses.

The sight and the smell drove us out, and George, standing at the door, said to me: " Our wives will be anxious; had we not better find somebody to tell them what has happened to us? "

But it was no use wishing or looking; there was nobody.

The officers' horses along the wall, their bridles loose, were quietly munching their feed, and ours, which were already tired, got nothing.

" Hey! " said I to the *feld-weibel*, who was overlooking the loading of the carts; " I hope you will not think of starting without giving a handful to our horses? "

" If you have got any money, you clown," said he, grinning, " you can give them hay, and even oats, as much as you like. There, look at the signboard before you: ' Hay and oats sold here.' "

That moment I heaped up more hatred against the Prussians than I shall be able to satiate in all my life.

" Come on," cried George, pulling me by the arm; for he saw my indignation.

And we went into the " Bay Horse," which was as full of people as the other, but larger and higher. We fed our horses; then, sitting alone in a corner

we ate a crust of bread and took a glass of wine,
watching the movements of the troops outside. I
went out to give my horses a couple of buckets of
water, for I knew that the Germans would never
take that trouble.

George called to him the little pedler Friedel, who
was passing by with his pack, to tell him to inform
our wives that we should not be home till to-morrow
morning, being obliged to go on to Sarreguemines.
Friedel promised, and went on his way.

Almost immediately, the word of command and
the rattle of arms warned us that the battalion was
about to march. We only had the time to pay and
to lay hold of the horses' bridles.

It was pleasant weather for walking—neither
too much sun nor too much shade; fine autumn
weather.

And since, in comparing the Germans with our
own soldiers as to their marching powers, I have
often thought that they never would have reached
Paris but for our railroads. Their infantry are just
as conspicuous for their slowness and their heavi-
ness as their cavalry are for their swiftness and
activity. These people are splay-footed, and they
cannot keep up long. When they are running,
their clumsy boots make a terrible clatter; which is
perhaps the reason why they wear them: they encourage each other by this means, and imagine they
dismay the enemy. A single company of theirs
makes more noise than one of our regiments. But

they soon break out in a perspiration, and their great delight is to get up and have a ride.

Toward evening, by five o'clock, we had only gone about three leagues from Droulingen, when, instead of continuing on their way, the commander gave the battalion orders to turn out of it into a parish road on the left. Whether it was to avoid the lodgings by the way, which were all exhausted, or for some other reason, I cannot say.

Seeing this, I ran to the commanding officer in the greatest distress.

" But in the name of heaven, captain," said I, " are you not going on to Sarreguemines? We are fathers of families; we have wives and children ! You promised that at Sarreguemines we might unload and return home."

George was coming, too, to complain; but he had not yet reached us, when the commander, from on horseback, roared at us with a voice of rage: " Will you return to your carts, or I will have you beaten till all is blue? Will you make haste back? "

Then we returned to take hold of our bridles, with our heads hanging down. Three hours after, at nightfall, we came into a miserable village, full of small crosses along the road, and where the people had nothing to give us; for famine had overtaken them.

We had scarcely halted, when a convoy of bread, meat, and wine arrived, escorted by a few hussars. No doubt it came from Alberstoff. Every soldier

WE CAME INTO A MISERABLE VILLAGE, FULL OF SMALL CROSSES ALONG
THE ROAD.

received his ration, but we got not so much as an onion: not a crust of bread—nothing—nor our horses either.

That night George and I alone rested under the shelter of a deserted smithy, while the Prussians were asleep in every hut and in the barns, and the sentinels paced their rounds about our carts, with their muskets shouldered; we began to deliberate what we ought to do.

George, who already foreboded the miseries which were awaiting us, would have started that moment, leaving both horses and carts; but I could not entertain such an idea as that. Give up my pair of beautiful dappled gray horses, which I had bred and reared in my own orchard at the back of the mill! It was impossible.

"Listen to me," said George. "Remember the Alsacians who have been passing by us the last fortnight: they look as if they had come out of their graves; they had never received the smallest ration: they would have been carried even to Paris if they had not run away. You see that these Germans have no bowels. They are possessed with a bitter hatred against the French, which makes them as hard as iron; they have been incited against us at their schools; they would like to exterminate us to the last man. Let us expect nothing of them; that will be the safest. I have only six francs in my pocket; what have you?"

"Eight livres and ten sous."

" With that, Christian, we cannot go far.   The nearer we get to Metz, the worse ruin we shall find the country in.   If we were but able to write home, and ask for a little money! but you see they have sentinels on every road, at all the lane ends: they allow neither foot-passengers, nor letters, nor news to pass.   Believe me, let us try to escape."

All these good arguments were useless.   I thought that, with a little patience, perhaps at the next village, other horses and other carriages might be found to requisition, and that we might be allowed quietly to return home.   That would have been natural and proper; and so in any country in the world they would have done.

George, seeing that he was unable to shake my resolution, lay down upon a bench and went to sleep. I could not shut my eyes.

Next day, at six o'clock, we had to resume the march; the Silesians well-refreshed, we with empty stomachs.

We were moving in the direction of Gros Tenquin.   The farther we advanced, the less I knew of the country.   It was the country around Metz, le pays Messin, an old French district, and our misery increased at every stage.   The Prussians continued to receive whatever they required, and took no further trouble with us than merely preventing us from leaving their company: they treated us like beasts of burden; and, in spite of all our economy, our money was wasting away.

Never was so sad a position as ours; for, on the fourth or fifth day, the officer, guessing from our appearance that we were meditating flight, quite unceremoniously said in our presence to the sentinels: "If those people stir out of the road, fire upon them."

We met many others in a similar position to ours, in the midst of these squadrons and these regiments, which were continually crossing each other and were covering the roads. At the sight of each other, we felt as if we could burst into tears.

George always kept up his spirits, and even from time to time he assumed an air of gayety, asking a light of the soldiers to light his pipe, and singing sea-songs, which made the Prussian officers laugh. They said: "This fellow is a real Frenchman: he sees things in a bright light."

I could not understand that at all: no, indeed! I said to myself that my cousin was losing his senses.

What grieved me still more was to see my fine horses perishing—my poor horses, so sleek, so spirited, so steady; the best horses in the commune, and which I had reared with so much satisfaction. Oh, how deplorable! . . . Passing along the hedges, by the roadside, I pulled here and there handfuls of grass, to give them a taste of something green, and in a moment they would stare at it, toss up their heads, and devour this poor stuff. The poor brutes could be seen wasting away, and this pained me more than anything.

Then the thoughts of my wife and Grédel, and their uneasiness, what they were doing, what was becoming of the mill and our village—what the people would say when they knew that their mayor was gone, and then the town, and Jacob—everything overwhelmed me, and made my heart sink within me.

But the worst of all, and what I shall never forget, was in the neighborhood of Metz.

For a fortnight or three weeks there had been no more fighting; the city and Bazaine's army were surrounded by huge earthworks, which the Prussians had armed with guns. We could see that afar off, following the road on our right. We could see many places, too, where the soil had been recently turned over; and George said they were pits, in which hundreds of dead lay buried. A few burnt and bombarded villages, farms, and castles in ruins, were also seen in the neighborhood. There was no more fighting; but there was a talk of francs-tireurs, and the Silesians looked uncomfortable.

At last, on the tenth day since our departure, after having crossed and recrossed the country in all directions, we arrived about three o'clock at a large village on the Moselle, when the battalion came to a halt. Several detachments from our battalion had filled up the gaps in other battalions, so that there remained with us only the third part of the men who had come from Droulingen.

After the distribution of provender, seeing that

the officers' horses had been fed, and that they were
putting their bridles on, I just went and picked up a
few handfuls of hay and straw which were lying on
the ground, to give to mine.   I had collected a small
bundle, when a corporal on guard in the neighborhood, having noticed what I was doing, came and
seized me by the whiskers, shaking me, and striking
me on the face.

"Ah! you greedy old miser!   Is that the way
you feed your beasts?"

I was beside myself with rage, and had already
lifted my whip-handle to send the rascal sprawling
on the earth, when Cousin George precipitated himself between us, crying: "Christian! what are you
dreaming of?"

He wrested the whip from me, and whilst I was
quivering in every limb, he began to excuse me to
the dirty Prussian; saying that I had acted hastily,
that I had thought the hay was to be left, that it
ought to be considered that our horses too followed
the battalion, etc.

The fellow listened, drawn up like a gendarme,
and said: "Well, then, I will pass it over this time;
but if he begins his tricks again, it will be quite another thing."

Then I went into the stable and stretched myself
in the empty rack, my hat drawn over my face, without stirring for a couple of hours.

The battalion was going to march again.   George
was looking for me everywhere.   At last he found

me. I rose, came out, and the sight of all these soldiers dressed in line, with their rifles and their helmets, made my blood run cold: I wished for death.

George spoke not a word, and we moved forward; but from that moment I had resolved upon flight, at any price, abandoning everything.

The same evening, an extraordinary event happened; we received a little straw! We lay in the open air, under our carts, because the village at which we had just arrived was full of troops. I had only twelve sous left, and George but twenty or thirty. He went to buy a little bread and eau-de-vie in a public-house; we dipped our bread in it, and in this way we were just able to sustain life.

Every time the corporal passed, who had laid his hand upon me, my knife moved of its own accord in my pocket, and I said to myself: " Shall an Alsacian, an old Alsacian, endure this affront without revenge? Shall it be said that Alsacians allow them•selves to be knocked about by such spawn as these fellows, whom we have thrashed a hundred times in days gone by, and who used to run away from us like hares? "

George, who could see by my countenance what I was thinking of, said: " Christian! Listen to me. Don't get angry. Set down these blows to the account of the Plébiscite, like the bonds for bread, flour, hay, meat, and the rest. It was you who voted all that: the Germans are not the causes! They are brute beasts, so used to have their faces slapped, that they catch every opportunity to give others the like, when there is no danger, and when they are ten to one.   These slaps don't produce the same effect on them as on us; they are felt only on the surface, no farther!   So comfort yourself; this monstrous beast never thought he was inflicting any disgrace upon you: he took you for one of his own sort."

But, instead of pacifying me, George only made me the more indignant; especially when he told me that the Germans, talking together, had told how Queen Augusta of Prussia had just sent her own cook to the Emperor Napoleon to cook nice little, dishes for him, and her own band to play agreeable music under his balcony!

I had had enough!   I lay under our cart, and all that night I had none but bad dreams.

We had always hoped that, on coming near a railway, the remains of the battalion would get in, and that we should be sent home; unhappily our men were intended to fill up gaps in other battalions: companies were detached right and left, but there were always enough left to want our conveyances, and to prevent us from setting off home.

We had not had clean shirts for a fortnight; we had not once taken off our shoes, knowing that we should have too much difficulty in getting them on again; we had been wetted through with rain and dried by the sun five and twenty times; we had suffered all the misery and wretchedness of hunger,

14

we were reduced to scarecrows by weariness and suffering; but neither cousin nor I suffered from dysentery like those Germans; the poorest nourishment still sustained us; but the bacon, the fresh meat, the fruits, the raw vegetables, devoured by these creatures without the least discretion, worked upon them dreadfully: no experience could teach them wisdom; their natural voracity made them devoid of all prudence.

As a climax to our miseries, the officers of our battalion were talking of marching on Paris.

The Prussians knew a month beforehand that Bazaine would never come out of his camp, and that he would finally surrender after he had consumed all the provisions in Metz; they said this openly, and looked upon Marshal Bazaine as our best general: they praised and exalted him for his splendid campaign. The only fault they could find was, that he had not shut himself up sooner; because then things would have been settled much earlier. They complained, too, of our Emperor, and affirmed that the best thing we could do would be to set him on his throne again.

George and I heard these things repeated a hundred times at the inns and public-houses where we halted. The French innkeepers made us sit behind the stove, and for pity, passed us sometimes the leavings of the soup; but for this, we should have perished of hunger. They asked us in whispers what the Germans were saying, and when we repeated their sayings, the poor people said to us: "Really, how fond the Prussians are of us! Certainly they do owe some comfort to the men who have surrendered! Every brave deed deserves to be rewarded."

One of the Lorraine innkeepers said this to us; he was also the first to tell us that Gambetta, having escaped from Paris in a balloon, was now at Tours with Glais-Bizoin and several others, to raise a powerful army behind the Loire. In these parts they got the Belgian papers, and whenever we heard a bit of good news it screwed up our courage a little.

Quantities of provisions and stores were passing: immense flocks of sheep and herds of oxen, cases of sausages, barrels of bread, wine, and flour; sometimes regiments also. The trains for the East were carrying wounded in heaps, stretched one over another in the carriages upon mattresses, their pale faces seeking fresh air and coolness at all the windows. German doctors with the red cross upon their arms were accompanying them, and in every village there were ambulances.

The heavy rains and the first frosts had come. A thousand rumors were afloat of great battles under the walls of Paris. The Prussians were especially wroth with Gambetta: "that Gambetta! the bandit!" as they called him, who was preventing them from having peace and bringing back Napoleon. Never have I seen men so enraged with an enemy because he would not surrender. The officers and soldiers talked of nothing else.

"That Gambetta," said they, "is the cause of all our trouble.   His francs-tireurs deserve to be strung up.   But for him, peace would be made.   We should already have got Alsace and Lorraine; and the Emperor Napoleon, at the head of the army of Metz, would have been on his way to restore order at Paris."

At every convoy of wounded their indignation mounted higher.   They thought it perfectly natural and proper that *they* should set fire to us, devastate our country, plunder and shoot us; but for us to defend ourselves, was infamous!

Is it possible to imagine a baser hypocrisy?   For they did not think what they were saying;   they wanted to make us believe that our cause was a bad one; yet how could there be a holier and a more glorious one?

Of course every Frenchman, from the oldest to the youngest—and principally the women—prayed for Gambetta's success, and more than once tears of emotion dropped at the thought that, perhaps, he might save us.   Crowds of young men left the country to join him, and then the Prussians burdened their parents with a war contribution of fifty francs a day.   They were ruining them; and yet this did not prevent others from following in numerous bands.

The Prussians threatened with the galleys whosoever should connive at the flight, as they called it, of these volunteers, whether by giving them money, or supplying them with guides, or by any other means. Violence, cruelty, falsehood—all sorts of means seemed good to the Germans to reduce us to submission; but arms were the least resorted to of all these means, because they did not wish to lose men, and in fighting they might have done so.

We had stopped three days at the village of Jametz, in the direction of Montmédy. It was in the latter part of October; the rain was pouring; George and I had been received by an old Lorraine woman, tall and spare, Mother Marie-Jeanne, whose son was serving in Metz. She had a small cottage by the roadside, with a little loft above which you reached by a ladder, and a small garden behind, entirely ravaged. A few ropes of onions, a few peas and beans in a basket, were all her provisions. She concealed nothing; and whenever a Prussian came in to ask for anything she feigned deafness and answered nothing. Her misery, her broken windows, her dilapidated walls and the little cupboard left wide open, soon induced these greedy gluttons to go somewhere else, supposing there was nothing for them there.

This poor woman had observed our wretched plight; she had invited us in, asking us where we were from, and we had told her of our misfortunes. She herself had told us that there remained a few bundles of hay in the loft and that we might take them, as she had no need for them; the Germans having eaten her cow.

We climbed up there to sleep by night and drew up the ladder after us, listening to the rain plashing on the roof and running off the tiles.

George had but ten sous left and I had nothing, when, on the third day, as we were lying in the hay-loft, about two in the morning, the bugle sounded. Something had happened: an order had come—I don't know what.

We listened attentively. There were hurrying footsteps; the butts of the muskets were rattling on the pavement: they were assembling, falling in, and in all directions were cries:

" The drivers! the drivers! where are they? "

The commander was swearing: he shouted furiously,

" Fetch them here! find them! shoot the vaga-bonds."

We did not stir a finger.

Suddenly the door burst open. The Prussians demanded in German and in French: " Where are the drivers—those Alsacian drivers? "

The aged dame answered not a word; she shook her head, and looked as deaf as a post, just as usual. At last, out they rushed again. The rascals had in-deed seen the trap-door in the ceiling, but it seems they were in a hurry and could not find a ladder without losing time. At last, whether they saw it or not, presently we heard the tramping of the men in the mud, the cracking of the whips, the rolling of the carts, and then all was silent.

The battalion had disappeared.

Then only, after they had left half an hour, the kind old woman below began to call us. You can come down," she said; "they are gone now."

And we came down.

The poor woman said, laughing heartily, "Now you are safe! Only you must lose no time; there might come an order to catch you. There, eat that."

She took out of the cupboard a large basin full of soup made of beans—for she used to cook enough for three or four days at a time—and warmed it over the fire.

"Eat it all; never mind me! I have got more beans left."

There was no need for pressing, and in a couple of minutes the basin was empty.

The good woman looked on with pleasure, and George said to her: "We have not had such a meal for a week."

"So much the better! I am glad to have done you any service! And now go. I wish I could give you some money; but I have none."

"You have saved our lives," I said. "God grant you may see your son again. But I have another request to make before we go."

"What is it, then?"

"Leave to give you a kiss."

"Ah, gladly, my poor Alsacians, with all my

heart!   I am not pretty as I used to be; but it is all the same."

And we kissed her as we would a mother.

When we went to the door, the daylight was breaking.

" Before you lies the road to Dun-sur-Meuse," she said, " don't take that; that is the road the Prussians have taken: no doubt the commander has given a description of you in the next village.   But here is the road to Metz by Damvillers and Etain; follow that.   If you are stopped say that your horses were worked to death, and you were released."

This poor old woman was full of good sense.   We pressed her hand again, with tears in our eyes, and then we set off, following the road she had pointed out to us.

I should be very much puzzled now to tell you all the villages we passed between Jametz and Rothalp. All that country between Metz, Montmédy and Verdun was swarming with cavalry and infantry, living at the expense of the people, and keeping them, as it were, in a net, to eat them as they were wanted. The troops of the line, and especially the gunners, kept around the fortresses; the rest, the Landwehr in masses, occupied even the smallest hamlets and made requisitions everywhere.

In one little village between Jametz and Damvillers, we heard on our right a sharp rattle of musketry along a road, and George said to me: " Behind there our battalion is engaged.   All I hope is that

the brave commander who talked of shooting us
may get a ball through him, and your corporal
too."

The village people standing at their doors said,
" It is the francs-tireurs! "

And joy broke out in every countenance, especially
when an old man ran up from the path by the cemetery, crying: " Two carriages, full of wounded, are
coming—two large Alsacian wagons; they are escorted by hussars."

We had just stopped at a grocer's shop in the market square, and were asking the woman who kept
this little shop if there was no watchmaker in the
place—for my cousin wished to sell his watch, which
he had hidden beneath his shirt, since we had left
Droulingen—and the woman was coming down the
steps to point out the spot, when the old man began
to cry, " Here come the Alsacian carts! "

Immediately, without waiting for more, we set
off at a run to the other end of the village; but near
to a little river, whose name I cannot remember, just
over a clump of pollard willows, we caught the glit-
ter of a couple of helmets, and this made us take a
path along the river-side, which was then running
over in consequence of the heavy rains.   We went
on thus a considerable distance, having sometimes
the water up to our knees.

In about half an hour we were getting out of
these reed beds, and had just caught sight, above the
hill on our left, of the steeple of another village,

when a cry of " Wer da! "* stopped us short, near a
deserted hut two or three hundred paces from the
first house.   At the same moment a Landwehr started out of the empty house, his rifle pointed at us,
and his finger on the trigger.

George seeing no means of escape, answered,
" Guter freund! "†

" Stand there," cried the German: " don't stir, or
I fire."

We were, of course, obliged to stop, and only ten
minutes afterward, a picket coming out of the village to relieve the sentinel, carried us off like va-
grants to the mayoralty-house.   There the captain of
the Landwehr questioned us at great length as to
who we were, whence we came, the cause of our departure, and why we had no passes.

We repeated that our horses were dead of overwork, and that we had been told to return home; but
he refused to believe us.   At last, however, as George
was asking him for money to pursue our journey,
he began to exclaim: " To the —— with you, scoundrels!   Am I to furnish you with provisions and
rations!   Go; and mind you don't come this way
again, or it will be worse for you! "

We went out very well satisfied.

At the bottom of the stairs, George was thinking
of going up again to ask for a pass; but I was so
alarmed lest this captain should change his mind,
that I obliged my cousin to put a good distance be-

* " Who goes there? "   † " A friend."

tween that fellow and ourselves with all possible
speed; which we did, without any other misad-
venture until we came to Etain.   There George sold
his gold watch and chain for sixty-five francs; making, however, the watchmaker promise that if he
remitted to him seventy-five francs before the end
of the month, the watch and chain should be returned to him.

The watchmaker promised, and cousin then taking me by the arm, said: " Now, Christian, come on;
we have fasted long enough, let us have a banquet."

And a hundred paces farther on, at the street corner, we went into one of those little inns where you
may have a bed for a few sous.

The men there, in a little dark room, were not
gentlemen; they were taking their bottles of wine,
with their caps over one ear, and shirt collars loose
and open; but seeing us at the door, ragged as we
were, with three-weeks' shirts, and beards and hats
saturated and out of all shape and discolored with
rain and sun, they took us at first for bear-leaders,
or dromedary drivers.

The hostess, a fat woman, came forward to ask
what we wanted.

" Your best strong soup, a good piece of beef, a
bottle of good wine, and as much bread as we can
eat," said George.

The fat woman gazed at us with winking eyes,
and without moving, as if to ask: " All very fine!
but who is going to pay me? "

George displayed a five-franc piece, and at once she replied, smiling: "Gentlemen, we will attend to you immediately."

Around us were murmurings: "They are Alsacians! they are Germans! they are this, they are that!"

But we heeded nothing, we spread our elbows upon the table; and the soup having appeared in a huge basin, it was evident that our appetites were good; as for the beef, a regular Prussian morsel, it was gone in a twinkling, although it weighed two pounds, and was flanked with potatoes and other vegetables. Then, the first bottle having disappeared, George had called for a second; and our eyes were beginning to be opened; we regarded the people in another light; and one of the bystanders having ventured to repeat that we were Germans, George turned sharply round and cried: "Who says we are Germans? Come let us see! If he has any spirit, let him rise. We Germans!"

Then he took up the bottle and shattered it upon the table in a thousand fragments. I saw that he was losing his head, and cried to him: "George, for Heaven's sake don't: you will get us taken up!"

But all the spectators agreed with him.

"It is abominable!" cried George. "Let the man who said we are Germans stand out and speak; let him come out with me; let him choose sabre, or sword, whatever he likes, it is all the same to me."

The speaker thus called upon, a youth rose and said: " Pardon me, I apologize; I thought——"

" You had no right to think," said George; " such things never should be said. We are Alsacians, true Frenchmen, men of mature age ; my companion's son is at Phalsbourg in the Mobiles, and I have served in the Marines. We have been carried away, dragged off by the Germans; we have lost our horses and our carriages, and now on arriving here, our own fellow-countrymen insult us in this way because we have said a few words in Alsacian, just as Bretons would speak in Breton and Provençals in Provençal."

" I ask your pardon," repeated the young man. " I was in the wrong—I acknowledge it. You are good Frenchmen."

" I forgive you," said George, scrutinizing him; " but how old are you? "

" Eighteen."

" Well, go where you ought to be, and show that you, too, are as good a Frenchman as we are. There are no young men left in Alsace. You understand my meaning."

Everybody was listening. The young man went out, and as cousin was asking for another bottle, the landlady whispered to him over his shoulder: " You are good Frenchmen; but you have spoken before a great many people—strangers, that I know nothing of. You had better go."

Immediately, George recovered his senses; he

laid a cent-sous piece on the table, the woman gave him two francs fifty centimes change, and we went out.

Once out, George said to me: " Let us step out: anger makes a fool of a man."

And we set off down one little street, then up another, till we came out into the open fields. Night was approaching; if we had been taken again, it would have been a worse business than the first; and we knew that so well, that that night and the next day we dared not even enter the villages, for fear of being seized and brought back to our battalion.

At last, fatigue obliged us to enter an enclosure. It was very cold for the season; but we had become accustomed to our wretchedness, and we slept against a wall, upon a bit of straw matting, just as in our own beds. Rising in the morning at the dawn of day, we found ourselves covered with hoar-frost, and George, straining his eyes in the distance, asked: " Do you know that place down there, Christian ? "

I looked.

" Why, it is Château-Salins! "

Ah! now all was well. At Château-Salins lived an old cousin, Desjardins, the first dyer in the country: Desjardins's grandfather and ours had married sisters before the Revolution. He was a Lutheran, and even a Calvinist; we were Catholics; but nevertheless, we knew each other, and were fond of each other, as very near relations.

CHAPTER X

WE arrived at the door of Jacques Desjardins about seven in the morning; he had just got up, and was taking coffee with his wife and his children.

At the first sight of us, Desjardins stood with his mouth wide open, and his wife and his children were preparing for flight, or to call for help; but when I said: " Good-morning, cousin; it is we," Desjardins cried: " Good heavens! it is Christian and George Weber! What has happened? "

" Yes, it is we, indeed, cousin," said George. " See what a condition the Prussians have brought us to."

" The Prussians! Ah, the brigands! " said Desjardins. " Lise, send to the butcher for some chops —get some wine up. Ah! my poor cousins. I think you must want to change your clothes, too."

" Yes," said George; " and to shave."

" Well, come then. While your breakfast is getting ready, you will change your shirts and clothes. You will put on mine, until yours have been washed. Good gracious! is it possible? "

He took us into a beautiful room upstairs; he opened the linen drawers. Cousin Lise was coming to fill our basins with clean warm water.

"Put on my shoes and stockings, too," said Desjardins. "Here are my razors. Make yourselves comfortable. Ah! those thieves and rogues of Germans! Did they, indeed, treat you in that way—a mayor, and a person of such respectability?"

Then she left the room, and we began to throw off our clothes. The sight of our stockings, our neckerchiefs, and our shirts, made this kind old Father Desjardins groan; for he was one of the best of men. He could hardly believe his eyes, and said: "My poor cousins! you have had a dreadful bad time."

Our first business was to get a good wash. The nice, clean white shirts were already spread open upon the bed; and I cannot tell you what pleasure I experienced in feeling this nice fresh linen next to my skin.

After this I shaved, while George was recounting our misfortunes to our cousin, who interrupted him at every moment, crying: "What! what! Did the barbarous creatures carry their cruelty to such a point? Then they are bandits indeed! Never has the like been seen!"

I wiped myself dry and comfortable, even to behind the ears, and passed the razor to George. Our Cousin Desjardins lent me a pair of stockings, trousers, a blouse, and nice dry shoes. We were about the same height, and never had I been more comfortable in my life.

Then George dressed; and just as we were finishing, the servant came tapping at the door, to announce breakfast; and we came down full of grateful feelings.

Cousin Lise and the children were waiting to embrace us; for they did not dare come near us before, and now they were anxious to excuse themselves for having received us so badly. But it was natural enough, and we did not feel hurt.

I need not tell you with what appetites we breakfasted. George began again the story of our misfortunes for Cousin Lise and the children, who were listening with eyes wide open with amazement, and cried: " Is it really possible? How much you must have suffered, and how happy you must be now you are safe! "

When we had finished she told us that all this was the doing of the Jesuits; that those people had sent abroad evil reports of the Protestants, and that now, the Prussians having proved victorious, they were preaching against Gambetta and Garibaldi. She told us that it was those people who had excited the Emperor to declare war, supposing that their Society would have nothing to lose and everything to gain by it; that if the French should conquer, they would crush the Lutherans; and that if the French lost, Chambord would be set up again, to restore to the Pope the ancient patrimony of St. Peter.

Thus spoke Cousin Lise, an elderly woman with

15

hair turning gray, and who took a pleasure in **dis-**
cussing these subjects.

But George, after emptying his glass, answered
that the true cause of all our misfortunes was the
army; that that army was not the army of the nation, but of the Emperor, who bestowed rank, honors, pensions, and grants of money; that the interests of such an army is ever opposed to that of
the country and the people, because the army wants
war, to get promotion; but the people want peace,
to work, bring up their children, and gain a livelihood.

Cousin Desjardins agreed with him; and when
coffee was brought, Lise and her children went out.
Pipes were lighted, and our cousin told us the latest
news.

Desjardins had many books, like most of the
Protestants, and received newspapers from all quarters; first of all, the *Indépendance Belge*, then papers from Cologne, Frankfort, Berne in Switzerland, Geneva, and elsewhere. At his age—having
a son fifty years old—he did not trouble himself
much now about dyeing or business, and spent his
time in reading.

He was therefore a better-informed man than
we were, and one in whom we could place full
confidence. It was from him that we heard of the
splendid defence of Chateaudun, the landing of
Garibaldi at Marseilles, and his appointment as
General of the Army of the Vosges, the march

of the Bavarians under Von der Tann upon the
Loire, and the arrival of the francs-tireurs in our
mountains, in the direction of Epinal and Raon-
l'Etape. He read to us that fine proclamation of
Gambetta to the French people, setting forth the
high purpose of the inhabitants of Paris, their in-
exhaustible means of defence, the organization of
the citizens as National Guards, the union and harmony of all in this moment of difficulty, and the
victualling of the city for several months, which
would raise the spirit of the provinces and give them
courage to follow so noble an example.

I still remember this passage, which stirred me
like a trumpet:

" Citizens of the departments, this position of affairs imposes important duties upon you. The first
of all is to allow no other occupation whatever to di-
vert your attention from the war—from a struggle
to the very last extremity; the second is, until
peace shall be made, loyally to accept the Republican power, which has sprung equally from necessity
and from right principle. You must have but one
thought: to rescue France from the abyss into
which it has been plunged by the Empire. There
is no want of men: all that is wanting is determination, decision, and continuity in the execution of
plans; what we have lost by the disgraceful capitulation of Sedan is arms. The whole of the resources of our nation had been directed upon Sedan,
Metz, and Strasbourg; and we might justly con-

clude that by one final and guilty plot, the author o.
all our disasters had schemed, in falling, to deprive
us of all means of repairing the ruin he had
caused!"

"He is quite capable," cried George. "Yes, I
am sure the *honest man* contrived to leave himself
a back door into Prussia."

Cousin Desjardins continued: "At this moment,
thanks to the extraordinary exertions of patriotic
men, arrangements have been concluded, the end
and object of which is to draw to ourselves all the
disposable muskets in all the markets of the globe.
The difficulty of effecting this negotiation was very
serious: it is now overcome. With regard to equip-
ments and clothing, manufactories and workshops
will be multiplied, and materials laid under requisition wherever needed; neither hands nor zeal on
the part of workers are wanting, nor will money be
lacking. All our immense resources must be called
into play, the lethargy of the rural districts shaken
into activity, partisan warfare spread in all directions. Let us, therefore, rise as one man, and suffer
death rather than submit to the disgrace of a parti-
tion of our country."

The enthusiasm of George rose with every sentence.

"Good! good!" cried he, "this is speaking to
some purpose. Once give the impulse, and the
object will soon be gained. Our youths will take
up arms *en masse.* One victory, only one, and all

France would rise; we should fall like hail on the backs of the scoundrels; they would be looked out for at every corner in the woods: not a man would live to get back again! ''

Cousin Desjardins, having folded up his papers, said nothing; I, too, was full of my own thoughts.

" And you, cousin," said I, " have you any confidence? "

And only after a minute's silence, and having taken a good pinch of snuff, to waken up his ideas— for he took snuff, like all the old folks, but did not smoke; after a minute he said: " No, Christian, I have no hope; but it is not the Germans that I fear: they have taken Strasbourg; after a time they will have Metz by starvation—that is already settled. They are besieging Verdun; Soissons has just fallen into their hands; they have invested Paris; they are advancing upon Orleans. Well, in spite of all this, it is not the Germans that I fear."

" Who then? " asked George.

Without noticing the question, he continued: " France is so strong, so brave, so rich, so intelligent, that in a few months she could have flung these barbarians across the Rhine again; but what alarms me, is the enemies in our midst."

" Nobody is moving," said I.

" It is just because no one is moving that the Germans are on the Loire," said he, fixing his clear, gray eyes upon me. " If the question was to re-

store Chambord, Ferdinand Philippe, or even
Bonaparte IV., you would see all the old councillors-general, all the councillors of the arrondisse-
ments, all the old préfets, sous-préfets, magistrates,
police inspectors, receivers of taxes, comptrollers,
gardes généraux, mayors, and deputy mayors in
the field. No matter which of the three, for the
principal object is to have a Monsieur who has
crosses, promotions, pensions, and perquisites to
give: whichever of the lot, it is all the same to
them; they only want just one such man! These
people would move heaven and earth for their man:
they would put the peasants into lines by thousands,
they would sing the Marseillaise, they would shout
the ' country is in danger!' And the bishops, the
priests, the curés, the vicars, would preach the holy
war; France would drive the Prussians to the farthest
corner of Prussia; arms, munitions of war, stores
would be found for every day! But as it is a Republic, and as the Republic demands the separation
of Church and State, free education, compulsory
military service; as it declares that all must con-
tribute to the public good, that a rich fool is not
a better man than a poor but able man; and because, on this principle, merit would be everything,
and intrigues and knavery go to the wall, they had
rather see France dismembered than consent to a
Republic! What would become of the good places
of the senators, the peers of France, prefects, cham-
berlains, squires, receivers-general, stewards, mar-

shals, influential deputies, and bishops under a Republic? They would all be put into one basket:
and they don't want that. They would rather
the King of Prussia than the Republic, if the
King of Prussia would only engage to keep all the
good places for them. Yes, in their eyes *la patrie*
means lucrative places and pensions. It is not the
first time that the Germans have been relied upon
to restore order in France. Marie Antoinette had
already ceded Alsace to Austria, to have her ante-
chambers filled again with smooth-faced, obsequious old servitors. Passing events bring back those
times again. Formerly the hunters after pensions,
the egotists who wanted to snap up everything and
leave nothing for the people, were called *nobles;*
now it is the *bourgeois* trained by the Jesuits. But
at that time the chiefs of the Republic were resolved upon the triumph of justice. They did not
leave the functionaries and the generals of Louis
XVI. at the head of the administrations and of the
armies. These great patriots had common-sense.
They established Republican municipalities in
every commune; they gave the command of our
armies to Republican generals; they restrained the
réactionnaires; and having cleared our territory of
Germans, they judged those who had called them
in; and France was saved.

" The same thing would happen to-day, in spite
of all the preparations of Germany, in spite of the
treason of Bonaparte, who, seeing his dynasty sacri-

ficed by his own incapacity, gave up our last army
at Sedan to stay the victory of the Republic.

" Yes, notwithstanding the egotism of this unhappy man, we might yet beat the Germans, if the
Royalists were not at the head of our affairs; but
they are everywhere. In Paris, they command the
National Guard and the army; in the provinces,
they are forming those famous councils-general,
whence have been drawn the juries to acquit Pierre
Bonaparte, and who would without shame sentence
Gambetta to death if they were assembled to try
him. Instead of helping this brave man, this good
patriot, to save France, they will obstruct him;
they will run sticks between the spokes of his
wheels; they will hinder him from getting the necessary levies; they will damp the enthusiasm of
the people. See what all these German papers say:
they cannot sufficiently abuse Gambetta, who is defending his country, nor sufficiently flatter the councils-general named under the Empire."

" But, then," said George, " must we surrender? "

" No," replied Desjardins. " Although we are
sure of being vanquished, we must show that we
are still the old race: that its roots are not dead,
and that the tree will sprout again. If we had
reeled and fallen under the blow of Sedan, the
contempt of Europe and of the whole world would
have covered us forever. The nation has risen
since. It seems incredible. Without armies, or

guns, or muskets, or victuals, or military stores, betrayed, surprised, overrun in all directions, this nation has risen again! It defends itself! One brave
man has been found sufficient to raise its courage.
What other nation would have done as much? I
am, therefore, of opinion that the struggle must be
maintained to the end, that the Germans may be
made, as it were, ashamed of their victory. They
have been fifty years preparing; they have hidden
themselves from us, to spy upon us in time of peace;
they have dissembled their hatred; they have
brought their whole power to bear upon us; they
have studied the question under every aspect; they
threw against us, at the opening of the campaign,
600,000 men against 220,000; they are going to
attack our raw conscripts with their best troops;
they will be five and six against one; they will call
Russia to their help if they want it; and then they
will proclaim, 'We are the conquerors!' They
will not be ashamed to say, 'We have vanquished
France. Now it is we who are *La Grande Nation!*'"

"All that," said George, "is possible. But in
the meantime, we may win a battle; and, if we
gain a victory, things will be different. We shall
gain fresh courage, and the Landwehr who are sent
against us—almost all fathers of families—will ask
no better than to return home."

"The Landwehr have not a word to say," replied Desjardins: "they are not consulted; those

fellows march where they are ordered; they have long been subject to military discipline. It is a machine: nothing but a machine; but a machine of crushing weight."

Then Cousin Desjardins told us that, having travelled long in Germany before and after 1848, on business, he had seen how these people detested us: that they envied us; that we were an offence to them; that hatred of the French was taught in their schools; that they thought themselves our superiors, on account of their religion, which is simple and natural; while ours, with all its ceremonies, its Latin chants, its tapers and its tinsel, induced them to look upon us as an inferior race, like the negroes, who are only fond of red, and hang rings in their noses; that, especially, they deemed their women more virtuous and more worthy of respect than ours: this they attribute also to their superior religion, which keeps them at home, while ours pass their time in all sorts of ceremonies, and neglect their first duties.

Desjardins had even had a serious dispute upon this subject with a school-master, being unable to hear an open avowal of such an opinion of French-women; amongst whom we number Jeanne d'Arc and other heroines, whose grandeur of character German women are unable to comprehend.

He told us that, from this point of view, the Germans, and especially the Prussians, considered us Alsacians and Lorrainers as exiles from fatherland, and unfortunate in being under the dominion of a debased race kept in ignorance by the priests.

George, on hearing this, became furious, and cried that we had more intelligence and more sense than all the Germans put together.

"Yes, I believe so, too," replied Cousin Desjardins; "only we ought to use it; we ought to set up schools everywhere; the lowest Frenchman should be able to read and write our own language; and this is exactly what the lovers of good places don't wish for. If the people had been educated, we should have known what was going on upon the other side of the Rhine; we should have had national armies, able generals, a watchful commissariat, a sound organization, enlightened and conscientious deputies; we should have had all that we are now wanting; we should not have placed the power of making war or peace in the hands of an imbecile; we should not have stupidly attacked the Germans, and the Germans, seeing us ready to receive them, would have been careful not to attack us. All our defeats, all our divisions, our internal troubles, our revolutions, our battles and massacres in the streets; the transportations, the hatred between classes—all this comes of ignorance; and this abominable ignorance is the doing of the selfish statesmen who have governed us for seventy years. Good sense, justice, and patriotism would lead them to inform the people; they preferred an alliance with the Jesuits to degrade the people; can any treason be worse?"

George, who had long entertained the same view, had nothing to add; but he still argued that we might gain a victory, and that then we should be saved.

Cousin Desjardins shook his head, saying: "Our forces are of too inferior a quality; Gambetta will never have time to organize them; and if the traitors thought that he would, they would deliver up Metz at once, in order that the second German army, Prince Frederick Charles's, might reach the Loire in time to prevent our army from raising the siege of Paris: for then, I think, the country might be saved. But this will not come to pass. When I saw generals coming out of Metz to go and consult the Empress in England, I knew that our cause was lost. And then the forces of King William are immense. Those 300,000 Russians who, as the papers tell us, are ready to march upon Constantinople, are only waiting the nod of the King of Prussia to start by the railways and come to overwhelm us, if the Germans don't think themselves numerous enough to vanquish us with 1,200,000 men. The decisive opinion of Europe is that there shall be no republic in France—no, not at any price; for, if the republic was established here, every monarchy would be shaken; the nations would all follow our example, and there would be an end of war; we should have a European confederation; kings, emperors, princes, courtiers, and professional soldiers might all be bowed off the stage. Only commerce, industry, science and arts would be thought of; to be anything, a man would have to know something. The talent of drawing up men in line to be mown down by cannon and mitrailleuses, would be relegated to the rear ranks; and a hundred years hence, men would hardly believe that such things have ever been; it would be too stupid."

Desjardins then told us how, in 1830, travelling about Solingen to buy dye-stuffs, he had noticed that the Prussians thought of nothing but war. From that very time they exhausted themselves to keep on foot, and ready to march, an army of 400,000 disciplined men. Since then, after their fusion with the forces of North Germany, Bavaria, Wurtemberg, and Baden, the total would amount to more than a million of men, without reckoning the landsturm: composed, it is true, of men in years, but who have all served, and can handle a rifle, load a gun, and ride well.

"Here, then, is what Monsieur Bonaparte has brought upon our shoulders without necessity," said he; "and it is against such a power that Gambetta is undertaking to organize in haste the youth that are left, and of whom the greater part have never served. I confess my hopes are small. God grant that I may be mistaken; but I fear that Alsace and Lorraine are for the time ingulfed in Germany. The war will continue for a time; treachery will go on working; and, finally, after all our sufferings, messieurs the sometime Ministers and councillors-general, the former préfets and sous-préfets, the old functionaries of every grade, in a word, all the egotists will be on the look-out, and will say: ' Let us make an arrangement with Bismarck. Let us make peace at the expense of Alsace and Lorraine; and let us name a king who shall find us first-rate places; France will still be rich enough to find us salaries and pensions.' "

Thus spoke Cousin Desjardins; and George, growing more and more angry, striking the table with his fist, said, "What I cannot understand is that the English desert us, and that they should allow the Prussians to extend their territory as they like."

" Ah," said Desjardins, smiling, " the English are not what they once were. They have become too rich; they cling to their comforts. Their great statesmen are no longer Pitts and Chathams, who looked to the future greatness of their nation and took measures to secure it: provided only that business prospers from day to day, future generations and the greatness of Britain give them no concern."

" Just so," said George. " If you had sailed, as I have done, in the North Sea and the Baltic, if you had seen what an enormous maritime power North Germany may possibly become in a few years, with her hundred and sixty leagues of sea-coast, her harbors of Dantzig, Stettin, Hamburg, and Bremen, whither the finest rivers bring all the best products of Central Europe, all kinds of raw material, not only from Germany and Poland, but also from Russia; if you had seen that population of sailors, of traders, which increases daily, you would be unable to understand the indifference of the English. Have they lost the use of their eyes? Has the love of Protestantism and comfort deprived them of all discernment? I cannot tell; but they must see that if King William and Bismarck want Alsace and Lorraine, it is not exactly for the love of us Alsacians and Lorrainers, but to hold the course of the Rhine from its source in the German cantons of Switzerland down to its outfall at Rotterdam; and that in holding this great river they will control all the commerce of our industrial provinces and be able to feed the Dutch colonies with their produce, which will make them the first maritime power on the Continent; and that, to carry out their purpose without being molested—whilst the Russians are attacking Constantinople, they will install themselves quietly in the Dutch ports, as they did in the case of Hanover, and will offer us Belgium, and perhaps even something more! All this is evident."

"No doubt, cousin," said Desjardins. "I also believe that every fault brings its own punishment: the English will suffer for their faults, as we are doing for ours; and the Germans, after having terrified the world with their ambition, will one day be made to rue their cruelty, their hypocrisy, and their robberies. God is just! But in the meantime, until that day shall arrive, we are confiscated, and all our observations are useless."

And so the conversation went on: I cannot remember it entirely, but I have given you the substance of it.

CHAPTER XI

WE remained with Cousin Desjardins all that day. Cousin Lise had our shirts washed, our clothes cleaned, and our shoes dried before the fire, after having first filled them with hot embers; and the next day we took our leave of these excellent people, thanking them from the bottom of our hearts.

We were very impatient to see our native place again, of which we had had no news for a month; and especially our poor wives, who must have supposed us lost.

The weather was damp; there were forebodings of a hard winter.

At Dieuze the rumor reached us that Bazaine had just surrendered Metz, with all his army, his flags, his guns, rifles, stores, and wounded, unconditionally!

The Prussian officers were drinking champagne at the inn where we halted. They were laughing! George was pale; I felt an oppression on my heart.

Some people who were there, carriers—German Jews, who followed their armies with carts, to load them with the clocks, the pots and pans,

the linen, the furniture, and everything which the
officers and soldiers sold them after having pillaged
them in our houses—told us how horses were given
away round Metz for nothing; that Arab horses
were sold for a hundred sous, but that nobody would
have them, horses' provender selling at an exorbi-
tant price; that these poor beasts were eating one
another—they devoured each other's hair to the
quick, and even gnawed the bark off trees to which
they were tied; that our captive soldiers dropped
down with hunger in the ditches by the roadside,
and then the Prussians abused them for drunkards.
We heard, also, that the inhabitants of Metz, on
hearing the terms of capitulation, had meant to rise
and put Bazaine to death, but that all through the
siege three mitrailleuses had been placed in front of
his head-quarters, and that he had escaped the day
before this shameful capitulation was to take place.

All this appeared to us almost impossible. Metz
surrender unconditionally! Metz, the strongest
town in France, defended by an army of a hundred
thousand well-seasoned troops: the last army left
to us after Sedan!

But it was true, nevertheless!

And in spite of all that can be said of the ignorance and the folly of the chiefs, to account for
this terrible disaster, I cannot but believe that our
honest man gave his orders to the very last; that
Bazaine obeyed, and that they did everything together. Besides, Bazaine went to join him imme-

diately at Wilhelmshöhe, where the cuisine was so excellent; there they reposed after their toils, until the opportunity should return of recommencing a campaign after the fashion of the 2d of December, in which men were entrapped by night in their beds, while they were relying upon *the honest man's* oath; or in the style of the Mexican war, where he ran away, deserting the men he had sworn to defend! In this sort of campaign, and if the people continue to have confidence in such men, as many assert will happen, they may begin again some fine morning, and once more get hold of the keys of the treasury; they will once more distribute crosses, and salaries, and pensions to their friends and acquaintances; and in a few years Bismarck will discover that the Germans possess claims upon Champagne and Burgundy.

Well, everything is possible; we have seen such strange things these last twenty years.

At Fénétrange, through which we passed about two o'clock, nothing was known.

At six in the evening we arrived upon the plateau of Metting, near the farm called Donat, and saw in the dim distance, two leagues from us, Phalsbourg, without its ramparts, and its demilunes; its church and its streets in ashes! The Germans were hidden by the undulations of the surrounding country, their cannon were on the hill-sides, and sentinels were posted behind the quarries.

There was deep silence: not a shot was heard:

it was the blockade! Famine was doing quietly what the bombardment had been unable to effect.

Then, with heads bowed down, we passed through the little wood on our left, full of dead leaves, and we saw our little village of Rothalp, three hundred paces behind the orchards and the fields; it looked dead too: ruin had passed over it—the requisitions had utterly exhausted it; winter, with its snow and ice, was waiting at every door.

The mill was working; which astonished me.

George and I, without speaking, clasped each other's hands; then he strode toward his house, and I passed rapidly to mine, with a full heart.

Prussian soldiers were unloading a wagon-load of corn under my shed; fear laid hold of me, and I thought, " Have the wretches driven away my wife and daughter? "

Happily Catherine appeared at the door directly; she had seen me coming, and extended her arms, crying, " Is it you, Christian? Oh! what we have suffered! "

She hung upon my neck, crying and sobbing. Then came Grédel; we all clung together, crying like children.

The Prussians, ten paces off, stared at us. A few neighbors were crying, " Here is the old mayor come back again! "

At last we entered our little room. I sat facing the bed, gazing at the old bed-curtains, the branch of box-tree at the end of the alcove, the old walls,

the old beams across the ceiling, the little window-
panes, and my good wife and my wayward daughter, whom I love. Everything seemed to me so
nice. I said to myself, "We are not all dead yet.
Ah! if now I could but see Jacob, I should be quite
happy."

My wife, with her face buried in her apron between her knees, never ceased sobbing, and Grédel,
standing in the middle of the room, was looking
upon us. At last she asked me: "And the horses,
and the carts, where are they?"

"Down there, somewhere near Montmédy."

"And Cousin George?"

"He is with Marie Anne. We have had to
abandon everything—we escaped together—we
were so wretched! The Germans would have let
us die with hunger."

"What! have they ill-used you, father?"

"Yes, they have beaten me."

"Beaten you?"

"Yes, they tore my beard—they struck me in
the face."

Grédel, hearing this, went almost beside herself;
she threw a window open, and shaking her fist at the
Germans outside, she screamed to them, "Ah, you
brigands! You have beaten my father—the best
of men!"

Then she burst into tears, and came up to kiss
me, saying, "They shall be paid out for all that!"
I felt moved.

My wife, having become calmer, began to tell me all they had suffered: their grief at receiving no news of us since the third day after the passage of the pedler; then the appointment of Placiard in my place, and the load of requisitions he had laid upon us, saying that I was a Jacobin.

He associated with none but Germans now; he received them in his house, shook hands with them, invited them to dinner, and spoke nothing but Prussian German. He was now just as good a servant of King William as he had been of the Empire. Instead of writing letters to Paris to get stamp-offices and tobacco-excise-offices, he now wrote to Bismarck-Bohlen, and already the good man had received large promises of advancement for his sons, and son-in-law. He himself was to be made super-intendent of something or other, at a good salary.

I listened without surprise; I was sure of this beforehand.

One thing gave me great pleasure, which was to see the mill-dam full of water: so the chest was still at the bottom. And Grédel having left the room to get supper, that was the first thing I asked Catherine.

She answered that nothing had been disturbed: that the water had never sunk an inch. Then I felt easy in my mind, and thanked God for having saved us from utter ruin.

The Germans had been making their own bread for the last fortnight; they used to come and grind at my mill, without paying a liard. How to get through our trouble seemed impossible to find out. There was nothing left to eat. Happily the Landwehr had quickly become used to our white bread, and, to get it, they willingly gave up a portion of their enormous rations of meat. They would also exchange fat sheep for chickens and geese, being tired of always eating joints of mutton, and Catherine had driven many a good bargain with them. We had, indeed, one cow left in the Krapenfelz, but we had to carry her fodder every day among these rocks, to milk her, and come back laden.

Grédel, ever bolder and bolder, went herself. She kept a hatchet under her arm, and she told me smiling that one of those drunken Germans having insulted her, and threatened to follow her into the wood, she had felled him with one blow of her hatchet, and rolled his body into the stream.

Nothing frightened her: the Landwehr who lodged with us—big, bearded men—dreaded her like fire; she ordered them about as if they were her servants: "Do this! do that! Grease me those shoes, but don't eat the grease, like your fellows at Metting; if you do, it will be the worse for you! Go fetch water! You sha'n't go into the store-room straight out of the stable! your smell is already bad enough without horse-dung! You are every one of you as dirty as beggars, and yet there is no want of water: go and wash at the pump."

And they obediently went.

She had forbidden them to go upstairs, telling them, " *I* live up there! that's my room. The first man who dares put his foot there, I will split his head open with my hatchet."

And not a man dared disobey.

Those people, from the time they had set over us their governor Bismarck-Bohlen, had no doubt received orders to be careful with us, to treat us kindly, to promise us indemnities. Captain Floegel went on drinking from morning till night, from night till morning; but instead of calling us rascals, wretches! he called us " his good Germans, his dear Alsacian and Lorraine brothers," promising us all the prosperity in the world, as soon as we should have the happiness of living under the old laws of Fatherland.

They were already talking of dismissing all French school-masters, and then we began to see the abominable carelessness of our government in the matter of public education. Half of our unhappy peasants did not know a word of French: for two hundred years they had been left grovelling in ignorance!

Now the Germans have laid hands upon us, and are telling them that the French are enemies of their race; that they have kept them in bondage to get all they could out of them, to live at their cost, and to use their bodies for their own protection in time of danger. Who can say it is not so? Are not all appearances against us? And if the Germans bestow on the peasants the education which all our governments have denied them, will not these people have reason to attach themselves to their new country?

The Germans having altered their bearing toward us, and seeking to win us over, lodged in our houses. They were Landwehr, who thought only of their wives and children, wishing for the end of the war, and much fearing the appearance of the francs-tireurs.

The arrival of Garibaldi in the Vosges with his two sons was announced, and often George, pointing from his door at the summit of the Donon and the Schneeberg, already white with snow, would say: " There is fighting going on down there ! Ah, Christian, if we were young again, what a fine blow we might deliver in our mountain passes! "

Our greatest sorrow was to know that famine was prevailing in the town, as well as small-pox. More than three hundred sick, out of fifteen hundred inhabitants, were filling the College, where the hospital had been established. There was no salt, no tobacco, no meat. The flags of truce which were continually coming and going on the road to Lützel-bourg, reported that the place could not hold out any longer.

There had been a talk of bringing heavy guns from Strasbourg and from Metz, after the surrender of these two places; but I remember that the *Haupt-mann* who was lodging with the curé, M. Daniel,

declared that it was not worth while; that a fresh
bombardment would cost his Majesty King William at least three millions; and that the best way was
to let these people die their noble death quietly, like
a lamp going out for want of oil.   With these words
the *Hauptmann* put on airs of humanity, continually repeating that we ought to save human life, and
economize ammunition.

And what had become of Jacob in the midst of
this misery?   And Jean Baptiste Werner?   I am
obliged to mention him too, for God knows what
madness was possessing Grédel at the thought that
he might be suffering hunger: she was no longer human; she was a mad creature without control over
herself, and she often made me wonder at the meek
patience of the Landwehr.   When one or another
wanted to ask her for anything, she would show them
the door, crying: " Go out; this is not your place! "

She even openly wished them all to be massacred;
and then she would say to them, in mockery: " Go,
then! attack the town! . . . go and storm the
place! . . . You don't dare! . . . You are afraid
for your skin!   You had rather starve people, bombard women and children, burn the houses of poor
creatures, hiding yourselves behind your heaps of
clay!   You must be cowards to set to work that way.
If ours were out, and you were in, they would have
been a dozen times upon the walls: but you are
afraid of getting your ribs stove in!   You are prudent men! "

And they, seated at our door, with their heads hanging down, spoke not a word, but went on smoking, as if they did not hear.

Yet one day these peaceable men showed a considerable amount of indignation, not against Grédel or us, but against their own generals.

It was some time after the capture of Metz. The cold weather had set in. Our Landwehr returning from mounting guard were squeezed around the stove, and outside lay the first fall of snow. And as they were sitting thus, thinking of nothing but eating and drinking, the bugle blew outside a long blast and a loud one, the echoes of which died far away in the distant mountains.

An order had arrived to buckle on their knapsacks, shoulder their rifles, and march for Orleans at once.

You should have seen the long, dismal faces of these fellows. You should have heard them protesting that they were Landwehr, and could not be made to leave German provinces. I believe that if there had been at that moment a sortie of fifty men from Phalsbourg, they would have given themselves up prisoners, every one, to remain where they were.

But Captain Floegel, with his red nose and his harsh voice, had come to give the word of command, " Fall in! "

They had to obey. So there they stood in line before our mill, three or four hundred of them, and

were then obliged to march up the hill to Mittelbronn, whilst the villagers, from their windows,
were crying, " A good riddance ! "

It was supposed, too, that the blockade of Phalsbourg would be raised, and everybody was preparing baskets, bags, and all things needful to carry
victuals to our poor lads.   Grédel, who was most
unceremonious, had her own private basket to carry.
It was quite a grand removal.

But where did this order to march come from?
What was the meaning of it all?

I was standing at our door, meditating upon this,
when Cousin Marie Anne came up, whispering to
me, " We have won a great battle: all the men at
Metz are running to the Loire."

" How do you know that, cousin? "

" From an Englishman who came to our house
last night."

" And where has this battle taken place? "

" Wait a moment," said she.   " At Coulmiers,
near Orleans.   The Germans are in full retreat;
their officers are taking refuge in the mayoralty-
office with their men, to escape being slaughtered."

I asked no more questions, and I ran to Cousin
George's, very curious to see this Englishman and
hear what he might have to tell us.

As I went in, my cousin was seated at the table
with this foreigner.   They had just breakfasted,
and they seemed very jolly together.   Marie Anne
followed me. .

" Here is my cousin, the former mayor of this village," said George, seeing me open the door.

Immediately the Englishman turned round. He was a young man of about five and thirty, tall and thin, with a hooked nose, hazel eyes full of animation, clean shaved, and buttoned up close in a long gray surtout.

" Ah, very good! " said he, speaking a little nasally, and with his teeth close, as is the habit of his countrymen. " Monsieur was mayor? "

" Yes, sir."

" And you refused to post the proclamations of the Governor, Bismarck-Bohlen? "

" Yes, sir."

" Very good—very good."

I sat down, and, without any preamble, this Englishman ran on with eight or ten questions: upon the requisitions, the pillaging, the number of carriages and horses carried away into the interior; how many had come back since the invasion; how many were still left in France; what we thought of the Germans: if there was any chance of our agreeing together: had we rather remain French, or become neutral, like the Swiss.

He had all these questions in his head, and I went on answering, without reflecting that it was a very strange thing to interrogate people in this way.

George was laughing, and, when it was over, he said, " Now, my lord, you may go on with your article."

The Englishman smiled, and said, " Yes, that will do!   I believe you have spoken the truth."

We drank a glass of wine together, which George had found somewhere.

" This is good wine," said the Englishman.   " So the Prussians have not taken everything."

" No, they have not discovered everything; we have a few good hiding-places yet."

" Ah! exactly so—yes—I understand."

George wanted to question him too, but the Englishman did not answer as fast as we; he thought well over his answers, before he would say yes or no!

It was not from him that Cousin George had learned the latest intelligence; it was from a heap of newspapers which the Englishman had left upon the table the night before as he went to bed—English and Belgian newspapers—which George had read hastily up to midnight: for he had learned English in his travels, which our friend was not aware of.

Besides the battle of Coulmiers, he had learned many other things: the organization of an army in the North under General Bourbaki; the march of the Germans upon Dijon; the insurrection at Marseilles; the noble declaration of Gambetta against those who were accusing him of throwing the blame of our disasters upon the army, and not upon its chiefs; and especially the declaration of Prince Gortschakoff " that the Emperor of Russia refused to be bound any longer by the treaty which was to restrain him from keeping in the Black Sea more than a certain number of large ships of war."

The Englishman had marked red crosses down this article; and George told me by and by that these red crosses meant something very serious.

The Englishman had a very fine horse in the stable; we went out together to see it; it was a tall chestnut, able no doubt to run like a deer.

If I tell you these particulars, it is because we have since seen many more English people, both men and women, all very inquisitive, and who put questions to us, just like this one; whether to write articles, or for their own information, I know not.

George assured me that the article writers spared no expense to earn their pay honorably; that they went great distances—hundreds of leagues—going to the fountain-head; that they would have considered themselves guilty of robbing their fellow-countrymen, if they invented anything: which, besides, would very soon be discovered, and would deprive them of all credit in England.

I believe it; and I only wish news-hunters of equal integrity for our country. Instead of having newspapers full of long arguments, which float before you like clouds, and out of which no one can extract the least profit, we should get positive facts that would help us to clear up our ideas: of which we are in great need.

So we thought we were rid of our Landwehr,

when presently they returned, having received coun-
ter orders, which seemed to us a very bad sign.

George, who had just accompanied his Englishman back to Sarrebourg, came into our house, and
sat by the stove, deep in thought.   He had never
seemed to me so sad; when I asked him if he had
received any bad news, he answered: " No, I have
heard nothing new; but what has happened shows
plainly that the German army of Metz has arrived
in time to prevent our troops from raising the blockade of Paris after the victory of Coulmiers."

And all at once his anger broke out against the
Dumouriez and the Pichegrus, men without genius,
who were selling their country to serve a false
dynasty.

" A week or a fortnight more, and we should have
been saved."

He smote the table with his fist, and seemed ready
to cry.   All at once he went out, unable to contain
himself any longer, and we saw him in the moonlight cross the meadow behind and disappear into
his house.

It was the middle of November; the frost grew
more intense and hardened the ground everywhere:
every morning the trees were covered with hoar-
frost.

We were now compelled to do forced labor; not
only to supply wood, but also to go and cleave it for
the Landwehr.   I paid Father Offran, who supplied

my place; it was an additional expense, and the day of ruin, utter ruin, was drawing close.

Of course the Landwehr, offended at having been hissed all through the village, had lost all consideration for us, and but for stringent orders, they would have wrung our necks on the spot; every time they were able to tell us a piece of bad news, they would come up laughing, dropping the butt-ends of their rifles on the stone floor, and crying: " Well, now, here's another crash!   There goes another stampede of Frenchmen!   Orleans evacuated!   Champigny to be abandoned!   Capital! all goes on right! Now, then, you people, is that soup ready?   Hurry! good news like these give one a good appetite! "

" Try to hold your tongues, if you can, pack of beggars," cried Grédel; " we don't believe your lies."

Then they grinned again, and said: " There is no need you should believe us, if only you get put into our basket; when you are there you will believe! Then look out!   If you stir a finger we'll nail you to the wall like mangy cats.   Aha! did you laugh and hiss when you saw us going? but there are more yet to come.   You will regret us, Mademoiselle Grédel; you will regret us some day; you will cry, ' if we had but our good Landwehr again! ' but it will be too late."

What surprises me is that Grédel never seems to have thought of poisoning them; luckily it was not the time of the year for the red toadstools: besides,

17

we were obliged to boil our soup in the same kettle; or these wary people would have had their suspicions, and obliged us to taste their meat, as they did at the Quatre Vents, the Baraques du Bois de Chênes, and in several other places.

They then drew their lines closer and closer round the place: upon all the roads which led to the advanced posts they placed guns, and watched by them day and night; they regulated their range and line of fire by day with pickets and with grooves cut in the ground, to enable them to change its direction and sweep the roads and paths, even in the dark nights, in case of an attack.

The snow was then falling in great flakes; all the country was covered with snow, and often at midnight or at one or two in the morning, the musketry opened, and they cried in the street: " A sortie! a sortie! "

And all the villagers, who still kept their cattle at home by order of the new mayor Placiard, were compelled to drive them to a distance, into the fields, to prevent the French, if they reached us, from finding anything in the stables.

Ah! that abominable, good-for-nothing scoundrel Placiard, that famous pillar of the Empire, what abominations he has perpetrated, what toils has he undergone to merit the esteem of the Prussians!

Does it not seem sad that such thieves should sometimes quietly terminate their existence in a good bed?

CHAPTER XII

ABOUT the end of November there happened an extraordinary thing, of which I must give you an account.

On the first fall of snow, our Landwehr had built on the hill, in the rear of their guns, huts of considerable size, covered with earth, open to the south and closed against the north wind. Under these they lighted great fires, and every hour relieved guard.

They had also received from home immense packages of warm clothing, blankets, cloaks, shirts, and woollen stockings; they called these love-gifts. Captain Floegel distributed these to his men, at his discretion.

Now, it happened that one night, when the Landwehr lodging with us were on guard, that I, knowing they would not return before day, had gone down to shut the back door which opens upon the fields. The moon had set, but the snow was shining white, streaked with the dark shadows of the trees; and just as I was going to lock up, what do I see in my orchard behind the large pear-tree on the left? A Turco with his little red cap over his ear, his blue jacket corded and braided all over, his belt and his gaiters. There he was, leaning in the attitude of attention, the butt-end of his rifle resting on the ground, his eyes glowing like those of a cat.

He heard the door open, and turned abruptly round.

Then, glad to see one of our own men again, I felt my heart beat, and gazing stealthily round for fear of the neighbors, I signed to him to draw near.

All were asleep in the village; no lights were shining at the windows.

He came down in four or five paces, clearing the fences at a bound, and entered the mill.

Immediately I closed the door again, and said : " Good Frenchman? "

He pressed my hand in the dark, and followed me into the back room, where my wife and Grédel were still sitting up.

Imagine their astonishment!

" Here is a man from the town," I said: " he's a real Turco. We shall hear news."

At the same moment we observed that the Turco's bayonet was red, even to the shank, and that the blood had even run down the barrel of his rifle; but we said nothing.

This Turco was a fine man, dark brown, with a little curly beard, black eyes, and white teeth, just as the apostles are painted. I have never seen a finer man.

He was not sorry to feel the warmth of a good fire. Grédel having made room for him, he took a

seat, thanking her with a nod of his head, and repeating: " Good Frenchman! "

I asked him if he was hungry; he said yes; and
my wife immediately went to fetch him a large
basin of soup, which he enjoyed greatly.   She gave
him also a good slice of bread and of beef; but instead of eating it he dropped it into his bag, asking
us for salt and tobacco.

He spoke as these people all do—thou-ing us.
He even wanted to kiss Grédel's hand.   She
blushed, and asked him, without any ceremony, before our faces, if he knew Jean Baptiste Werner?

" Jean Baptiste! " said he.   " Bastion No. 3—
formerly African gunner.   Yes, I know him.
Good man! brave Frenchman! "

" He is not wounded? "

" No."

" Not ill? "

" No."

Then Grédel began to cry in her apron; and
mother asked the Turco if he knew Jacob Weber, of
the 3d company of Mobiles; but the Turco did not
know our Jacob; he could only tell us that the
Mobiles had lost very few men, which comforted
my wife and me.   Then he told us that a captain in
the Garde Mobile, a Jew named Cerfber, sent as a
flag of truce to Lützelbourg, had taken the opportunity to desert, and that the German general, being disgusted at his baseness, had refused to receive
him, upon which the wretch had gone into Ger-

many. I was nowise surprised at this. I knew Cerfber; he was mayor of Niederwillen, at four leagues from us, and more Bonapartist than Bonaparte himself. Unable to surrender the rest, as his master had done at Sedan, he had surrendered himself.

Grédel had gone out while the Turco was telling us these news; she returned presently with a large quantity of provisions. She had taken all my tobacco, and begged the Turco to take it to Jean Baptiste and Jacob. She had not quite the face to say before me that it was for Jean Baptiste alone; that would have been going a little too far; but she said, "It is for the two." The Turco promised to perform this commission; then Grédel gave him several things for himself; but he wanted especially salt, and fortunately we possessed enough to fill his bag. My wife stood sentinel in the passage. Thank God there was no stir for a whole hour; during which this Turco answered, as well as he was able, all the questions we asked him.

We understood that there was much sickness in the town; that several articles of consumption were utterly exhausted, among others, meat, salt, and tobacco; and that the inhabitants were weary of being shut in without any news from outside.

About one in the morning, the wind, having risen, was shaking the door, and we fancied we could hear the Landwehr returning. The Turco noticed it, and made signs to us that he would go.

THERE HE WAS, LEANING FORWARD TO LISTEN.

We could have wished to detain him, but the danger was too great. He therefore took up his rifle again, and asked to kiss my wife's hand, just as the gypsies do in our country. Then pointing to his bag, he said: " For Jacob and Jean Baptiste! "

I took him back through the orchard. The weather was frightful; the air was full of snow, whirled into drifts by a stormy wind; but he knew his way, and began by running with his body bending low as far as the tall hedge on the left; a moment after he was out of sight. I listened a long while. The watch-fires of the Landwehr were shining on the hill, above Wechem; their sentinels were challenging and answering each other in the darkness; but not a shot was fired.

I returned. My wife and Grédel seemed happy; and we all went to bed.

Next day we learned that two Landwehr had been found killed—one near the Avenue des Dames, between the town and the Quatre Vents, the other at the end of Fiquet, both fathers of families. The unfortunate men had been surprised at their posts.

What a miserable thing is war! The Germans have lost more men than we have; but we will not be so cruel as to rejoice over this.

And now, if I am asked my opinion about the Turcos, against whom the Germans have raised such an outcry, I answer that they are good men and true! Jacob and Jean Baptiste have received everything

that we sent to them.   This Turco's word was worth
more than that of the lieutenant and the feld-weibel
who had promised to pay me for my wine.

No doubt, amongst the Turcos there are some bad
fellows; but the greater part are honest men, with a
strong feeling of religion: men who have known
them at Phalsbourg and elsewhere acknowledge
them to be men of honor.   They have stolen nothing, robbed nobody, never insulted a woman.   If
they had campaigned on the other side of the Rhine,
of course they would have twisted the necks of ducks
and hens, as all soldiers do in an enemy's country:
the Landwehr put no constraint upon themselves in
our country.   But the idea would never have occurred to the Turcos, as it had to German officers and
generals, of sending for packs of Jews to follow them
and buy up, wholesale, the linen, furniture, clocks
—in a word, anything they found in private individuals' houses.   This is simple truth!   Monsieur
de Bismarck may insult the Turcos as much as he
pleases before his German Parliament, which is
ready to say " Amen " every time he opens his
mouth.   He might as well not talk at all.   Thieves
are bad judges of common honesty!   I am aware
that Monsieur le Prince de Bismarck thinks himself
the first politician in the world, because he has deceived a simpleton; but there is a wide difference
between a great man and a great dishonest man.
By and by this will be manifest, to the great misfortune of Europe.

But it was a real comfort to have seen this **Turco**; and for several days, when we were alone, my wife and Grédel talked of nothing else; but sad reflections again got the upper hand.

No one can form an idea of the misery, the feeling of desolation which takes possession of you, when days and weeks pass by in the midst of enemies without the least word reaching you from the interior; then you feel the strength of the hold that your native land has upon you. The Germans think to detach us from it by preventing us from learning what is taking place there; but they are mistaken. The less you speak the more you think; and your indignation, your disgust, your hatred for violence, force, and injustice is ever on the increase. You conceive a horror for those who have been the cause of such sufferings. Time brings no change; on the contrary, it deepens the wound: one curse succeeds another; and the deepest desire left is either for an end of all, or vengeance.

Besides, it is perfectly evident the Lorrainers and the Alsacians are a bold, brave nation; and all the fine words in the world will not make them forget the treatment they have suffered, after being surprised defenceless. They would reproach themselves as cowards, did they cease to hope for their revenge. I, Christian Weber, declare this, and no honest man can blame me for it. Abject wretches alone accept injustice as a final dispensation; and we have ever God over us all, who forbids us to believe

that murder, fire, and robbery may and ought to prevail over right and conscience.

Let us return to our story.

Cousin George had seen in the Englishman's
newspapers that the circulation of the *Indépendance
Belge* and the *Journal de Genève* had doubled and
trebled since the commencement of the war, because
they filled the place of all the other journals which
used to be received from Paris; and without loss of
time he had written to Brussels to subscribe.

The first week, having received no answer, he had
sent the money in Prussian notes in a second letter;
for we had at that time only Prussian thalers in
paper, with which the Landwehr paid us for whatever they did not take by force. We had no great
confidence in this paper, but it was worth the trial.

The newspaper arrived. It was the first we had
seen for four months, and any one may understand
the joy with which George came to tell me this good
news.

Every evening from that time I went to hear the
newspapers read at Cousin George's. We could
hardly understand anything at first, for at every line
we met with new names. Chanzy had the chief
command upon the Loire, Faidherbe in the north.
And these two men, without any soldiers besides
Mobiles and volunteers, held the open country.
They even gained considerable advantages over an
enemy that far outnumbered them; whilst the marshals of the Empire had suffered themselves to be

vanquished and annihilated in three weeks, with our best troops.

This shows that, in victories, generals have no more than half the credit.

Of all the old generals, Bourbaki was the only one left.

As for Garibaldi, we knew him, and we could tell by the restless movements of our Landwehr that he was approaching our mountains about Belfort. He was the hope of our country: all our young men were going to join him.

We also learned that the Government was divided between Tours and Paris; that Gambetta was bearing all the burden of the defence of the country, as Minister of War; that he was everywhere at once, to encourage the dispirited; that he had set up the chief place of instruction for our young soldiers at Toulouse, and that the Prussians were pursuing their horrible course in the invaded countries with renewed fury; that a party of francs-tireurs having surprised a few Uhlans at Nemours, a column of Germans had surrounded the town on the next day, and set fire to it to the music of their bands, compelling the members of the committee for the defence to be present at this abominable act; that M. de Bismarck had laid hands upon certain bourgeois of the interior, in reprisal for the captures made by our ships five hundred leagues away in the North Sea; that Ricciotti Garibaldi, having defeated the Prussians at Chatillon-sur-Seine, those atrocious wretches had delivered the innocent town over to plunder, and laid it under contribution for a million of francs; that respectable persons belonging to the Grand Duchy of Baden, private individuals, were crossing the Rhine with horses and carts to come and pillage Alsace with impunity—all the towns and villages being occupied by their troops.   In a word, many other things of the kind; which plainly prove that with the Prussians, war is an honest means of growing rich, and getting possession of the property of the inoffensive inhabitants.

At St. Quentin, one of their chiefs, the Colonel de Kahlden, gave public notice to the inhabitants, that "if a shot was fired upon a German soldier, *six inhabitants should be shot;* and that every individual compromised or *suspected* would be punished with death."

Everywhere, everywhere these great philosophers plundered and burned without mercy whatever towns or villages dared resist!

George said that these beings were not raised above the beasts of prey, and that education only does for them what spiked collars do for fighting dogs.

We also heard of the capitulation of Thionville, after a terrible bombardment, in which the Prussians had refused to allow the women and children to leave the place!   We heard of the first encounters of Faidherbe in the north with Manteuffel; and the battles of Chanzy with Frederick Charles, near Orleans.

In spite of the inferiority of our numbers, and the inexperience of our troops, we often got the upper hand.

These news had restored us to hope.   Unhappily, the heaviest blow of all was to come.   Phalsbourg, utterly exhausted by famine, was about to surrender, after a resistance of five months.

Oh! my ancient town of Phalsbourg, what affliction sank into our hearts, when, on the evening of the 9th December, we heard your heavy guns fire one after another, as if for a last appeal to France to come to your rescue!   Oh! what were then our sufferings, and what tears we shed!

"Now," said George, "it is all over!   They are calling aloud to France, our beloved France, unable to come!   It is like a ship in distress, by night, in the open sea, firing her guns for assistance, and no one hears: she must sink in the deep."

Ah! my old town of Phalsbourg, where we used to go to market; where we used to see our own soldiers—our red-trousered soldiery, our merry Frenchmen!   We shall never more see behind our ramparts any but heavy Germans and rough Prussians!   And so it is over!   The earth bears no longer the same children; and men whom we never knew tell us, "You are in our custody: we are your masters!"

Can it be possible?   No! ancient fortress of Vauban, you shall be French again: "Nursery of brave men," as the first Bonaparte called you.   Let our sons come to manhood, and they shall drive from thy walls these lumpish fellows who dare to talk of Germanizing you!

But how our hearts bled on that day! Every one went to hide himself as far back in his house as he could, murmuring, " Oh! my poor Phalsbourg, we cannot help thee; but if our life could deliver thee, we would give it."

Yes! I have lived to behold this, and it is the most terrible sensation I have ever experienced: the thought of meeting Jacob again was no comfort; Grédel herself was listening with pale cheeks, and counting the reports from second to second; and then the tears fell and she cried: " It is over! "

Next day, all the roads were covered with German and Prussian officers galloping rapidly to the *place;* the report ran that the entry would take place the same evening; every one was preparing a small stock of provisions for his son, his relations, his friends, whom he dreaded never more to see alive.

On the morning of the 11th of December, leave was given to start for the town; the sentinels posted at Wechem had orders to allow foot-passengers to pass.

Phalsbourg, with its fifteen hundred Mobiles and its sixty gunners, disdained to capitulate; it surrendered no rifles, no guns, no military stores, no eagles, as Bazaine had done at Metz! The Commander Taillant had not said to his men: " Let us, above all, for the reputation of our army, avoid all acts of

indiscipline, such as the destruction of arms and material of war; since, according to military usage,
strong places and arms will return to France when
peace is signed." No! quite the contrary; he had
ordered the destruction of whatever might prove
useful to the enemy: to drown the gunpowder,
smash rifles, spike the guns, burn up the bedding in
the casemates; and when all this was done, he had
sent a message to the German general: " We have
nothing left to eat! To-morrow I will open the
gates! Do what you please with me! "

Here was a man, indeed!

And the Germans ran, some laughing, others
astonished, gazing at the walls which they had won
without a fight: for they have taken almost every
place without fighting; they have shelled the poor
inhabitants instead of storming the walls; they have
starved the people. They may boast of having
burnt more towns and villages, and killed more
women and children in this one campaign, than all
the other nations in all the wars of Europe since the
Revolution.

But, to be sure, they were a religious people, much
attached to the doctrines of the Gospel, and who
sing hymns with much feeling. Their Emperor
especially, after every successive bombardment, and
every massacre—whilst women, children, and old
men are weeping around their houses destroyed by
the enemy's shells, and from the battle-fields strewn
with heaps of dead are rising the groans and cries of

thousands and thousands of sufferers whose lives are crushed, whose flesh is torn, whose bodies are rent and bleeding!—their Emperor, the venerable man, lifts his blood-stained hands to heaven and thanks God for having permitted him to commit these abominable deeds! Does he look upon God as his accomplice in crime?

Barbarian! one day thou shalt know that in the sight of the Eternal, hypocrisy is an aggravation of crime.

On the 11th of December, then, early in the morning, my wife, Grédel, Cousin George, Marie Anne and myself, having locked up our houses, started, each carrying a little parcel under our arms, to go and embrace our children and our friends—if they yet survived.

The snow was melting, a thick fog was covering the face of the country, and we walked along in single file and in silence, gazing intently upon the German batteries which we saw for the first time, in front of Wechem, by Gerbershoff farm, and at the *Arbre Vert*.

Such desolation! Everything was cut down around the town; no more summer-arbors, no more gardens or orchards, only the vast, naked surface of snow-covered ground, with its hollows all bare; the bullet marks on the ramparts, the embrasures all destroyed.

A great crowd of other village people preceded and followed us; poor old men, women, and a few children; they were walking straight on without paying any attention to each other: all thought of the fate of those they loved, which they would learn within an hour.

Thus we arrived at the gate of France; it stood open and unguarded. The moment we entered, the ruins were seen; houses tottering, streets demolished, here a window left alone, there up in the air a chimney scarcely supported; farther on some doorsteps and no door. In every direction the bombshells had left their tracks.

God of heaven! did we indeed behold such devastation? we did in truth. We all saw it: it was no dream!

The cold was piercing. The townspeople, haggard and pale, stared at us arriving; recognitions took place, men and women approached and took each other by the hand.

"Well?" "Well," was the reply in a hollow whisper, in the midst of the street encumbered with blackened beams of wood. "Have you suffered much?" "Ah! yes."

This was enough: no need for another word; and then we would proceed farther. At every street corner a new scene of horror began.

Catherine and I were seeking Jacob; no doubt Grédel was looking for Jean Baptiste.

We saw our poor Mobiles passing by, scarcely recognizable after those five months. All through the fearful cold these unhappy men had had noth-

ing on but their summer blouses and linen trousers.
Many of them might have escaped and gained their
villages, for the gates had stood open since the evening before; but not a man thought of doing so; it was
not supposed that Mobiles would be treated like
regular soldiers.

On the *place*, in front of the fallen church filled
with its own ruins, we heard, for the first time, that
the garrison were prisoners of war.

The cafés Vacheron, Meyer, and Hoffmann, riddled with balls, were swarming with officers.

We were gazing, not knowing whom to ask after
Jacob, when a cry behind us made us turn round;
and there was Grédel in the arms of Jean Baptiste
Werner!   Then I kept silence; my wife also.
Since she would have it so, well, so let it be; this mat-
ter concerned her much more than it did us.

Jean Baptiste, after the first moment, looked em-
barrassed at seeing us; he approached us with a pale
face, and as we spoke not a word to him, George
shook him by the hand, and cried: " Jean Baptiste,
I know that you have behaved well during this
siege; we have learned it all with pleasure: didn't
we, Christian? didn't we, Catherine? "

What answer could we make?   I said " yes "—
and mother, with tears in her eyes, cried: " Jean
Baptiste, is Jacob not wounded? "

" No, Madame Weber; we have always been very
comfortable together.   There is nothing the matter.   I'll fetch him: only come in somewhere."

" We are going to the Café Hoffmann," said she.
" Try to find him, Jean Baptiste."   And as he
was turning in the direction of the mayoralty-house:

" There," said he, " there he is coming round the
corner by the chemist Rèbe's shop."   And we began
to cry " Jacob! "

And our lad ran, crossing the *place*.

A minute after, we were in each other's arms.

He had on a coarse soldier's cloak, and canvas
trousers; his cheeks were hollow; he stared at us,
and stammered: " Oh, is it you?   You are not all
dead? "

He looked stupefied; and his mother, holding him,
murmured: " It is he! "

She would not relinquish her hold upon him, and
wiped her eyes with her apron.

Grédel and Jean Baptiste followed arm-in-arm,
with George and Marie Anne.   We entered the
Café Hoffmann together; we sat round a table in the
room at the left, and George ordered some coffee,
for we all felt the need of a little warmth.

None of us wished to speak; we were downcast,
and held each other by the hand, gazing in each
other's faces.

The young officers of the Mobiles were talking
together in the next room; we could hear them saying that not one would sign the engagement not to
serve again during the campaign; that they would
all go as prisoners of war, and would accept no other
lot than that of their men.

This idea of seeing our Jacob go off as a prisoner of war, almost broke our hearts, and my wife began to sob bitterly, with her head upon the table.

Jacob would have wished to come back to the mill along with us; I could see this by his countenance; but he was not an officer, and his *parole* was not asked for. And, in spite of all, hearing those spirited young men, who were sacrificing their liberty to discharge a duty, I should myself have said " No: a man must be a man! "

Werner was talking with my cousin: they spoke in whispers; having, no doubt, secret matters to discuss. I saw George slip something into his hand. What could it be? I cannot say; but all at once Jean Baptiste rising from his seat and kissing Grédel without any ceremony before our faces, said that he was on service; that he would not see us again very soon, as after the muster their march would begin, so that we should have to say good-by at once.

He held out both his hands to my wife and then to Marie Anne, after which he went out with George and Grédel, leaving us much astonished.

Jacob and Marie Anne remained with us; in a couple of minutes Grédel and my cousin returned; Grédel, whose eyes were red, sat by the side of Marie Anne without speaking, and we saw that her basket of provisions was gone.

The stir upon the *place* became greater and greater. The drums beat the assembly. the officers

of the Mobiles were coming out.   I then thought I
would ask Jacob what had become of Mathias Heitz;
he told us that the wretched coward had been trembling with fright the whole time of the siege, and
that at last he had fallen ill of fear.   Grédel did
not turn her head to listen; she would have nothing
to do with him!   And, in truth, on hearing this, I
felt I should prefer giving our daughter to our ragman's son than to this fellow Mathias.

The review was then commencing under the tall
trees on the *place*, and Jacob appeared with his
comrades.   No sadder spectacle will ever be seen
than that of our poor lads, about half a hundred
Turcos and a few Zouaves, the remnants of Froeschwiller, all haggard and pale, and their clothes falling to pieces.   They were unarmed, having destroyed their arms before opening the gates.

Presently Jacob ran to us, crying that they were
ordered to their barracks, and that they would have
to start next day before twelve.

Then his eyes filled with tears.   His mother and
I handed him our parcels, in which we had en-
closed three good linen shirts, a pair of shoes almost
new, woollen stockings, and a strong pair of
trousers.

I was wearing upon my shoulders my travelling
cape; I placed it upon his.   Then I slipped into his
pocket a small roll of thalers, and George gave him
two louis.   After this, the tears and lamentations

of the women recommenced; we were obliged to promise to return on the morrow.

The garrison was defiling down the street; Jacob ran to fall in, and disappeared with the rest, near the barracks.

As for Jean Baptiste Werner, we saw him no more.

The German officers were coming and going up and down the town to distribute their troops amongst the townspeople. It was twelve o'clock, and we returned to our village, sadder and more distressed than ever.

And now we knew that Jacob was safe; but we knew also that he was going to be carried, we could not tell where, to the farthest depths of Germany.

My wife arrived home quite ill; the damp weather, her anxiety, her anguish of mind, had cast her down utterly. She went to bed with a shivering fit, and could not return next day to town, nor Grédel, who was taking care of her, so I went alone.

Orders had come to take the prisoners to Lützelbourg. On reaching the square, near the chemist Rèbe's shop, I saw them all in their ranks, moving by twos down the road. The inhabitants had closed their shutters, not to witness this humiliation; for Hessian soldiers, with arms shouldered, were escorting them: our poor boys were advancing between them, their heads hanging sorrowfully down.

I stopped at the chemist's corner, and waited,

"GOOD-BY, MY FATHER! GOOD-BY, MY MOTHER!"

being unable to discern Jacob in the midst of that crowd. All at once I recognized him, and I cried, "Jacob!"' He was going to throw himself into my arms; but the Hessians repulsed me. We both burst into tears, and I went on walking by the side of the escort, crying, "Courage! . . . Write to us. . . . Your mother is not quite well. . . . She could not come. . . . It is not much!"

He answered nothing; and many others who were there had their friends and relations before or behind them.

We wanted to accompany them to Lützelbourg; unhappily, at the gate the Prussians had posted sentinels, who stopped us, pointing their bayonets at us. They would not even allow us to press our children's hands.

On all sides were cries: "Adieu, Jean!" "Adieu, Pierre!" and they replied: "Adieu! Farewell, father!" "Adieu! Farewell, mother!" and then the sighs, the sobs, the tears. . . .

Ah! the Plébiscite, the Plébiscite!

I was compelled to stay there an hour; at last they allowed me to pass. I resumed my way home, my heart rent with anguish. I could see, hear nothing but the cry, "Adieu! Adieu!" of all that crowd; and I thought that men were made to make each other miserable; that it was a pity we were ever born; that for a few days' happiness, acquired by long and painful toil, we had years of endless misery; and that the people of the earth, through their folly, their idleness, their wickedness, their trust in consummate rogues, deserved what they got.

Yes, I could have wished for another deluge: I should have cared less to see the waters rise from the ends of Alsace and cover our mountains, than to be bound under the yoke of the Germans.

In this mood I reached home.

I took care not to tell my wife all that had happened; on the contrary I told her that I had embraced Jacob in my arms for her and for us all; that he was full of spirits, and that he would soon write to us.

CHAPTER XIII

WE were now rid of our Landwehr, who were garrisoned at Phalsbourg, but a part of whom were sent off into the interior. They were indignant, and declared that if they had known that they were to be sent farther, the blockade would have lasted longer; that they would have let the cows, the bullocks, and the bread find their way in, many a time, in spite of their chiefs; and that it was infamous to expose them to new dangers when every man had done his part in the campaign.

There was no enthusiasm in them; but, all the same, they marched in step in their ranks, and were moved some on Belfort, some on Paris.

We learned, through the German newspapers, that they had severer sufferings to endure round Belfort than with us; that the garrison made sorties, and drove them several leagues away; that their dead bodies were rotting in heaps, behind the hedges, covered with snow and mud; that the commander, Denfert, gave them many a heavy dig in the ribs; and every day people coming from Alsace told us that such an one of the poor fellows whom we had known had just been struck down by a ball,

maimed by a splinter or a shell, or bayoneted by our
Mobiles. We could not help pitying them, for they
all had five or six children each, of whom they were
forever talking; and naturally, for when the par-
ent-bird dies the brood is lost.

And all this for the honor and glory of the King
of Prussia, of Bismarck, of Moltke, and a few
heroes of the same stamp, not one of whom has had
a scratch in the chances of war.

How can one help shrugging one's shoulders and
laughing inwardly at seeing these Germans, with
all their education, greater fools than ourselves?
They have won! That is to say, the survivors; for
those who are buried, or who have lost their limbs,
have no great gain to boast of, and can hardly rejoice over the success of the enterprise. They have
gained—what? The hatred of a people who had
loved them; they have gained that they will be
obliged to fight every time their lords or masters
give the order; they have gained that they can say
Alsace and Lorraine are German, which is absolutely no gain whatever; and besides this they have
gained the envy of a vast number of people, and the
distrust of a vast many more, who will end by agreeing together to fall upon them in a body, and treat
them to fire and slaughter and bombardment, of
which they have set us the example.

This is what the peasants, the artisans, and the
bourgeois have gained: as for the chiefs, they have
won some a title, some a pension or an épaulette:

others have the satisfaction of saying, "I am the great So-and-So! I am William, Emperor of Germany; a crown was set on my head at Versailles, whilst thousands of my subjects were biting the dust!"

Alas! notwithstanding all this, these people will die, and in a hundred years will be recognized as barbarians; their names will be inscribed on the roll of the plagues of the human race, and there they will remain to the end of time.

But what is the use of reasoning with such philosophers as these? In time they will acknowledge the truth of what I say!

Now to our story again.

They were fighting furiously round Belfort; our men did not drop off asleep in casements; they occupied posts at a distance all round the place: their sortie from Bourcoigne, and their slaughter of the Bavarians at Haute-Perche, were making a great noise in Alsace.

We learned from the *Indépendance* the battles of Chanzy at Vendôme against the army of Mecklenburg; the fight by General Crémer at Nuits against the army of Von Werder; the retreat of Manteuffel toward Amiens, after having overwhelmed Rouen with forced contributions; the bayonet attack upon the villages around Pont-Noyelles, in which Faidherbe had defeated the enemy; and especially the grand measures of Gambetta, who had at last dissolved the Councils-General named by the Prefects of the Empire, and replaced them by really Republican departmental commissions.

Cousin George highly approved of this step. This was of more importance in his eyes than the decrees of our Prussian Préfet Henckel de Bonnermark; though he had inflicted heavy fines upon the fathers and mothers of the young men who had left home to join the French armies, and had laid Lorraine, already ruined by the invasion, under a contribution of 700,000 livres to compensate the losses suffered by the German mercantile marine; plundering decrees which went nigh to tearing the bread out of our mouths.

Then George passed on to the campaign of Chanzy; for what could be grander than this struggle of a young, inexperienced army, scarcely organized, against forces double their number, commanded by the great Prussian general who had been victorious at Woerth, Sedan, and Metz, over the whole of the Imperial troops?

George especially admired the noble protest of Chanzy, proclaiming to the world the ferocity of the Germans, and pointing out with pride the falsehoods of their generals, who invariably claimed the victory.

" The Commander-in-Chief lays before the army the subjoined protest, which he transmits, under a flag of truce, to the commander of the Prussian troops at Vendôme, with the assurance that his in-

dignation will be shared by all, as well as his desire
to take signal revenge for such insults.

" To the Prussian commander at Vendôme:

" I am informed that unjustifiable acts of violence have been committed by troops under your
orders upon the unoffending inhabitants of St.
Calais. In spite of our humane treatment of your
sick and wounded, your officers have exacted money
and commanded pillage. Such conduct is an abuse
of power, which will weigh heavily upon your consciences, and which the patriotism of our people will
enable them to endure; but what I cannot permit
is, that you should add to these injuries insults
which you know full well to be entirely gratuitous.

" You have asserted that we were defeated; that
assertion is false. We have beaten you and held
you in check since the 4th of this month. You
have presumed to attach the name of coward to
men who are prevented from answering you; pretending that they were coerced by the Government
of National Defence, which, as you said, compelled
them to resist when they wanted peace, and you
were offering it. I deny this: I deny it by the
right given me by the resistance of entire France
and this army which confronts you, and which you
have been hitherto unable to vanquish. This communication reaffirms what our resistance ought already to have taught you. Whatever may be the
sacrifices still left us to endure, we will struggle to
the very end, without truce or pity; since now we

are resisting the attacks not of loyal and honorable enemies but of devastating bands who aim solely at the ruin and disgrace of a nation, which itself is striving to maintain its honor, rank, and independence. To the generous treatment we have accorded to your prisoners and wounded, your reply is insolence, fire, and plunder. I therefore protest, with deep indignation, in the name of humanity and the rights of men, which you will trample underfoot.

" The present order will be read before the troops at three consecutive muster-calls.

" CHANZY, *Commander-in-Chief.*

"HEAD-QUARTERS, *Le Mans, 26th December, 1870.*"

These are the words of an honorable man and a patriot, words to make a man lift up his head.

And as Manteuffel, whose only merit consists in having been during his youth the boon companion of the pious William; as this old courtier followed the same system as Frederick Charles and Mecklenburg, of lowering us to raise themselves, and to get their successes cheap; General Faidherbe also obliged him to abate his pride after the affair of Pont-Noyelles.

" The French army have left in the hands of the enemy only a few sailors, surprised in the village of Daours. It has kept its positions, and has waited in vain for the enemy until two o'clock in the afternoon of the next day."

This was plain speaking, and it was clear on which side good faith was to be looked for.

Thus, after having opposed a million of men to 300,000 conscripts, these Germans were even now obliged to lie in order not to discourage their armies.

Of course they could not but prevail in the end: France had had no time to prepare anew, to arm, and to recover herself after this disgraceful capitulation of the *honest man* and his friend Bazaine; but still she resisted with terrible energy, and the Prussians at last became anxious for peace too, and wished for it, perhaps, even more than ourselves.

The proof of this is the numberless petitions of the Germans entreating King William to bombard Paris.

Humane Germans, fathers of families, pious men, seated quietly by their counters at Hamburg, Cologne, or Berlin, in every town and village of Germany, eating and drinking heartily, warming their fat legs before the fire during this winter of unexampled severity, cried to their king at Christmas time to bombard Paris, and set fire to the houses—to kill and burn fathers and mothers of families like themselves, but reduced to famine in their own dwellings!

Have any but the Germans ever done the like?

We too have besieged German towns, but never have petitions been sent up like this under the Republic, or under the Empire, to ask our soldiers to do more injury than war between brave men re-

quires. And since that period we have never use-
lessly shelled houses inhabited by inoffensive persons; and even when we have had to bombard
walled towns, warning was given, as at Odessa and
everywhere else, to give helpless people time to de-
part for the interior, if they did not want to run
the risk of meeting with stray bullets; and permission was given to old men, women, and children
to come out—a privilege never granted by the
Prussians.

Ah! the French may not be so pious, so
learned, and so good as the *good German people*,
but they have better hearts and feelings of compassion; they have less of the Gospel upon their
lips, but they have it in the bottoms of their souls.
They are not hypocrites, and therefore we Alsacians and Lorrainers had rather remain French than
belong to the *good German people*, and be like
them.

Indignities without a precedent have been committed by them: " Shell—bombard—burn, in the
name of Heaven! Set fire everywhere with petroleum bombs!—You are too gracious a king!—Your
scruples betray too much weakness for this Babylon: Bombard quick: Bombardments have succeeded better than anything else. Sire, your good
and faithful people entreat you to bombard everything—leave nothing standing! "

Oh! scoundrels!—rascals!—if you have so often
played the saint for fifty years; if you have talked

so edifyingly about friendship, brotherhood, and
the alliance of nations, it was because you did not
then think yourselves the strongest; now that you
think you are, you piously bombard women, old
men, and children, in the name of the Saviour!
Faugh! it is simply disgusting!

Every time that Cousin George read these assas-
sins' petitions, he would spring off his chair and
cry: " Now I know what to think of fanatics of
every religion. These men have no need to play
the hypocrite: their religion does not oblige them
to it. Well, they play the Jesuit for the love of it,
better than we do by profession. May they be
execrated and despised perpetually."

Then he dilated with much warmth of feeling
upon the kind reception which the Parisians, in former days, used to accord to the Germans, for forty
years and more. Men who came to seek a livelihood among us, without a penny, lean, humble,
half-clad, with a little bundle of old rags under their
arms, asking for credit, even in George's and Marie
Anne's little inn, for a basin of broth, a bit of meat,
and a glass of wine, were kindly received; they
were cheered up, and situations found for them:
everybody was anxious to put them in the right way,
to explain to them what they did not know. Soon
they grew fat and flourishing, and gained assurance; by servility they would win the confidence
of the head-clerk, who showed them all about the
business; and then some fine morning it was noised

19

about that the head-clerk was discharged and the
German was in his place. He had had a private
interview with the head partner, and had proposed
to do the work for half the salary. Of course the
partners are always glad to have good workmen,
humble and obsequious, and, above all, cheap.

George had witnessed this fifty times.

But people did not get angry; they would say,
" The poor fellow must earn a living somehow.
The other is a Frenchman: he will very soon secure
another place."

And it was thus that the Germans slipped quietly
into the shoes of those who had received them kindly and taught them their trade.

A few old clerks used to get angry; but they
were always held to be in the wrong. " *That good
German*" was justified! He had not meddled;
everything had gone on simply and naturally.

And twenty, thirty, fifty thousand Germans
used thus to come and prosper in Paris; and then
they would get a holiday to take a turn home and
exhibit the flesh and fat they had gained, and their
gold trinkets.

If they happened to be professors of languages
or newspaper correspondents, they were sure to
break out down there against the corruption of manners in this " modern Babylon." Great hulking
fellows they were, with long hooded cloaks, and
gold or silver spectacles, who had scandalized even
their doorkeepers by bringing home night after

night "princesses" of Mabile and elsewhere, singing, drinking like a sponge, shaking all the house,
and preventing people from sleeping; bringing,
besides, other colleagues of the same stamp, and
leading disgraceful lives!

But it is the fashion in Germany to cry out
against "modern Babylon." It flatters the secret
envy of the Germans, and establishes the character of the speaker for seriousness, gravity, and influence; as a man worthy of every consideration,
and who may hope—if his situation in Paris is
permanent—for the hand of "Herr Rector's" or
"Herr Doctor's" fair daughter: for in that country they are all doctors in something or other. He
had gone off as cold and comfortless as the stones in
the street; he would have become a school-master,
or a small clerk at a couple of hundred thalers all
his life, in old Germany. He weighed heavily
upon his poor father, encumbered with a dozen
children; but he had grown fat, well-feathered,
and well-trained in Paris; and there he is now virt-
uously indignant against our own townswomen:
against the degenerate race which has given him
his daily bread, and pulled him out of the mire, instead of kicking him downstairs.

This German fellow used to be republican, so-
cialist, communist, etc. He had fled from Cologne,
or elsewhere, in consequence of the events of 1848.
Nothing in our opinion was sufficiently strong, de-
cided, or advanced for him. He spouted about his

sacrifices for the universal Republic, his terrible campaign in the Duchy of Baden against the Prussians, the loss of his place, of his property. We thought, what sufferings he has endured! Surely, the Germans are the first Democrats in the world!

But now this very same gentleman is the most faithful servant of his Majesty William, King of Prussia, Emperor of Germany. No doubt he talks at Berlin of the sacrifices which he has made to the noble cause of Germany, the battles he has fought in the public-houses amongst the broken bottles of beer which he has been swallowing by the dozen, to reclaim old Alsace, where lie deep the roots of the Germanic tongue. He abounds in indignation against the " modern Babylon; " his name stands at the head of the earliest petitions that Babylon should be burned, till nothing but ashes were left: that that race of madmen should be exterminated; and as during his residence in France he has rendered police services to Bismarck, he is pretty sure to obtain a post in Alsace-Lorraine, where all these old German spies are swooping down to Germanize us.

Thus spoke George, in his indignation; and Marie Anne, after listening to him, said: " Ah, it is too true! Those men did deceive us; and they did not even pay their debts. Some fine morning, when their bill had run up, three-fourths of them would make a start, and they were never heard of again. I have never had any confidence in any of them, except the crossing-sweepers and the shoe-blacks: one knew where to find them; but as for the professors, the newspaper correspondents, the inventors, the book-worms—they have done us too many bad turns; and they were too overbearing. They were filled with hatred and envy of our nation."

Since the departure of the Landwehr, we were able to speak more freely: those sulky eavesdroppers were no longer spying upon us, and we felt the relief.

Paris, as we saw in the *Indépendance*, was making sorties. The Gardes Mobiles and the National Guards were being drilled and becoming better skilled in the use of arms. Our sailors, in the forts, were admirable. But the Germans grew stronger from day to day; they had brought such enormous guns—called Krupp's—that the railways were unable to bear them, the tunnels were not high enough to give them passage, and the bridges gave way under their ponderous mass. This proves that if the bombardment had not yet commenced, in spite of the innumerable petitions of *the good Germans*, it was not for want of will on the part of his Majesty King William, Messieurs Moltke, Bismarck, and all those good men. Oh, no! our forts and our sorties hampered them a good deal in gaining their positions!

At last, about the end of December, " by the grace of God," as the Emperor William said, they began by bombarding a few forts, and were soon enabled to reach houses, hospitals, churches, and museums.

George and Marie Anne knew all these places by name, and these ferocious acts drew from them cries of horror. I, my wife, and Grédel could not understand these accounts: having never been in Paris, we could not form an idea of it.

The German news-writers knew them, however; for daily they told us how great a misfortune it was to be obliged to shell such rich libraries, such beautiful galleries of pictures, such magnificent monuments, and gardens so richly stocked with plants and rare collections; that it made their hearts bleed: they professed themselves inconsolable at being driven to such an extremity by the evil dispositions of those who presumed to defend their property, their homes, their wives, their children, contrary to every principle of justice! They pitied the French for their want of common-sense; they said that their brains were addled; that they were in their dotage, and uttered similar absurdities.

But every time that they lost men, their fury rose: " The Germans are a sacred race! Kill Germans! a superior race! it is a high crime. The French, the Swiss, the Danes, the Dutch, Belgians, Poles, Hungarians, even the Russians, are destined to be successively devoured by the Germans." I have heard this with my own ears! Yes, the Russians, too, they cannot dispense with the Germans;

their manufactures, their trade, their sciences come
to them from Germany; they, too, belong to an
inferior race. The renowned Gortschakoff is unworthy to dust the boots of Monsieur Bismarck, and
the Emperor of Russia is most fortunate in being
allied by marriage to the Emperor William: it is a
glorious prerogative for him!

The captain, Floegel, used often to repeat these
things; and besides, the Germans all say the same
at this time; you have but to listen to them: they are
too strong now to need to hide their ambition. They
think they are conferring a great honor upon us
Alsacians and Lorrainers in acknowledging us as
cousins, and gathering us to themselves out of love.
We were a superior race in "that degenerate
France;" but we are about to become little boys
again amongst the noble German people. We are
the last new-comers into Germany, and shall require
time to acquire the noble German virtues: to become hypocrites, spies, bombarders, plunderers; to
learn to receive slaps and kicks without winking.
But what would you have? You cannot regenerate
a people in a day.

The Prussians had announced that Paris would
surrender after an eight-days' bombardment; but as
the Parisians held out; as there were passing by Saverne innumerable convoys of wounded, scorched,
maimed, and sick by thousands; as General Faidherbe had gained a victory in the North, the victory
of Bapaume, in which we had driven the Prussians

from the field of battle all covered with their dead, and in which the enemy had left in our hands not only all their wounded, but a great number of prisoners; as the inhabitants of Paris had only one fault to find with General Trochu, that he did not lead them out to the great battle, and they were raising the cry of " victory or death; " since Chanzy, repulsed at Le Mans, was falling back in good order, while in the midst of the deep snows of January and the severest cold, Bourbaki was still advancing upon Belfort; and Garibaldi with his francs-tireurs was not losing courage; since the Germans were suffering from exhaustion; and it takes but an hour, a minute, to turn all the chances against one; and if Faidherbe had gained his victory nearer to Paris a great sortie would have ensued, which might have entirely changed the face of things—for these and other reasons, I suppose, all at once there was much talk of humanity, mildness, peace; of the convocation of an assembly at Bordeaux, where the true representatives of the nation might settle everything, and restore order to our unhappy France.

As soon as these rumors began to spread, George said that Alsace and German Lorraine were to be sacrificed; that our egotists had come to an understanding with the Germans; that all our defeats had been unable to cast us down, and the Prussians were better pleased than ourselves to come to an end of it, for they needed peace, having no reserves left to throw into the scale; that Gambetta's enthusiasm

and courage might at once win over the most timid,
and that then the Germans would be lost, because a
people that rises in a body, and at the same time pos-
sesses arms and munitions of war in a third of our
provinces, such a nation in the long run would crush
all resistance.

I could say nothing.   Even to-day I do not know
what might have happened.   When Cousin George
spoke, I was of his opinion; and then, left to my own
reflections, when I saw that immense body of prisoners delivered by Bonaparte and Bazaine all at
once; all our arms surrendered at Metz and Strasbourg, and our fortresses fallen one after another;
then the ill-will, to say the least of all the former
place-holders under the Empire, three-fourths of
whom were retaining their posts—I thought it quite
possible that we might wage against the Germans a
war much more dangerous than the first; that we
might destroy many more of the enemy at the same
time with ourselves; but, if I had been told to
choose, I should have found it hard to decide.

Of course, if the Prussians had been defeated in
the interior, before abandoning our country, they
would have ruined us utterly, and set fire to every
village.   I have myself several times heard a
Hauptmann at Phalsbourg say, " You had better
pray for us!   For woe to you, if we should be repulsed!   All that you have hitherto suffered would
be but a joke.   We would not leave one stone upon
another in Alsace and Lorraine.   That would be

our defensive policy.   So pray for the success of our armies.   If we should be obliged to retire, you would be much to be pitied! "

I can hear these words still.

But I would not have minded even that: I would have sacrificed house, mill, and all, if we could only have finally been victorious and remained French; but I was in doubt.   Misery makes a man lose, not courage, but confidence; and confidence is half the battle won.

About that time we received Jacob's first letter; he was at Rastadt, and I need not tell you what a relief it was to his mother to think that she could go and see him in one day.

Here is the letter, which I copy for you:

" MY DEAR FATHER AND MY DEAR MOTHER,—
" THANK God, I am not dead yet; and I should be glad to hear from you, if possible.   You must know that, on arriving at Lützelbourg, we were sent off by railway in cattle-trucks.   We were thirty or forty together; and we were not so comfortable as to be able to sit, since there were no seats, nor to breathe the air, as there was only a small hole to each side.   Those of us who wanted to breathe or to drink, found a bayonet before our noses, and charitable souls were forbidden to give us a glass of water. We remained in this position more than twenty hours, standing, unable even to stoop a little.   Many were taken ill; and as for me, my thigh bones seemed

to run up into my ribs, so that I could scarcely breathe, and I thought with my comrades that they had undertaken to exterminate us after some new fashion.

" During the night we crossed the Rhine, and then we went on rolling along the line, and travelling along the other side as far as Rastadt, where we are now. The hindmost trucks, where I was, remained; the others went on into Germany. We were first put into the casemates under the ramparts; damp, cold vaults, where many others who had arrived before us were dying like flies in October. The straw was rotting—so were the men. The doctors in the town and those of the Baden regiments were afraid of seeing sickness spreading in the country; and since the day before yesterday those who are able to walk have been made to come out. They have put us into large wooden huts covered in with tarred felt, where we have each received a fresh bundle of straw. Here we live, seated on the ground. We play at cards, some smoke pipes, and the Badeners mount guard over us. The hut in which I am—about three times as large as the old market-hall of Phalsbourg—is situated between two of the town bastions; and if by some evil chance any of us took a fancy to revolt, we should be so overwhelmed with shot and shell that in ten minutes not a man would be left alive. We are well aware of this, and it keeps our indignation within bounds against these Badeners, who treat us like cattle. We get food twice a day—a little haricot or millet soup, with a very small piece of meat about the size of a finger: just enough to keep us alive. After such a blockade as ours, something more is wanted to set us up; our noses stand out of our faces like crows' bills, our cheeks sink in deeper and deeper; and but for the guns pointed at us, we should have risen a dozen times.

"I hope, however, I may get over it; father's cloak keeps me warm, and Cousin George's louis are very useful. With money you can get anything; only here you have to pay five times the value of what you want, for these Badeners are worse than Jews; they all want to make their fortunes in the shortest time out of the unhappy prisoners.

"I use my money sparingly. Instead of smoking, I prefer buying from time to time a little meat or a very small bottle of wine to fortify my stomach; it is much better for my health, and is the more enjoyable when your appetite is good. My appetite has never failed. When the appetite fails, comes the typhus. I do not expect I shall catch typhus. But, if it please God to let me return to Rothalp, the very first day I will have a substantial meal of ham, veal pie, and red wine. I will also invite my comrades, for it is a dreadful thing to be hungry. And now, to tell you the truth, I repent of having never given a couple of sous to some poor beggar who asked me for alms in the winter, saying that he had eaten nothing. I know what hunger is now, and

I feel sorry. If you meet one in this condition,
father or mother, invite him in, give him bread, let
him warm himself, and give him two or three sous
when he goes. Fancy that you are doing it for your
son; it will bring me comfort.

"Perhaps mother will be able to come and see
me: not many people are allowed to come near us;
a permit must be had from the commandant at Rastadt. These Badeners and these Bavarians, who
were said to be such good Catholics, treat us as hardly as the Lutherans. I remember now that Cousin
George used to say that was only part of the play:
he was right. Instead of only praising and singing
to our Lord, they would much better follow His example.

"Let mother try! Perhaps the commandan
may have had a good dinner; then he will be in a
good temper, and will give her leave to come into
the huts: that is my wish. And now, to come to
an end, I embrace you all a hundred times; father,
mother, Grédel, Cousin George, and Cousin Marie
Anne.

"Your son,
"JACOB WEBER.

"I forgot to tell you that several out of our battalion escaped from Phalsbourg before and after the
muster-call of the prisoners: in the number was Jean
Baptiste Werner. It is said that they have joined
Garibaldi: I wish I was with them. The Germans

tell us that if they can catch them they will shoot them down without pity; yes, but they won't let themselves be caught; especially Jean Baptiste; he is a soldier indeed!   If we had but two hundred thousand of his sort, these Badeners would not be bothering us with their haricot-soup, and their cannons full of grape-shot.

"RASTADT, *January* 6, 1871."

From that moment my wife only thought of seeing Jacob again; she made up her bundle, put into her basket sundry provisions, and in a couple of days started for Rastadt.

I put no hindrance in her way, thinking she would have no rest until she had embraced our boy.

Grédel was quite easy, knowing that Jean Baptiste Werner was with Garibaldi.   I even think she had had news from him; but she showed us none of his letters, and had again begun to talk about her marriage-portion, reminding me that her mother had had a hundred louis, and that she ought to have the same.   She insisted upon knowing where our money was hidden, and I said to her, "Search; if you can find it, it is yours."

Girls who want to be married are so awfully selfish; if they can only have the man they want, house, family, native land, all is one to them.   They are not all like that; but a good half.   I was so annoyed with Grédel that I began to wish her Jean Baptiste

would come back, that I might marry them and
count out her money.

But more serious affairs were then attracting the
eyes of all Alsace and France.

Gambetta had been blamed for having detached
Bourbaki's army to our succor by raising the blockade of Belfort. It has been said that this movement enabled the combined forces of Prince Frederick Charles, and of Mecklenburg, to fall upon
Chanzy and overwhelm him, and that our two
central armies ought to have naturally supported
each other. Possibly! I even believe that Gambetta committed a serious error in dividing our
forces: but, it must be acknowledged, that if the
winter had not been against us—if the cold had not,
at that very crisis of our fate, redoubled in intensity,
preventing Bourbaki from advancing with his guns
and warlike stores with the rapidity necessary to prevent De Werder from fortifying his position and
receiving reinforcements—Alsace would have been
delivered, and we might even have attacked Germany itself by the Grand Duchy of Baden. Then
how many men would have risen in a moment!
Many times George and I, watching these movements, said to each other: " If they only get to
Mutzig, we will go! "

Yes, in war everything cannot succeed; and when
you have against you not only the enemy, but frost,
ice, snow, bad roads; whilst the enemy have the railroads, which they had been stupidly allowed to take

at the beginning of the campaign, and are receiving without fatigue or danger, troops, provisions, munitions of war, whatever they want; then if good plans don't turn out successful, it is not the last but the first comers who are to be blamed.

But for the heavy snows which blocked up the roads, Bourbaki would have surprised Werder. The Germans were expecting this, for all at once the requisitions began again. The Landwehr, this time from Metz, and commanded by officers in spectacles, began to pass through our villages; they were the last that we saw; they came from the farthest extremity of Prussia. I heard them say that they had been three days and three nights on the railway; and now they were continuing their road to Belfort by forced marches, because other troops from Paris were crowding the Lyons railway.

George could not understand how men should come from Paris, and said: " Those people are lying! If the troops engaged in the siege were coming away, the Parisians would come out and follow them up."

At the same time we learned that the Germans were evacuating Dijon, Gray, Vesoul, places which the francs-tireurs of Garibaldi immediately occupied; that Werder was throwing up great earthworks against Belfort; things were looking serious; the last forces of Germany were coming into action.

Then, too, the *Indépendance* talked of nothing but peace, and the convocation of a National Assem-

bly at Bordeaux; the English newspapers began
again to commiserate our loss, as they had done at
the beginning of the war, saying that after the first
battle her Majesty the Queen would interpose between us. I believe that if the French had conquered, the English Government would have cried,
"Halt—enough! too much blood has flown already."

But as we were conquered, her Majesty did not
come and separate us; no doubt she was of opinion
that everything was going on very favorably for her
son-in-law, the good Fritz!

So all this acting on the part of the newspapers
was beginning again; and if Bourbaki's attempt had
prospered, the outcries, the fine phrases, the tender
feelings for our poor human race, civilization and
international rights would have redoubled, to prevent us from pushing our advantages too far.

Unhappily, fortune was once more against us.
When I say fortune, let me be understood: the Germans, who had no more forces to draw from their
own country, still had some to spare around Paris,
which they could dispose of without fear: they felt
no uneasiness in that quarter, as we have learned
since.

If General Trochu had listened to the Parisians,
who were unanimous in their desire to fight, Manteuffel could not have withdrawn from the besieging
force 80,000 men to crush Bourbaki, 120 leagues
away; nor General Van Goeben 40,000 to fall upon

20

Faidherbe in the north; nor could others again have joined Frederick Charles to overwhelm Chanzy. This is clear enough!   The fortune of the Germans at this time was not due to the genius of their chiefs,, or the courage and the number of their men; but to the inaction of General Trochu!   Yes, this is the fact!   But it must also be owned that Gambetta, Bourbaki, Faidherbe, and Chanzy ought to have allowed for this.

However, France has not perished yet; but she has been most unfortunate!

The cold was intense.   Bourbaki was approaching Belfort; he took Esprels and Villersexel at the point of the bayonet; then all Alsace rejoiced to hear that he was at Montbéliard, Sar-le-Château, Vyans, Comte-Hénaut and Chusey; retaking all this land of good people, more ill-fated still than we, since they knew not a word of German, and that bad race bore them ill-will in consequence.

Our confidence was returning.   Every evening George and I, by the fireside, talked of these affairs; reading the paper three or four times over, to get at something new.

My wife had returned from Rastadt full of indignation against the Badeners, for not having allowed her to see Jacob, or even to send him the provisions she had brought.   She had only seen, at a distance, the wooden huts, with their four lines of sentinels, the palisades, and the ditches that surrounded them.   Grédel, Marie Anne, and she, talked only of these poor prisoners; vowing to make a pilgrimage to Marienthal if Jacob came back safe and sound.

Fatigue, anxiety, the high price of provisions, the fear of coming short altogether if the war went on, all this gave us matter for serious reflection; and yet we went on hoping, when the *Indépendance* brought us the report of General Chanzy upon the combats at Montfort, Champagne, Parigné, l'Evêque, and other places where our columns, overpowered by the 120,000 men of Frederick Charles and the Duke of Mecklenburg, had been obliged to retire to their last lines around Le Mans.   That evening, as we were going home upon the stroke of ten, George said: " I don't believe much in pilgrimages, although several of my old shipmates in the *Boussole* had full confidence in our Lady of Good Deliverance: I have never made any vows; these are no part of my principles; but I promise to drink two bottles of good wine with Christian in honor of the Republic, and to distribute one for every poor man in the village if we gain the great battle of to-morrow. According to Chanzy our army is driven to bay; it has fallen back upon its last position, and the great blow will be struck. Good-night."

" Good-night, George and Marie Anne."

We went out by moonlight, the hoar-frost was glittering on the ground; it was the 15th of January, 1871.

The next day no *Indépendance* arrived, nor the next day; it often had missed, and would come three or four numbers together. Fresh rumors had spread; there was a report of a lost battle; the Land-wehr at Phalsbourg were rejoicing and drinking champagne.

On the 18th, about two in the afternoon, the foot-postman Michel arrived. I was waiting at my cousin's. We were walking up and down, smoking and looking out of the windows; Michel was still in the passage, when George opened the door and cried: "Well?" "Here they are, Monsieur Weber."

My cousin sat at his desk. "Now we will see," said he, changing color.

But instead of beginning with the first, he opened the second, and read aloud that report of Chanzy's in which he said that all was going on well the evening before; but that a panic which seized upon the Breton Mobiles had disordered the army, without the possibility of either he or the Vice-Admiral Jaurréguiberry being able to check or stop it; so that the Prussians had rushed pell-mell into the unhappy city of Le Mans, mingled with our own troops, and taken a large body of prisoners.

I saw the countenance of my cousin change every moment; at last, he flung the journal upon the table, crying: "All is lost!"

It was as if he had pierced my heart with a knife. Yet I took up the paper and read to the end.

Chanzy had not lost all hope of rallying his army at Laval, and Gambetta was hastening to join him, to support him with his courageous spirit.

" There now," said George, " look at that! "

Placiard was passing the house arm-in-arm with a Landwehr officer, followed by a few men; they were making requisitions, and entered the house opposite. " There is the Plébiscite in flesh and blood. Now that scoundrel is working for his Imperial Majesty William I., for the Germans have their emperor, as we have had ours; they will soon learn the cost of glory; each has his turn! By and by, when the reins are tightened, these poor Germans will be looking in every direction to see if the French are not revolting; but France will be tranquil: they themselves will have riveted their own chains, and their masters will draw the reins tighter and tighter, saying: ' Now, then, Mechle!* Attention! eyes right; eyes left. Ah! you lout, do you make a wry face? I will show you that might is right in Germany, as everywhere else, if you don't know it already. Whack ! how do you like that, Mechle? Aha! did you think you were getting victories for German Fatherland and German liberty, idiot? You find out now that it was to put yourself again under the yoke, as after 1815; just to show you the difference between the noble German lord and a brute of your own sort. Get on, Mechle! ' "

* Nickname for the Germans, answering to the English " John Bull," and the French " Jaques Bonhomme."

George exclaimed: " How miserable to be surprised and deluged as we have been daily by six hundred thousand Germans, and to have our hands
bound like culprits, without arms, munitions, orders,
chiefs, or anything! Ah! the deputies of the majority who voted for war would not demand compulsory service; they feared to arm the nation.
They would not risk the bodies of their own sons;
the people alone should fight to defend their places,
their salaries, their châteaux, their property of every
sort! Miserable self-seekers! they are the cause of
our ruin! their names should be exposed in every
commune, to teach our children to execrate them."

He was becoming embittered, and it is not sur-
prising, for every day we heard of fresh reverses :
first the surrender of Veronne, just when Faidherbe
was coming to deliver it, and the retreat of our army
of the North upon Lille and Cambrai, before the
overwhelming forces of Van Goeben, fresh from
Paris; then the grand attack of Bourbaki from
Montbéliard to Mont Vaudois, which he had pur-
sued three successive days, the 15th, 16th, and 17th
January without success, on account of the reinforcements which Werder had received, and the horrible state of the roads, broken up by the rain and
the snow; lastly, the arrival of Manteuffel, with his
80,000 men, also from Paris—to cut off his retreat.

Then we understood that the Landwehr had been
right in telling us that they were getting reinforcements from Paris; and George, who understood such

things better than I, suddenly conceived a horror for those who were commanding there.

" Either," he said, " the Parisians are afraid to fight—which I cannot believe, for I know them— or the men in command are incapable—or traitors. Hitherto relieving armies have been sent in support of a besieged city; now we see the besiegers of a city twice as strong as themselves in men, arms, and munitions of every kind, detaching whole armies to crush our troops fighting in the provinces: the thing is incredible! I am certain that the Parisians are demanding to be led out, especially as they are suffering from famine. Well, if sorties were taking place, the Germans would want all their men down there, and would be unable to come and overwhelm our already overtasked armies."

Let them explain these things as they will, George was right. Since the Germans were able to send away from Paris 40,000 men in one direction, and 80,000 in another, evidently they were free to undertake what they pleased; instead of surrounding the city with troops, they might have set helmets and cloaks upon sticks all round, for scarecrows, as they do to keep sparrows out of a corn-field.

Here, then, is how we have lost: it was the incapacity of the man who was commanding at Paris, and the weakness of the Government of Defence— and especially of Monsieur Jules Favre!—who, when they ought to have replaced this orator by a man of action, as Gambetta demanded, had not the courage to fulfil their duty.   Everybody knows this; why not say it openly?

The only thing which cheered us a little about the end of this terrible month of January, was to learn that the francs-tireurs had blown up the bridge of Fontenoy, on the railroad between Nancy and Toul. But our joy was not of long duration; for three or four days after, proclamations posted at the door of the mayoralty-house gave notice that the Germans had utterly consumed the village of Fontenoy, to punish the inhabitants for not having denounced the francs-tireurs; and that all we Lorrainers were condemned, for the same offence, to pay an extraordinary contribution of ten millions to his Majesty, the Emperor of Germany.   At the same time, as the French workmen were refusing to repair this bridge, the Prussian prefect of La Menotte wrote to the Mayor of Nancy:

"If to-morrow, Tuesday, January 24, at twelve o'clock, five hundred men from the dockyards of the city are not at the station, first the foremen, then a certain number of the workmen, will be arrested and shot immediately."

This prefect's name was Renard—"Count Renard."

I mention this that his name may not be forgotten.

But all this was nothing, compared with what was to follow.   One morning the Prussians had given me a few sacks of corn to grind; I dared not refuse

to work for them, as they would have crushed me
with blows and requisitions: they might have carried me off nearly to Metz again, they might even
have shot me. I had pleaded the snow, the ice, the
failure of the water, which prevented me from
grinding; unfortunately, rain had fallen in abundance, the snow was melting, the mill-dam was full,
and on the 2d or 3d of February (I am not sure
which, I am so confused) I was piling up the sacks
of that wicked set in my mill; Father Offran and
Catherine were helping; Grédel, upstairs, was dress-
ing herself, after sweeping the house and lighting
the kitchen fire. It was about eight o'clock in the
morning, when looking out into the street by
chance, where the water was rattling down the gut-
ters, I saw George and Marie Anne coming.

My cousin was taking long strides, his wife coming after him; farther on a Landwehr was coming
too: the people were sweeping before their doors,
without caring how they bespattered the passers-by.
George, near the mill, cried out, " Do you know
what is going on? "

" No—what? "

" Well, an armistice has been concluded for
twenty-one days; the Paris forts are given up: the
Prussians may set fire to the city when they please.
Now they may send all their troops and all their
artillery against Bourbaki; for the armistice does
not extend to the operations in the east."

George was pale with excitement, his voice shook.

Grédel, at the top of the stairs, was hastily twisting her hair into a knot.

" Look, Christian," said my cousin, pulling a paper out of his pocket; " the armies of Bourbaki and Garibaldi are surrendered by this armistice. Manteuffel has come down from Paris with 80,000 men to occupy the passes of the Jura in their rear: the unfortunate men are caught as in a vice, between him and Werder; and all who have escaped from the hands of the Prussians and taken service again, like our poor Mobiles of Phalsbourg, will be shot! "

While cousin was speaking, Grédel had come downstairs, without even putting on her slippers; she was leaning against him, as pale as death, trying to read over his shoulder; when suddenly she tore the paper from his hands. George wished he had said nothing; but it was too late!

Grédel, after having read with clinched teeth, ran off like a mad woman, uttering fearful screams: " Oh! the wretches! . . . Oh! my poor Jean Baptiste! . . . Oh! the thieves! . . . Oh! my poor Jean Baptiste! "

She seemed to be seeking something to fight with. And as we stood confounded at her outcries, I said: " Grédel, for Heaven's sake don't scandalize us in this way. The people will hear you from the other end of the village! " She answered in a fury: " Hold your tongue! You are the cause of it all! "

" I! " said I, indignantly.

"Yes, you!" she shrieked, with a terrible flashing in her eyes: "you, with your Plébiscite; deceiving everybody by promising them peace! You deserve to be along with Bazaine and the rest of them."

And my wife cried: "That girl will be the death of us."

She had sat down upon the stairs. Marie Anne, with her hands clasped, said: "Do forgive her; her mind is going."

Never had I felt so humbled; to be treated thus by my own daughter! But Grédel respected nothing now; and Cousin George, trying to get in a word, she exclaimed: "You! you! an old soldier! Are you not ashamed of staying here, instead of going to fight? The Landwehr are as old as you, with their gray hairs and their spectacles; they don't make speeches; they all march. And that's why we are beaten!"

At last I became furious; and I was looking for my cowhide behind the door, to bring her to her senses, when, unfortunately, a Landwehr came in to ask if the flour was ready. The moment Grédel caught sight of him, she uttered such a savage shriek that my ears still tingle with it, and in a second she had laid hold of her hatchet; George had scarcely time to seize her by her twisted back hair, when the hatchet had flown from her hand, whizzing through the air, and was quivering three inches deep in the door-post.

The Landwehr, an elderly man, with great eyes and a red nose, had seen the steel flash past close to his ear; he had heard it whiz, and as Grédel was struggling with George, crying: " Oh, the villain; I have missed him! " he turned, and ran off at the top of his speed. I ran to the mill-dam, supposing he was going to the mayor's, but no, he ran a great deal farther than that, and never stopped till he reached Wechem.

Then Grédel became aware that she had made a mistake; she went up into her room, put on her shoes, took her basket, went into the kitchen for a knife and a loaf, and then she left the house; running down the other side of the hill to gain the Krapenfelz, where our cow was with several others, under the charge of the old rag-dealer.

" This is a very bad business," said George, fixing his eyes upon me; " that Landwehr will denounce you: this evening the Prussian gendarmes will be here. I'm sure I don't know, my poor Christian, where you got that girl from; amongst those who have gone before us, there must have been some very different from your poor mother, and grandmother Katherine."

" What would you have," said Marie Anne; " she is fond of her Jean Baptiste." And I thought: " If he but had her now; it is not I would refuse them permission to marry now; no, not I. I only wish they were married already! "

I was thinking how I might settle this dangerous business. George said we must overtake the Landwehr, and slip three or four cent-sous pieces in his hand, to induce him to hold his tongue: the Prussians are softened with money. But where could he be found now? How was he to be overtaken? I had no longer my two beautiful nags. So I resolved to leave it all to Providence.

To my great surprise, the Landwehr never returned. That same day two other Germans, with Lieutenant Hartig, came to take an invoice of the flour, without mentioning that affair: one would have thought that nothing had occurred. The next day, and the day after that, we were still in painful expectation; but that man gave no sign of appearing. No doubt he must have been a marauder; one of those base fellows who enter houses without orders, to receive requisitions of every kind, to sell again in the neighboring villages; such things had been done more than once since the arrival of the Germans. This is the conclusion I came to by and by; but at that time the fear of seeing that fellow returning with the gendarmes, left me no peace; every minute my wife, standing at the door, would say: "Christian, run! Here are the Prussian gendarmes coming!"

For a cow, or a Jew astride upon a donkey at the end of the road, she would throw one into fits.

Grédel remained a week in the woods in the Krapenfelz. Every day the woodman brought her news of what was going on in the village. At last she came back, laughing; she went up into her room to change her clothes, and resumed her work without any allusion to the past. We did not want to start the subject of Jean Baptiste again; but she herself, seeing us dispirited, at last said to us: "Pooh! it's all right now. There; look at that!"

It was a letter from Jean Baptiste Werner, which she had received among the rocks on the Krapenfelz. In that letter, which I read with much astonishment, Werner related that he had at first wished to join Garibaldi at Dijon; but that for want of money he had been obliged to stop at Besançon, where the volunteers of the Vosges and of Alsace were being organized; that upon the arrival of Bourbaki, he had enlisted as a gunner in the 20th corps. Two days after there were engagements at Esprels and Villersexel, where more than four thousand Prussians had remained on the field. The cold was extraordinary. The Prussians, repulsed by our columns, had retired from village to village, on the other side of the Lisaine, between Montbéliard and Mont Vaudois. There Werner, behind a deep ravine, had mounted batteries of twenty-four-pounders, well protected, on three stages, one over another; his army and his reinforcements were concentrated and securely intrenched. In spite of this, Bourbaki, wanting to relieve Belfort and descend into Alsace, had given orders for a general assault, and all that country, for three days, resembled a sea of smoke and flame under the tremendous fire of the hostile armies. Unhappily, the passage could not be forced; and the exhaustion of munitions, the fatigue, the sharp sufferings of cold and hunger—for there were no stores of clothing and provisions in our rear—all these causes had compelled us to retire, but in the hope of renewing the assault; when all at once the news spread that another German army was standing in our line of retreat, near Dôle: a considerable army, from Paris. They had hurried to get clear as far as possible by gaining Pontarlièr; but these fresh troops had a great advantage over us. Werder, also, was following us up; and we were going to be surrounded on all sides around Besançon. Jean Baptiste went on to say that then Bourbaki had attempted his own life, and was seriously wounded; that General Clinchamp had then assumed the command-in-chief; but that all these disasters would not have hindered us from arriving at Lyons, across the Jura, if the Maires of the villages had not published the armistice, causing the army to neglect to secure a line of retreat; that a great number had even lain down their arms and withdrawn into the villages; that the Prussians had kept advancing, and that only in the evening, when they had occupied all the passes, General Manteuffel declared that the armistice did not extend to operations in the east, and that our army must lay down their arms, as those of Sedan and Metz had done! But the soldiers of the Republic refused to surrender, and they had made a passage through the ice, the snow, and thousands of Prussian corpses, to Switzerland.

Jean Baptiste Werner related, in this long letter, full particulars of all that he had suffered; the attacks delivered by the corps of General Billot, who was charged to protect the retreat, upon the rocks, at the foot of precipices, in all the deep passes where the enemy lay in wait to cut off our retreat; how many of our poor fellows had perished of cold and hunger!   And then the admirable reception given to our unhappy soldiers by the noble Swiss, who had received them not as strangers, but as brothers: every town, village, and house, was opened to them with kindness.   It is manifest that the Swiss are a great people; for greatness is not to be measured by the extent of a country, and the number of the inhabitants, as the Germans suppose; but by the humanity of the people, the elevation of their character, their respect for unsuccessful courage, their love of justice and of liberty.

How much help have the Swiss sent us in succor, in money, in clothing, in food, in seed corn, for our poor fellow-countrymen ruined by the war! It came to Saverne, to Phalsbourg, to Petite Pierre —everywhere.   Ah, we perceived then that heaven and earth had not altogether deserted us; we saw that there were yet brave hearts, true republicans; that all men were not born for fire, pillage, and slaughter; that there are men in the world besides

IT IS CLEAR THAT THE SWISS ARE A GREAT PEOPLE.

hypocrites—true Christians, inspired by Him who said to men: " love one another; ye are brethren." He would not have invented petroleum bombshells, or declared that brute-force dominated over right, like those barbarians from the other side of the Rhine.

That letter of Jean Baptiste Werner's pleased me; it was clear that he was a brave man and a good patriot. But in the meanwhile, the policy of Bismarck and Jules Favre went on its way. The order of the day was, " elect deputies to sit in the assembly at Bordeaux," which was to decide for peace, or the continuance of the war: the twenty-one days' armistice had no other object, it was said.

So those who did not care to become Prussians took up arms, George and I the first; myself with the greatest zeal, for every day I reproached myself with that abominable Plébiscite as a crime. And now began the old story again: no Legitimists, no Bonapartists, no Orleanists could be found; all cried: " We are Republicans. Vote for us! "

But in every part of the country through which the Prussians had gone, the Plébiscite was remembered; the people were beginning to understand that this unworthy farce was our ruin, and that men should be judged by their actions, not their words.

At Strasbourg, at Nancy, all who desired to remain French nominated two lists of old republicans,

21

who immediately started for Bordeaux. Gambetta
was elected by us and by La Meurthe; he was also
elected in many other departments, with Thiers,
Garibaldi, Faidherbe, Chanzy, etc.

These elections once more revived our hopes.
We supposed that everything had taken place in
the West and the South as with us.

Gambetta, who never lost his sound judgment
in critical moments, had declared that all the old
official deputies of Bonaparte, all the senators,
councillors of State, and prefects of the Empire,
were disqualified for election. George commended
him. " When a spendthrift devours all his living
in debauchery, he is put under restraint; much
more, therefore," he urged, " ought men to be restrained who have devoured the wealth of the nation and put our two finest provinces in jeopardy.
All these men ought forever to be held incapable of
exercising political functions."

But Bismarck, who relied chiefly on the old Imperial functionaries, by way of testifying his gratitude to the *honest man* for all he had done for
Prussia—for his noble behavior at Sedan, and his
gift of Metz to his Majesty, William—protested
against this manifesto by Gambetta: he declared
that the elections would not then be free, and that
liberty was so dear to his heart, that he had rather
break the armistice than in any way cramp the freedom of the elections.

George, on hearing this, broke out into a rage.

" What," he cried, " this Bismarck, who has warned
the Prussian deputies to be careful of their expres-
sions in speaking of the nobleness and the majesty
of King William, ' because laws exist in Prussia
against servants who presume to insult their masters '—this very Bismarck comes here to defend
liberty, and support the accomplices of Bonaparte!
Oh! these defenders of liberty! "

Unhappily, all this was useless; the Prussians
were already in the forts of Paris, and the menaces
of Bismarck had more weight in France than the
words of Gambetta.   Therefore, once more we had
to yield to his Majesty, William, and many of our
deputies are indebted to him for their admission
into the Chambers of Bordeaux.

These defenders of the Republic immediately
showed that they were not ungrateful to Bismarck;
for they hissed Garibaldi, who had come from Italy,
old, sick, and infirm, with his two sons, to fight the
enemies of France, and uphold justice, when all
Europe held aloof!

Garibaldi was not even allowed to reply: these
representatives of the people hissed him down!   He
calmly withdrew!

The Sunday following—I am ashamed to say
it—our curé Daniel, and many other curés in our
neighborhood, preached that Garibaldi was a *ca-
naille*.   I am not condemning them; I am simply
stating a fact.   They had received orders from their
bishops, and they obeyed;   for the poor country

priest is at his bishop's mercy, and under his orders, like a whip in a driver's hand; if he disobeys, he is turned out! I know that many would rather have been silent than said such things, and I pity them!

Well, Bismarck might well laugh; he had more friends among us than was believed. Those who want to make their profits out of nations, always come to an understanding; their interests and their enemies are the same.

Then the Assembly of Bordeaux voted peace. No hard matter; only involving the sacrifice of Alsace and Lorraine, and five milliards as an indemnity for the trouble which the Prussians had taken in bombarding, devastating, and stripping us!

Then our unhappy deputies of Alsace and Lorraine were declared to be German by their French brothers, against every feeling of justice; for nobody in the world had the right to make Germans of us; to rend us from the body of our French mother-country, and fling us bleeding into the barbarian's camp, as a lump of living flesh is thrown to a wild beast, to satisfy it; no, no one in the world had this right. We alone freely ought to choose, and decide by our own votes, whether we would become Germans or remain French. But with Bismarck and William, right, liberty, and justice are powerless; might is everything. Our sorrowing deputies at last protested:

" The representatives of Alsace and Lorraine,

previous to any negotiations for peace, have laid upon the table of the National Assembly a declaration, by which they affirm, in the clearest and most emphatic language, that their will and their right is to remain Frenchmen.

"Delivered up, in contempt of justice, and by a hateful exercise of power, to the dominion of the foreigner, we have one last sad duty to fulfil.

"We again declare null and void a compact which disposes of us against our consent.

"The revindication of our rights remains forever open to each and all, after the form and in the measure which our consciences may dictate.

"In taking leave of this Chamber, in which it would be a lowering of our dignity to sit longer, and in spite of the bitterness of our sorrow, our last impulse is one of gratitude for the men who for six months have never ceased to defend us; and we are filled with a deep and unalterable love for our mother-country, from which we are violently torn.

"We will ever follow you with our prayers; and with unshaken confidence we await the future day when regenerated France shall resume the course of her high destiny.

"Your brothers of Alsace and Lorraine, separated at this moment from the common family, away from their home, will ever cherish a filial affection for their beloved France, until the day when she shall come to reclaim her place among us."

These were their words.

Monsieur Thiers asked them if they knew any other way of saving France? No reply was made. Unfortunately there was none: after the capitulation of Paris, the sacrifice of an arm was needful to save the body.

Half the deputies were already thinking of other things; peace made, they only thought of naming a king, and of decapitalizing Paris, as the newspapers said, to punish it for having proclaimed the Republic! All these people, who had presented themselves before the electors with professions of republicanism, were royalists.

Gambetta, having accepted the representation of the Bas Rhin (Alsace), left the chamber with the deputies; and other old republicans, contemptuously hissed whenever they opened their mouths, gave in their resignations.

Paris was agitated. A rising was apprehended.

About that time, early in March, 1871, Prussian tax-collectors, controllers, *gardes généraux*, and other functionaries, came to replace our own; we were warned that the French language would be abolished in our schools, and that the brave Alsacians who felt any wish to join the armies of the King of Prussia, would be met with every possible consideration; they might even be admitted into the guard of his Royal and Imperial Majesty. About this time, an old friend of Cousin George's, Nicolas Hague, a master saddler, a

wealthy and highly respectable man, came to see
him from Paris.

Nicolas Hague had bought many vineyards in
Alsace; he had planned, before the war, to retire
amongst us, as soon as he had settled his affairs;
but after all the cruelties perpetrated by the Germans, and seeing our country fallen into their hands,
he was in haste to sell his vineyards again, not caring to live amongst such barbarians.

George and Marie Anne were delighted to receive this old friend; and immediately an upstairs
room was got ready for him, and he made himself
at home.

He was a man of fifty, with red ears, a kind of
collar of beard around his face, large, velvet waistcoat adorned with gold chains and seals; a thorough
Alsacian, full of experience and sound common-
sense.

His wife, a native of Bar-le-Duc, and his two
daughters were staying with their relations; they
were resting, and recruiting their strength after
the sufferings and agonies of the siege; he was
as busy as possible getting rid of his property; for
he looked upon it as a disgrace to bring into the
world children destined to have their faces slapped
in honor of the King of Prussia.

I remember that on the second day after his
arrival, as we were all dining together at my cousin's, after having explained to us his views, Nicolas
Hague began telling us the miseries of the siege of

Paris. He told us that during the whole of that long winter, every day, were seen before the bakers' shops and the butchers' stalls strings of old men half clothed, and poor women holding their children, discolored with the cold, close in their arms, waiting three or four hours in rain, snow, and wind, for a small piece of black bread, or of horse flesh; which often never came! Never had he heard any of these unhappy people expressing any desire to surrender; but superior officers and staff officers had shamelessly declared, from the earliest days of the siege, that Paris could not hold out! And these men, formerly so proud of their rank, their epaulettes, and their titles, who were solely charged to defend us, and to uphold the honor of the nation, discouraged by their language those who were trusting in them, and whose bread they had eaten for years passed in useless reviews and parades, in frivolous fêtes at St. Cloud, at Compiègne, the Tuileries, and elsewhere.

According to Nicolas Hague, all our disasters, from Sedan to the capitulation of Paris, were attributable to the disaffection of the staff officers, the committees, and those former Bonapartist place-holders, who knew well that if the Republic drove out the Prussians, nobody in the world would be able to destroy it; and as they did not care for the Republic, they acted accordingly.

"There is a great outcry at the present moment against General Trochu," said he, "principally got

up by the Bonapartists, who, in their hearts, reproach him with having supported France rather
than their dynasty. They make him responsible
for all our calamities; and many Republicans are
simple enough to believe them. But, when it is
remembered that this man arrived only at the last
moment, when all was lost already; when the Prussians were advancing by forced marches upon Paris;
when MacMahon was forsaking the capital, *by
order of the Emperor*, to go to Sedan, to get the
army crushed down there which was to have
covered us; when it is remembered that at that moment Paris had no arms, no munitions of war, no
provisions, no troops; that the whole neighborhood,
men, women, and children, were taking refuge in
the city; that wagons full of furniture, hay, and
straw were choking the streets; that order had to be
restored amidst this abominable confusion, the forts
armed, the National Guard organized, the inhabitants put upon rations, etc.; and, then, that all
those thousands of men, who did not know even
how to keep in ranks, were to be taught to handle
a musket, to march, and, finally, led under fire;—
when all these things are remembered, it must be
acknowledged that, for one man, it was too much,
and that, if faults have been committed, it is not
General Trochu who is to be blamed, but the miserable men who brought us to such a pass. Above
all, let us be just. It is quite clear that, if General
Trochu had had under his orders real soldiers, com-

manded by real officers, he might have made great
sorties, broken the lines, or at least kept the Germans busy round the place. But how could I, Nicolas Hague, saddler, Claude Frichet, the grocer
round the corner, and a couple of hundred thousand others like us, who did not even know the
word of command—how could we fight like old
troops? We were not wanting in good will, nor in
courage; but every man to his trade. As for our
percussion rifles, and our flint locks, and a hundred
other discouraging things, you feel utterly cast
down when you know that the enemy are well
armed and supported by a terrible artillery. Trochu was well aware of these things; and I believe
that neither he, nor Jules Favre, nor Gambetta,
nor any of those who declared themselves Republicans on the 4th of September, are responsible for our
misfortunes, but only Bonaparte and his crew!"

At last, having heard Nicolas Hague explain his
views, seeing that we had been delivered up by
selfish men—as Cousin Jacques Desjardins had
foreseen four months before—but that the Republic was in existence, and that no doubt justice would
be done upon all who had brought us into this sad
condition, by which means we might rise some day
and get our turn, I had resolved to sell my mill, my
land, and everything that belonged to me in the
country, and go and settle in France; for the sight
of Placiard and the other Prussian functionaries,
who were fraternizing together, and shouting,

" Long live old Germany! " made my blood boil.
I could not stand it.

Cousin George, to whom I mentioned my de-
sign, said: " Then, if all the Alsacians and Lorrainers go, in five or six years all our country will
be Prussian. Instead of going to America, the Germans will pour in here by hundreds of thousands;
they will find in our country, almost for nothing,
fields, meadows, vineyards, hop-grounds, noble forests, the finest lands, the richest and most produc-
tive in Central Europe. How delighted would Bismarck and William be if they saw us decamping!
No, no; I'll stay. But this does not mean that I
am becoming a Prussian—quite the contrary. But
in this ill-drawn treaty there are two good articles;
the first affirms that the Alsacians and the Lorrainers, dwelling in Alsace and Lorraine, may, up
to the month of October, 1872, declare their inten-
tion of remaining French, on condition of possessing
an estate in France; the second affirms that the
French may retain their landed estates in Germany.

" Well, I at once elect to remain a Frenchman,
and I take up my abode in Paris with my friend
Nicolas Hague, who will be happy to do me this
service. I don't want to become a burgomaster, a
municipal councillor, or anything of that kind; it
will be enough for me to possess good land, a
thriving business, and a pleasant house. Yes—I
intend to declare at once; and if all who are able to
secure an abode in France will do as I am doing, we

shall have German authorities over us, it is true, but the land and the people will remain French and the land and the men are everything.

" Were not the old préfets and sous-préfets of the *honest man* intruders, just as much as these men are? Did they care for anything but making us pay what the chambers had voted, and compelling us to elect for deputies old fogies who would be safe to vote whichever way the Emperor required them? Did they trouble themselves about us, our commerce, our trade, any farther than merely to draw from us the best part of our profits for themselves, their friends, their acquaintances, and all the supporters of the dynasty of the perjurer?

" These new préfets, these *kreis-directors,* these burgomasters, set over us to defend the Prussian dynasty, will not concern us much more than the others did. At first they will try mildness; and as we have been well able to remain French under the préfets of Bonaparte, so we may live and remain French under those of Emperor William.

" My principal concern is that a large majority should declare as I am about to do. The fear is lest the Placiards, and other mayors of the Empire kept in their places by the Prussians, will be able to turn aside the people from declaring themselves as Frenchmen, by intimidating them with threats of being looked upon suspiciously, or even of being expelled; the fear is lest these fellows

should keep back day after day those who are afraid
of deciding: for when once the day is past, those
who have not declared for France will be Prussians
—their children will serve and be subject to blows
at the age of twenty, for old Germany; and those
who have already fled into France will be forced
to return or renounce their inheritance forever.

" My chief hope now is that the French journals,
which are always so busy saying useless things, will
now, without fail, warn the Alsacians and Lorrainers of their danger, and explain to them that if
they declare for France their persons and their
property will be guaranteed in safety by the treaty;
but if they neglect to do so, their persons and their
property fall under the Prussian laws. They would
even do well to furnish a clear and simple form of
declaration. By this step, all who are interested
would be clearly informed, and these papers would
have done the greatest service to France.

" As for me, here I stay! I am here upon my
own land; I have bought it; I have paid for it with
the sweat of my brow. I will pay the taxes; I will
hold my tongue, that I may be neither worried nor
driven away. I will sell my crops to the Germans
as dearly as I can; I will employ none but Frenchmen; and if the Republic acquires strength, as I
hope it will—for now the people see what Mon-
archies have been able to do for us—if the nation
transacts its own business wisely, sensibly, with
moderation, good order, and reflection, she will soon

rise again, and will once more become powerful. In ten years our losses will be repaired: we shall possess well-informed constituencies, national armies, upright administrations, a commissariat, and a staff very different from that which we have known.

"Then let the French return; they will find us, as before, ready to receive them with open arms, and to march at their sides.

"But if they pursue their old course of *coups d'état* and revolutions; if the adventurers, the Jesuits, and the egotists form another coalition against justice; if they recommence their disgraceful farces of plébiscites and constitutions by yes and no, with bayonets pointed at people's throats and with electors of whom one-half cannot read; if they bestow places again by patronage and recommendation of friends, instead of honestly throwing them open to competition; if they refuse elementary education and compulsory military service; if they will have, as in past times, an ignorant populace, and an army filled with mercenaries, in order that the sons of nobles and bourgeois may remain peaceably at home, whilst the poor labor like beasts of burden, and go and meet their deaths upon battle-fields for masters they have no concern with:— in a word, if they overthrow the Republic and set up Monarchy again, then what miseries may we not expect? Poor France, rent by her own children, will end like Poland; all our conquests of '89 will be lost. Switzerland, Italy, Belgium, Holland, all the free nations of the Continent will share our fate; the great splay feet of the Germans will overspread Europe, and we unhappy Alsacians and Lorrainers will be forced to bow the head under the yoke, or go off to America."

This speech of George's made me reflect, and I resolved to wait.

Many Alsacians and Lorrainers have thought the same; and this is why M. Thiers was right in saying that the Republic is the form of government which least divides us: it is also the only one which can save us. Any other form of government upon which Legitimists, Orleanists, and Bonapartists could well meet on common ground, would end in our destruction. If it should happen that one of these parties succeeds in placing its prince upon the throne, the next day all the others would unite and overthrow it; and the Germans, taking advantage of our division, would seize upon the Franche Comté and Champagne.

The Deputies of the Right ought to reflect well upon this. It is to reinstate the country, not a party, that they are at Versailles; it is to restore harmony to our distracted country, and not to sow fresh dissensions. I appeal to their patriotism, and, if this is not enough, to their prudence. New *coups d'état* would precipitate us into fresh revolutions more and more terrible. The nation, whose desire is for peace, labor, order, liberty, education, and justice for all, is weary of seeing itself torn to pieces by Emperors and Kings; the nation might become exasperated against these anglers after Kings in troubled waters, and the consequences might become terrible indeed.

Let them ponder well; it is their duty to do so.

And all these princes, too—all these shameless pretenders, who make no scruple of coming to divide us at the crisis when union alone can save us— when the German is occupying all the strong places on the frontier, and is watching the opportunity to rend away another portion of our country! These men who slip into the army through favor; whose disaffected newspapers impede the revival of trade, in the hope of disgusting the people with the Republic! These princes who one day pledge their word of honor, and the day after withdraw it, and who are not ashamed to claim millions in the midst of the general ruin. Yes, these men must conduct themselves differently, if they don't wish to call to remembrance their father Louis Philippe, intriguing with the Bonapartists to dethrone his benefactor Charles X.; and their grandfather, Philippe Egalité, intriguing with the Jacobins and voting the death of Louis XVI. to save his fortune, whilst his son was intriguing in the army of the North with the traitor Dumouriez to march upon Paris and overthrow the established laws.

But the day of intrigues has passed by!

Bonaparte has stripped many besides these Princes of Orleans; he has shot, transported, totally ruined fathers of families by thousands; their wives and their children have lost all! Not one of these unhappy creatures claim a farthing; they would be ashamed to ask anything of their country at such a time as this: the Princes of Orleans, alone, claim their millions.

Frankly, this is not handsome.

I am but a plain miller; by hard work I have won the half of what I possess: but if my little fortune and my life could restore Alsace and Lorraine to France, I would give them in a moment; and if my person were a cause of division and trouble, and dangerous to the peace of my country, I would abandon the mill built by my ancestors, the lands which they have cleared, those which I have acquired by work and by saving, and I would go! The idea that I was serving my country, that I was helping to raise it, would be enough for me. Yes, I would go, with a full heart, but without a backward glance.

And now let us finish the story of the Plébiscite.

Jacob returned to work at the mill; Jean Baptiste Werner also came back to demand Grédel in marriage. Grédel consented with all her heart; my wife and I gave our consent cordially.

But the dowry? This was on Grédel's mind. She was not the girl to begin housekeeping without her hundred livres! So I had again to run the water out of the sluice to the very bottom, get into the mud again, and once more handle the pick and spade.

Grédel watched me; and when the old chest came to the light of day with its iron hoops, when I had set it on the bank, and opened the rusty padlock, and the crowns all safe and sound glittered in her eyes, then she melted; all was well now; she even kissed me and hung upon her mother's neck.

The wedding took place on the 1st of July last; and in spite of the unhappy times, was a joyful one.

Toward the end of the fête, and when they were uncorking two or three more bottles of old wine, in honor of M. Thiers and all the good men who are supporting him in founding the Republic in France, Cousin George announced to us that he had taken Jean Baptiste Werner into partnership in his stone quarry. Building stone will be wanted; the bombardments and the fires in Alsace will long furnish work for architects, quarrymen, and masons: it will be a great and important business.

My cousin declared, moreover, that he, George Weber, would supply the money required; that Jean Baptiste should travel to take orders and work the quarries, and they would divide the profits equally.

M. Fingado, notary, seated at the table, drew the deeds out of his pocket, and read them to us, to the satisfaction of all.

And now things are in order, and we will try to regain by labor, economy, and good conduct, what Bonaparte lost for us by his Plébiscite.

My story is ended; let every one derive from it such reflections and instruction as he may.